S0-BFB-149

The
Spanish
Queen

ALSO BY CAROLLY ERICKSON

HISTORICAL ENTERTAINMENTS

The Unfaithful Queen
The Hidden Diary of Marie Antoinette
The Last Wife of Henry VIII
The Secret Life of Josephine
The Tsarina's Daughter
The Memoirs of Mary Queen of Scots
Rival to the Queen
The Favored Queen

NONFICTION

The Records of Medieval Europe
Civilization and Society in the West
The Medieval Vision
Bloody Mary
Great Harry
The First Elizabeth
Mistress Anne
Our Tempestuous Day
Bonnie Prince Charlie
To the Scaffold
Her Little Majesty
Arc of the Arrow
Great Catherine
Josephine
Alexandra
Royal Panoply
Lilibet
The Girl from Botany Bay

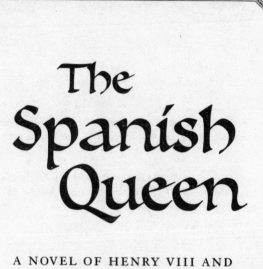

The Spanish Queen

A NOVEL OF HENRY VIII AND
CATHERINE OF ARAGON

CAROLLY ERICKSON

St. Martin's Griffin ❧ New York

This is a work of fiction. All of the characters, organizations, and events portrayed in this novel are either products of the author's imagination or are used fictitiously.

THE SPANISH QUEEN. Copyright © 2013 by Carolly Erickson. All rights reserved. Printed in the United States of America. For information, address St. Martin's Press, 175 Fifth Avenue, New York, N.Y. 10010.

www.stmartins.com

The Library of Congress has cataloged the hardcover edition as follows:

Erickson, Carolly, 1943–
    The Spanish queen : a novel of Henry VIII and Catherine of Aragon / Carolly Erickson. — First Edition.
        p. cm.
    ISBN 978-1-250-00012-5 (hardcover)
    ISBN 978-1-250-03838-8 (e-book)
    1. Catharine, of Aragon, Queen, consort of Henry VIII, King of England, 1485–1536—Fiction.   2. Great Britain—History—Henry VIII, 1485–1509—Fiction.   3. Queens—Great Britain—Fiction.   I. Title.
    PS3605.R53S73 2013
    813'.6—dc23

                                                                    2013020799

ISBN 978-1-250-04911-7 (trade paperback)

St. Martin's Griffin books may be purchased for educational, business, or promotional use. For information on bulk purchases, please contact Macmillan Corporate and Premium Sales Department at 1-800-221-7945, extension 5442, or write specialmarkets@macmillan.com.

First St. Martin's Griffin Edition: October 2014

10 9 8 7 6 5 4 3 2 1

To my friends in Chelan, Washington,
and in loving remembrance of
Omar Carl Kiger
Edna Maree Webber Kiger
Morton Webber Kiger

In any retreat, the wounded are left behind.
Their suffering is the price of victory.
—Queen Isabella of Castile

The
Spanish
Queen

1

IT WAS THE HISS AND CRACKLE OF THE EVENING CAMP FIRES THAT I remember most vividly, when I think of my childhood. The sounds of the soldiers singing together and the boy choristers of the royal chapel chanting as the bishop carried the host in procession through the camp, the soldiers bowing low in reverence. The horizon turning to fiery red and then to blue in the gathering dusk. The sparks flying up from the fires into the night sky as the first of the stars came out.

And most of all, I remember my mother, warming herself at the fire along with her soldiers, praising them for their courage, scolding them when they drank too freely of the coarse wines of the south, smiling and nodding when they cheered for her. I remember her, her face alight with happiness, her thick curling red-brown hair coming free from under her headdress, her skin aglow, contentment in her eyes.

I can almost hear her clear, strong voice as she gathered her commanders and gave them their orders for the following day.

"How many more men are we going to need?" she would ask, her expression serious, her tone urgent. "The guns," she would say. "How are the guns? What defenses do they have? What of their supplies? How long can they hold out against us?"

My valiant mother, Queen Isabella of Castile, was already famed as a warrior queen when I was very young. But what I remember far better than her renown—for what is that to a young child?—is how she often took me aside, as the camp fires were snapping and hissing, and told me my favorite story.

It was the story of how, during the long series of battles against the heathen Moors, she had continued to put on her heavy armor and lead her army, exhorting the men to attack bravely for the cause of Christ, even when she knew she was carrying me in her belly.

"I carried you for nearly nine long months, Catalina," she would say. "All through that hot spring season and the baking hot summer, with the scorching sun drying up every drop of moisture from the barren plains of Andalus, and the mules dying from thirst, and our enemies growing ever stronger. I carried you when my belly swelled larger and larger and I had to have my armorer make me new cuirasses to fit over my swollen shape.

"We had been fighting against the enemies of Christendom for four strenuous, exhausting years, your father and I, and our fight was nowhere near its end. Its outcome was uncertain, though we never lost hope.

"With all the strain and hardship I knew I might lose you, Catalina, as I had lost many of the babes I carried. Only your brother and your three sisters lived, out of all the times I hoped for a child, and I was very much afraid that you would never live to take your first breath."

Even though I had heard the story again and again, I always listened keenly for every word, watching the expressions of worry and sadness and courageous hope cross my mother's everchanging face. I could not wait for the last part of the story. The best.

"When raw weather came in the fall," she said, "and the rains came, and strong winds began to blow across the plains, I received a message from the Archbishop of Toledo. Come to my castle at Alcala de Henares, he wrote. It is a strong fortress. You will be safe there behind its old stone walls. Rest there until your child is born.

"So I did," she went on, tenderly cupping my cheeks in her hands as she spoke, and smiling. "I traveled north to Alcala, and rested there as winter began. And in the Advent season, you were born. Oh, Catalina, that was a wild night! With the winds keening around the castle walls, and the fires burning low, and the air so very cold. All the midwives prayed for me—and for you. But at last I heard you cry, and cough, and then I heard someone say 'A girl.' And then I began to cry, I was so very weary, and my pains had been so great."

Telling this part of the story always brought tears to her green eyes, with their hint of blue. And seeing her tears, I always cried with her.

But that was not the end of her tale. There was always one last part.

"When your father heard you were a girl, and not the son he wanted, he blamed me. He took his revenge. Oh yes, he took his revenge! Her name was Francesca, and she had breasts like ripe melons and the face of an angel. She was only nineteen."

She lowered her voice. "I wanted to scratch that angel's face with my nails, Catalina, until she screamed for mercy. But I couldn't. He protected her. So I nursed you, and prayed that you would live. And you did! Long before you were weaned, your father had found another girl. And so it has gone ever since."

I have said it was my favorite story, this tale of my birth. But I must add that I took no pleasure in hearing of my mother's sadness, and seeing her sorrow etched on her face. She had paid a heavy price for my birth, in weariness and pain. At times I wished, for her sake, that I had been born a boy. But more often I wished for the chance to meet the angel-faced Francesca, and shout at her, and call on the royal guardsmen to seize her and throw her into my mother's dungeons where she would starve, alone and in darkness.

But of course I never did meet her, and if I had, I would have tried to follow Our Lord's teaching and forgive her. Whether my mother ever forgave her, I cannot say.

My early memories of my father are quite different from those of
my mother. I saw much less of him, and he rarely talked to me or
even took much notice of me when I was very young. My brother
Juan was his favorite. My splendid, handsome, athletic, chivalrous
brother, who was the heir to Castile and Aragon and all my
father's lesser kingdoms combined. It was not until Juan died that
my father, angry that his only son should be taken from him when
he was barely nineteen, began to look at me and say a few words
to me.

He sent for me early one morning when he was preparing to go
hawking.

"Catalina," he said in his abrupt way, taking in at a glance my
compact, sturdy young body and the earnest look on my face—my
habitual expression at that age—"Catalina, you are aware, I trust, of
what will soon be expected of you. Not long from now the time
will come when you must be sent to England."

I had always known that I would one day leave my family and
make the long journey to England, which I believed to be a distant
cold island full of warlike people. There I would become the wife of
Prince Arthur, Prince of Wales. I dreaded that day, knowing that it
would mean leaving my mother. Sometimes I prayed that I would not
have to leave. That something would happen to make it possible for
me to stay home. But I knew very well where my duty lay. My father
did not need to remind me.

"Yes, father. I am well aware of it."

"Prince Arthur will soon be fourteen years old, and he expects
to marry you then."

"Yes, father. I know."

Something in my tone of voice must have irritated him, for he
turned to look at me then, and I thought I saw in his usually dull
brown eyes a flicker of irritation.

I had often heard it said that my father was a fine-looking man,
but I never thought him so. He had a hefty, strong body, a body

that served him well to deflect the buffeting of blows in the tiltyard and to dodge weapons hurled at him from the high walls of fortresses by enemies. But his face was fleshy and jowly, his eyes set close together and his thick black hair fell untidily over his short forehead and wide cheeks. I remember feeling glad that I did not resemble him. I was especially thankful that I did not inherit his large nose or his full red lips. My sister Juana, the beauty of our family, did resemble him, so perhaps he was a fine-looking man after all.

"It would be a shame to have to send you away, perhaps to Azuaga, to await your departure for England," he said curtly. "But I assure you that is what will happen if I hear the least hint of defiance or sulking from you."

He knew that I dreaded Azuaga, a lonely castle in the barren hills far from our court at Granada to which only criminals and outcasts were sent. He knew how to alarm me.

"No, father," I answered, my voice tremulous. "Of course not, father." I looked down at the tiled floor. I waited a moment, then added, "I am eager to go to my new home, and to meet my husband."

He turned back to his pier glass and put on his velvet cap with its trailing feathers.

"Indeed I have many questions about my new home," I added, doing my best to keep any hint of defiance out of my tone.

"What is it really like there? Have you ever been to England? Is it as cold as they say? Is the court there as splendid as ours? Does it move from place to place as we do, and do the English have to fight against the enemies of Christ as we do?"

With a final glance at his image in the pier glass my father turned to me and held up one plump hand, the many rings on his fingers glittering.

"Remember, Catalina, that you are being sent to England for only one purpose: to have sons. Sons that will one day rule that realm—and be yoked by blood to our own lands of Aragon and Castile. That is all that matters: not the weather, or the splendor of the court—though they do say that the English king is very rich—or anything else. You will marry the prince and strive to obey and please him and bear his sons."

And with that he shouted for his grooms and strode from the room, without another word to me.

I did my best not to anger my father over the next few months, as the preparations for my journey were made. There was a great deal to do, from the choosing of my many attendants and servants to the sewing of my wedding clothes to the packing of my possessions in heavy trunks. But while all this was under way, I continued to have questions, not only about England but about the prince I was pledged to marry.

I went to my almoner John Reveles, a tall, good-looking Englishman who had been sent to our court to join my household and to teach me the English tongue.

"Master Reveles, have you seen Prince Arthur?"

"Indeed I have, many times," was his answer.

I hesitated. "Can you tell me what he is like? I have the letters he sends me, as you know. But they are so formal, so very polite and full of praise. They do not tell me anything about the prince, how he is different from all others."

"You have his portrait as well as his letters, do you not?" he answered with a smile. "That should tell you much."

A portrait had been sent to me two years earlier, of a young blond boy with a thin face and pale skin. A boy with frightened eyes, I thought, though I was not going to say that to the almoner.

"Can you not see a future king in that portrait?" Master Reveles asked.

I did not know how to answer him. At length he sighed and led me to a window embrasure where we both sat.

"The prince is very unlike his father King Henry," he began. "The king is forceful, while the prince is—thoughtful. The king scowls and bellows, while Arthur—plays chess, and reads."

"What does he read?"

"Tales of chivalry, I believe. Unless I am mistaken, he also writes them."

"But that pleases me very much!" I cried. "I have always loved the old romances, ever since my mother first read them to me. What else does he like to do?"

"He has been trained in the joust, he has some fine Barbary horses in his stables, he dances a little—"

"But is he daring, and strong, yet kind, like my brother Juan was?" I wanted to know.

The almoner took his time in replying. In the end he said, "He is amusing."

"Amusing! Do you mean that he is like a fool? Like one of my mother's dwarves, that dresses up in ridiculous gowns and turns somersaults?"

"Not like that. The prince is witty. He likes puns, and word-play."

I was stunned into silence.

"Your mother would like him. Your father—" He made an equivocal gesture, and frowned. His meaning was clear.

"But then, the prince is young yet," Master Reveles went on, putting his hands on his knees and getting up from where we sat. "He will grow into manhood, and become kingly."

He looked at me. "Until then, I hope you will keep what I have confided to you locked away in your heart."

I nodded.

There was another visitor to our court who had seen my future husband. A Siennese, Maestre Antonio. He had been summoned to England by the English king, my future father-in-law, to paint the walls of a chapel. When I asked him about the prince he seemed reluctant to answer me—and not only because his grasp of our Castilian tongue was limited.

"Ah, Infanta Catalina," he answered with a shrug, "what can I say? The fair young prince—"

"Yes, yes?"

"Is—" He looked uncomfortable, unable to say what he thought, and apologetic for thinking it.

"Have you seen him riding in the tiltyard?"

"No, Infanta."

"Riding to the hunt?"

"No, Infanta."

"Would you say he is amusing, that his company is lively?"

The Siennese shook his head slowly while keeping his eyes on my face.

"There must be something you can remember about him!"

"When I saw him," he said softly after a long pause, "they were carrying him in a litter. There were three physicians with him, in long black gowns."

I took this in, but did not know what to make of it.

"Perhaps he was injured in the tiltyard," I managed to say. "My sister's husband was thrown from his horse while competing in the lists. It is often the bravest and most daring of jousters who suffer injury."

But Maestre Antonio merely shrugged again, and told me nothing more.

In the end most of my questions about Prince Arthur and England went unanswered. I realized I would just have to wait and find the answers for myself once I arrived.

At last all the preparations for my journey were complete. My officials and servants were assembled, their possessions packed, our supplies loaded onto carts, the archers and knights of my escort armed and alerted, awaiting the order to move northward.

All that remained was for me to say my goodbyes to those I was leaving behind.

To my surprise my duenna, Doña Elvira Manuel, came to me with a message.

Doña Elvira, who had known me and looked after me since I was a baby, was a plump woman with quick brown hands that were never still and bright searching eyes. She was restless that afternoon, and her strong voice held a slight quaver.

"Your mother asks for you, Infanta Catalina," she said.

"What is it? Is she not ready to leave?"

Much to my comfort, my mother was to accompany my traveling party to La Coruña, where our ships were waiting to cross the sea to England. We were to have several more weeks to be together. Her serving women had been busying themselves making ready for her departure for many days.

"I do not know, mistress. All I know is that she is asking for you."

I got up from where I had been sitting and went toward the doorway.

"If you please, mistress," Doña Elvira said, "I know it will delight her to see you—wearing your wedding gown."

I was puzzled. No one but my dresser, Maria de Caceres, and Doña Elvira, and my dressmaker and seamstresses had seen me in the full-skirted gown of heavy white silk, its many yards of softly shimmering tissue belling out from bodice and sleeves as well as from my waist.

"But everyone knows it is bad fortune to wear a wedding dress before the wedding day! No one must see it but the seamstress and fitters!"

"I have seen it," Doña Elvira reminded me mildly.

"You do not count. You are my shadow."

She was quiet a moment. When she spoke again her voice was soft.

"I believe you must do this, Infanta Catalina."

"Why? What is wrong?"

Instead of answering she summoned Maria de Caceres, who stood, eyes downcast, waiting for me to speak. I could tell that both women knew something, or sensed something, and that I needed to heed their unspoken urging.

"Very well, bring me my wedding dress. But be quick! All the carts are loaded and we are ready to leave!"

My mother was waiting for me in the Alhambra, in the cool green garden of the Court of Myrtles, sitting on a marble bench in the shade of a tall palm. Fountains plashed nearby, their waters sparkling in the afternoon sunshine. From the city spread out below us, in the distance, came the first sound of the call to prayer—for

Granada was home to many Moors and despite my parents' warmaking, not all of them had yet become converts to the Christian faith.

"Ah! Catalina! My angel!"

Seeing me dressed in my wedding gown so overwhelmed my dear mother that tears came into her eyes, and she held out her arms to me.

We embraced—awkwardly, for the gown's wide sleeves were an obstacle—and it was a moment or two before either of us could speak.

"You are so beautiful, little bride," she said, her voice tender. "How I wish I could be with you on your wedding day."

"Why not come with me then, not just to La Coruña but all the way to England?"

She shook her head slowly, sadness in her eyes. I saw then how pale she was, her face lined and drawn. I remembered that she was old, at least fifty years old, though no one at court ever mentioned her age in her presence. She could still ride, and walk briskly enough through the palace gardens. But she coughed ceaselessly during the winter, and her once vivid red-brown hair had long since gone gray.

"If only I could. I have waited as long as I dared to make this hard decision. Dr. Carriazo tells me I must rest, I am not strong enough for the rigors of traveling. I am often unwell," she went on, "I am overcome at times by dizziness. If I ride in a swaying litter I feel ill."

Church bells rang, we heard them as we sat side by side in the midst of the lush green garden. Suddenly I realized that I would have to say goodbye, not only to mother, but to the Alhambra, the lovely enclave of palaces I had come to know so well, with their brilliantly colored tiles and intricately carved ceilings, their mosaics and marble columns. This place where we had spent the past few years, the closest thing I had ever known to a home. Where would I ever find such loveliness again? How could I bear to leave it?

"I did not want to trouble you by telling you this earlier," mother was saying. "I hoped my weakness would pass. Instead I am growing weaker. Losing Juan was hard, so very hard. Then I lost my Isabella—"

She could not go on. My oldest sister, mother's namesake Isabella, had died three years earlier. Though she was much older than I was, nearly fifteen years older, I too mourned her passing and often pondered her fate.

Isabella had been sent away to Portugal to marry Prince Alfonso, who was the heir to his father's throne. But the prince had died very soon after the wedding, and Isabella's grief went on for years. I remembered her as a mournful, veiled recluse, living at our court but shut away from the world like a nun, growing thinner and more melancholy year after year. In her widowhood she had languished, until our father ordered her to marry again. Her new husband was Prince Alfonso's cousin Manuel.

Yet once again fate turned against her—or, as the archbishop preferred to say, she was punished for her sins, though what those sins may have been I had no idea, for she was a grave and thoughtful woman, not at all inclined to vice or folly. She became pregnant and gave birth to a son. Within days she was dead of the terrible sickness that so often afflicts mothers as soon as their babies are born, and her little boy died too.

It was no wonder mother was ill. She carried a heavy burden in her heart, especially since my other two sisters, Juana and Maria, had gone away, Juana to her husband's court in Burgundy and Maria to Portugal. I was the only one of her children left—and now I too was about to depart. It might well be, I thought with a pang, that we would never see each other again.

I did my best to recover my composure.

"The physician is right," I told mother. "You need to rest, not to be jounced along on dusty roads. It is best that you stay here. I will miss your company, and think of you every hour."

"We will pray for one another," she promised, giving me one last kiss and managing to smile. "I know you will be brave, Catalina, and make me proud."

"I will make a pilgrimage to the shrine of St. James at Compostela for you, and pray to the saint to make you well again."

It was not long before I discovered that there was another reason, besides her illness, that had made mother decide not to travel with me.

We had hardly begun our journey when a very angry, red-faced Doña Elvira brought me news.

"That woman!" she sputtered. "He's made that woman head of your traveling household!"

I was in no mood to be confronted with yet another trouble. I missed my mother terribly and Doña Elvira could be tiresome when in one of her moods. Still, in as calm a voice as I could manage, I said, "What woman?"

Instead of answering me directly, Doña Elvira cocked her head in the direction of a cluster of carts. I heard shouting, and saw that the entire traveling party had come to a halt.

"Tell the Count de Cabra to come to me," I said to Doña Elvira. The count was in command of my escort, seventy knights and archers.

Looking flustered, Doña Elvira made me the briefest of bows and went in search of the commander. Before long he came riding toward us, proud and erect on his splendid mount, his crimson velvet doublet and feathered cap dusty from the road. He had been a valiant fighter in the wars against the Moors, his reputation for bravery was unmatched, so mother always said. But he was an old man. At that moment, a very impatient old man.

The shouting and commotion was growing louder.

The count rode up, dismounted with the agility of a much younger man, and threw up his hands in a gesture of exasperation.

"Infanta Catalina, she is insisting on having her own escort! She says the king your father has appointed her to be head of your traveling household, and that she has his permission to do anything she likes."

"Who says this?"

"The Lady Aldonza Ruiz de Iborre y Alemany!"

At once I understood why my mother, ill and weak as she was, had chosen not to travel with me. She did not want to contend with the Lady Aldonza, my father's mistress and the most imperious woman at our court.

"Bring her to me at once."

"But Infanta, she will not come."

"Then she must be forced. Bring her at once!"

"Yes, Infanta." He squared his shoulders, bowed to me, and prepared to do his duty—though I could see how crestfallen he was.

When at last Doña Aldonza, carried in her gold-trimmed litter, emerged from its curtains and stood before me, her dissatisfaction was plain to see. She stood, tall and proud, as aloof in her ripe beauty as she was imperious, looking down at me. Her slight bow and small, forced smile did nothing to soften the severity of her expression. She lifted one eyebrow critically as she waited for me to speak to her.

I took my time, as I had seen my mother do when faced with an overbearing nobleman or, more rarely, noblewoman.

"Doña Aldonza," I said presently, "let it be understood that Doña Elvira Manuel is head of my traveling household, and will remain so."

Doña Aldonza drew herself up to her full height.

"That is not your father's wish."

"Then let him convey his wish directly to me. Until he does, Doña Elvira will retain her post."

Doña Aldonza made a huffing sound. A sound of contempt.

"You will obey my wishes in this, or you will be placed under guard, and sent back to Granada."

For a moment I thought she would defy me. I saw a flash of pure malice in her black eyes. Instead, she drew from a pocket of her gown a folded document, which she proceeded to unfold. She handed it to me. I saw that it bore the royal seal.

"What is this?"

She did not answer, she merely continued to hold the document out. Incensed by her rudeness, but curious nonetheless, I took it from her. I unfolded it further and began to read.

"Be it known that my beloved daughter Maria Juana Ruiz de Iborre y Alemany, who is also the daughter of Doña Aldonza Ruiz de Iborre y Alemany, is appointed principal maid of honor to the Infanta Catalina. She is to accompany the Infanta Catalina to England, to serve her there. It is my wish that a man of due rank and fortune be found in England who will become her husband. The Infanta Catalina will provide a suitable dowry."

The document was signed with my father's familiar signature, and beneath it his secretary had written his titles and the date— which was the day of my departure, May the twenty-first, in the Year of Our Lord 1501.

Try as I might, I could not hide my astonishment. I knew that Doña Aldonza was my father's mistress, and had been for many years. It was whispered that she had borne his children, though at our Catholic court no one was permitted to say such things aloud, and I knew nothing of these whispered children, and had certainly never seen any of them.

Before I could react or speak, Doña Aldonza was walking rapidly toward her litter. With a flourish she pulled open the curtains and drew out a girl. A girl who looked to be about my own age.

She was dark, slim, with a supple, seductive body and masses of deep brown curling hair that flowed from under her cap. She had her mother's height, and as Doña Aldonza took her by the hand and led her toward me I could see that she had more than a little of her mother's acid manner as well.

I am a king's daughter too, her dull brown eyes seemed to be saying. I am your equal, whatever you may think.

She is indeed my father's daughter, I thought to myself. She has his eyes, set close together. His broad, fleshy cheeks. Even his full red lips. And she has her mother's beauty and sensuality. No, I cannot doubt that she carries the blood of the royal house of Trastamara. But she is no infanta.

I looked from Maria Juana to Doña Aldonza and back again. I

had seen a gleam of triumph in Doña Aldonza's eyes, and the slight smile that crossed her lips. She thinks she has won, I said to myself. Aloud I said, "I will honor my father's wishes. The Infanta of Spain can do no less."

2

THE SCORCHING SUN BEAT DOWN WITH RELENTLESS FORCE THAT summer, as our long caravan of carts and wagons, litters and horsemen wound along the narrow dirt roads that seemed to stretch endlessly before us. I felt well protected, and much honored; nearly every town we reached, it seemed, decorated its crooked streets with garlands of parched greenery and noisy crowds of townspeople greeted me with cries of "Long live the Infanta Catalina!" "Long live the Princess of Wales!"

Toasts were drunk to my health and fruitfulness, oxen were roasted whole and feasts prepared, even in the poorest towns. Officials in their long gowns and ceremonial cloaks made speeches, religious processions filed slowly past and children's choirs sang. In each town prayers were offered for my forthcoming marriage to Prince Arthur, and I was presented with gifts: embroidered shawls and jars of unguent, prayer books, songbirds in cages. I thanked the townspeople as graciously as I could, and told Master Reveles to give out alms in generous measure.

At the end of each long, hot day, both Doña Elvira and Master Reveles assured me that I was doing well, that my mother would be proud of me.

I tried to ignore the pricking of the thorn in my side—the distressing complication caused by Doña Aldonza and her daughter. I announced that Maria Juana was appointed to be my principal maid of honor—much to the chagrin of my eleven other waiting maids—and Doña Aldonza continued to thrust herself forward in precedence over Doña Elvira. I heard harsh words exchanged between them from time to time, but did not intervene. It was too hot, and our progress too slow, to add more difficulties.

After many weeks we arrived at La Coruña, where the ships were waiting to take my traveling party to England. It was cooler in the port, a welcome wind arose to freshen the air and we all breathed more easily.

But we had no sooner embarked and set out from shore than the wind strengthened, a storm quickly blew up and our frail vessels were yawing dangerously in the rising seas.

At first we were almost too ill to be frightened. We clung to the masts, to the timbers, to one another as the ships rose and plunged like maddened bulls or rearing horses. I had never felt so sick. My stomach heaved. My head ached terribly. I was far too dizzy to stand. I tried to sleep, but when I closed my eyes I felt even worse. Surely seasickness is God's curse to mankind, I thought: and when I felt my worst, I wanted to die.

I wanted to die—but it was not long before I realized that we all might very well die, and soon, not because of illness but by drowning, the storm was so violent.

Then the terrible screaming began, and the desperate whinnying and bleating of the animals, the cries and prayers of the sailors—all of it soon lost in the wild roaring of the incessant wind.

There was no safety anywhere, but Doña Elvira did her best to lash me to the mast, and the Count de Cabra and his men locked arms and formed a ring around me and the other women, though our protectors slipped and slid with each sudden lurch and drop of the ship, and before long it was all they could do to find something or someone to cling to.

Barrels, trunks, chests of provisions went flying, striking everyone and everything in their path. I shuddered each time I heard a scream and saw a body, arms and legs flailing, go over the ship's side and plunge into the foaming sea. Then, without warning, the wind tore a sail to shreds and as it fell to the deck, I heard a woman's wail.

It was Doña Aldonza.

She had been struck on the head. She was bleeding. Staggering, she managed to reach out her hand toward me. Just then the ship began to rock and plunge, and she lost her footing. I could see that she was headed for the railing.

"Infanta! Infanta!" she screamed. "Save me, Infanta!"

I reached toward her, as far as I could, but I was tied where I was, and my arms were not long enough. Others tried to grasp Doña Aldonza's arms, her long hair as it flew in the wind, the hem of her gown.

But she slipped by too quickly. In an instant she knew that she was lost. She gave a strangled cry, and then she began to curse.

"Damn you to hell, Infanta Catalina! And may all the devils drag you to your death!"

Her last words were only a wail, and then a moan, and I heard, over the shrieking of the wind, Maria Juana's loud anguished scream as she saw her mother fall into the sea.

We were fortunate. We were saved. Our ship did not founder, and the first thing we did once we were back in port—we returned to La Coruña—was to go to the shrine of Santa Fe and give thanks.

We were saved, but many in my traveling party had been lost, not only Doña Aldonza but ten knights and nearly as many archers, some sailors, most of the livestock and some fine horses, along with nearly all of our provisions.

"It is an omen," I overheard people whispering. "The infanta is not meant to go to England."

I did my best to hush such superstitious talk. But it was hard to control; people love to gossip, and fear gives rise to all sorts of extravagant thoughts.

As it happened, just at the time we encountered the fearful storm, and then made our pilgrimage to the shrine of Santa Fe to give thanks, all the wells in the area went dry. They went dry, in fact, because the summer had been very hot and no rains had yet fallen. But many of my servants and officials, the memory of the storm and its damage, and especially of Doña Aldonza's curse, fresh in their minds, chose to imagine that the dry wells were just one more omen of bad luck to come.

Maria Juana was among the most outspoken in spreading this poisonous talk. I knew that she blamed me for her mother's death, though in truth I had tried to save her, and had done all I could. I made certain Maria Juana was there when I instructed my almoner Master Reveles to have a hundred masses said for the soul of Doña Aldonza, and to ensure that a suitable tombstone be inscribed in her memory.

Yet I was only too aware of the hostile looks Maria Juana gave me, the darkness in her eyes every time she glanced my way. Now that she was my principal maid of honor I had no choice but to speak to her, to give her instructions or answer her questions. She obeyed me, but unwillingly. When she spoke to me her words had a bitter edge.

As we prepared to embark once again for England I dreaded the voyage, knowing that it would bring fresh memories of all that we had suffered, and renewed fears, and that for Maria Juana, there would be renewed blame and anger directed at me.

One thing I had saved from the destructive storm had been my small chest of keepsakes, containing jewels my mother had given me and miniatures of my sisters and brother, an amulet that had belonged to my grandmother and other precious things. In the chest were my letters from Prince Arthur.

On the night before we embarked for the second time I brought out these letters and read them several times. He said that he longed to see me, to embrace me. That he loved me with a burning love.

How every time he thought of me the thought was sweet. He called me his dearest wife.

Reading the letters warmed me. Surely once we were in England, all would be well. All difficulties and friction would be put behind us. The prince would love me, and I him.

I tried to imagine him writing the letters, a tall slender blond boy with a winning smile. A boy looking forward to seeing me and embracing me. I brought to mind what Master Reveles had told me about my future husband, that he was amusing and that he wrote tales of chivalry. That my mother would like him.

With these happy thoughts I went to sleep, putting aside my awareness that we would embark the following afternoon, with the outgoing tide.

Our embarkation day was sunny. The sun was low, the horizon a blaze of red when we set out on calm seas. To my relief the seas remained calm for days, and I had almost ceased to worry when on the fourth day our pilot called out that the coast of England was in sight.

Eager for the first glimpse of my new home, I peered over the ship's railing—only to see, instead of a verdant land, a line of gray clouds. Storm clouds.

"Not again," I muttered to myself. "Please God, not again."

But as we sailed on toward the land, lightning flashed and we heard the booming of thunder and soon afterward came drenching rain. The sea became unsettled, then broke into peaks and valleys and our ship began to creak and groan with each assault of the waves.

Lurching from side to side, the ship pressed on, as we wallowed in water up to our knees.

"The rocks! Rocks ahead!" I heard a lookout shout.

Before long two massive fingers of wet gray rock loomed up in front of us, and I thought for certain our ship would collide with them. I held my breath, shut my eyes and murmured a prayer.

But before the worst could happen, I felt the ship buck sharply

under me, seeming to rear up like a stubborn horse. I opened my eyes
and saw that we were caught in the backwash coming off the jagged
rocks. It was this that had prevented our ship from breaking to bits
against the giant obstacles in our path.

Soon after this I heard the cry of "Land ho" from the sailors,
and through the thick veil of rain, saw Plymouth harbor coming
into view.

Drenched by the rain, my gown and cloak soaked and ruined, I
went ashore on the arm of the Count de Cabra, as the townsfolk of
Plymouth cheered me. They too were wet to the skin, and had been
waiting many hours to receive me. Knowing this, and grateful for
their welcome, I wanted to thank them. I asked the count to lift me
up onto a low rock wall where I could be seen and, I hoped, heard.
I am small of stature but my voice is low and carries well.

"Good people of Plymouth!" I began, doing my best to recall the
English words Master Reveles had been teaching me over the past
several years and aware that I spoke them with a Castilian accent.

"I thank you all," I went on, "I bring you greeting from the
court of Spain." As I watched, I could see the surprise—indeed
astonishment—on the faces of my listeners. The Infanta of Spain
was, after a fashion, speaking in their tongue.

"I am glad to be among you," I said. "I pray for your wealth and
happiness."

I could think of nothing more. But I had no need to go on, for
my hearers burst into shouts of acclaim.

"God bless the Princess of Wales!" came the cry. "God bless her
sweet face!"

Just then the clouds parted, and a thin ray of sunlight shone
down on the wave-frothed waters of the harbor. I could not help
but smile at the sight, cheered by the warmth of the welcome I was
being given, certain that this break in the clouds was an omen of
good things to come.

I was told that the king and Prince Arthur would be meeting me
soon, perhaps in London, the renowned capital of my new country
of England. As soon as we were able, we resumed our journey,

traveling toward the capital along roads muddy from the fall rains. So this is England, I thought, this misty green countryside with its gentle sloping grass-covered hills and clear running streams, rocky beaches and overcast skies.

I observed the prosperous-looking villages tucked between the hills, smoke rising from their roofs, animals grazing in their common pasturelands. Villagers came out to see us as we passed by, excited and full of well wishes. They were not like the ragged, half-starved, sun-baked peasants of Castile. These English peasants, shouting and waving eagerly, were well fed and rosy-cheeked, and looked to be in good spirits.

We were not far from London when a messenger rode up with an urgent announcement for the Count de Cabra. The king and Prince Arthur were on their way and would meet us at the palace of the Bishop of Bath.

"But they must not!" was Doña Elvira's horrified cry. "She must be veiled! She cannot be seen by her future relatives until after the wedding!"

It was the custom throughout my parents' realms that the bride be shielded from view until the moment she became a wife in the eyes of God, through repeating her wedding vows. But that moment would be weeks away, and I was impatient.

"Doña Elvira!" I burst out. "I must see my prince! I must see Prince Arthur! I have been waiting so very long."

Her face set and grim, my duenna took me firmly by my arm and fastened on my veil. A heavy, thick veil such as Moorish women wear, and was quite often worn at my parents' court. I could barely see through it.

"There," she said. "Now you are properly attired to meet His Highness King Henry—and his son!"

I heard the sound of muffled laughter, and saw that it was Maria Juana, covering her mouth with her hand.

We rode on the short distance to Dogmersfield, where the bishop's palace was, and where we were expecting to spend the night. A large suite of rooms had been prepared for me and my women, with a spacious bedchamber and several anterooms. Doña Elvira hurried me inside, and shut the wide door, standing with her back to it as if to guard me.

It was not long before we heard a pounding of fists on the far side of the thick oak door.

Doña Elvira shrieked—but did not move. She braced herself.

The pounding came again.

"His Majesty King Henry sends greetings and requires the Infanta Catalina to join him for a collation in the great hall."

"She—she is resting after her long journey," Doña Elvira answered. "She cannot come."

"Waken her!"

"She—is not prepared. She will require time—to bathe and dress."

"One hour," came the voice on the other side of the door. "One hour. No more."

We heard the sound of boots—more than one pair of boots—passing along the corridor. Then silence.

I removed the heavy veil.

"So, the king wishes to inspect the goods he has bought before he lets his son marry them!" It was Maria Juana, speaking more boldly and rudely than ever before.

I glanced at her, and would have slapped her had Doña Elvira not been too quick. In two steps Doña Elvira was slapping Maria Juana's fleshy cheeks and threatening to send her back to Spain.

"Wretched girl! Wretched daughter of a miserable whore! If you dare speak so again you will be whipped!"

Maria Juana, tears of anger in her eyes, ran from the room.

Meanwhile there was another knock on the door, this time a much softer, more polite knock.

"No," Doña Elvira responded firmly, "the infanta cannot come now. She is resting—I mean bathing."

We heard a boy's voice say, "Pardon, mistress. I am David, King Henry's valet. I bring the king's apologies, and a gift for the infanta."

It was a gentle, melodious voice. Something in the gentleness of it unlatched my heart.

"Cannot the king's valet come in, Doña Elvira?" I pleaded. "Surely there is nothing in our old Castilian customs to prevent a mere valet from seeing me? Especially as he has brought me a gift."

Doña Elvira looked suspicious, but then relented. "I suppose not," she said after a time. She gave a heavy sigh. Her whole body seemed to sag. The confrontation was sapping her strength.

I called to Maria de Caceres, my dresser. "Maria, will you accompany Doña Elvira to an inner chamber where she can lie down?"

Doña Elvira made only the most feeble of protests as Maria, tactful and empathetic, persuaded her to go with her into another room. When they had gone I went to the heavy oak door and undid the lock. I pulled the door open.

There before me stood a smiling blond boy, amusement in his light blue eyes.

"Infanta Catalina," he said, holding out a small golden cask.

I recognized him at once. It was Prince Arthur.

As soon as he stepped across the threshold he took me in his arms and kissed me lightly on the mouth as I had seen the English do.

"I am so very glad to see you—" I started to say, in my accented English, aware that I was blushing, my face hot. No boy had ever kissed me before. Doña Elvira would never have allowed it.

But he put one finger over my lips.

"I am the king's valet, David. I bring you the king's gift." Once again he held out the small chest. "Shall we open it together?"

We smiled at one another, a conspiratorial smile. We sat side by side on a cushioned bench. I couldn't speak. I was confused, yet overjoyed. All my composure had abandoned me.

"The king is eager to see you," he began. "He hopes you will join him, as do I. He sends you this token"—he lifted a string of pearls from the chest and fastened them around my neck—"and my mother, I mean the queen, also sends you a token of her love." He brought from the chest a ring with a large pearl and slipped it onto my finger, very gently.

"Please thank His Majesty for me, David. And Her Majesty the queen as well. And please tell the prince that, at this moment, my heart is full of joy."

"I think he knows that already, Infanta."

Once again he reached for my hand and put it to his lips.

Then, before any of my women could interrupt us, he stood and bowed and took his leave.

I called for my servants and quickly bathed and had Maria de Caceres dress me in a gown of russet silk with wide cream-colored sleeves. I knew that the gown flattered me, bringing out the rich auburn shade of my hair and the fairness of my skin. When my hair had been brushed and carefully bound beneath my jeweled headdress, I put on the long string of pearls the king had sent me, looping it twice so that it fell nearly to my waist, and added the pearl ring. I hoped my future parents—for that is how I thought of them, as a second father and mother—would find me acceptable.

While I was dressing Doña Elvira emerged from the antechamber where she had been resting. As I expected, she sputtered and fumed when I told her, calmly and firmly (though inwardly I was anything but calm) that I was going to meet the king as he had requested, and join him for a light meal.

"This is his realm, Doña Elvira. We are not in Spain now, and his word is supreme here. I must learn to adapt and be gracious."

She tried to argue with me, but I silenced her. Then I made my way, full of excitement, to the great hall.

Over the next few days, while we remained at Dogmersfield, Arthur and I saw each other several times and exchanged a few words under the careful vigilance of others. These were formal meetings, filled with protocols to be observed and restrictions on what we could do or say.

But we also found ways to meet and talk in private, without the constraints of Doña Elvira's protective presence and without any court formalities. Arthur took pleasure in arranging these quiet meetings, and I, who had never been without the scrutiny not only of my duenna but of my mother, or her servants, or of any of the dozens of members of the royal household, felt liberated from a lifelong burden.

We could not talk for very long, to be sure. And we had to be watchful ourselves, to be certain we were not discovered. But this only added to our enjoyment. We shared a secret, and that brought us even closer together.

"My father would bellow at me if he caught us," Arthur confided with an almost gleeful tone in his voice. I could believe what he told me, for having dined with King Henry on the afternoon of our arrival I saw how wrathful he could be. His anger was not directed at me, to be sure, but at a servant who displeased him by bringing him a dish of food he disliked.

"Eels! Eels!" he shouted, pushing the platter away.

"These are lampreys, Your Majesty," was the servant's cautious reply.

"Eels! Lampreys! Have you no sense? Don't you know that a king of England once dined on eels, and died the next day?"

His voice rose, his face grew so red it was almost purple. He reached out to strike the servant, but the man was already running from the room. With an oath the king sat down again and ordered the offending platter of lampreys removed. Before long his anger had begun to subside, though all the servants remained tense and no one dared to say a word. The only sound was the hiss and crackle of the fire in the hearth, and now and then the heavy thud of a log falling amid a shower of brilliant sparks.

"I have seen your father's anger," I told Arthur. "I hope I never displease him."

"Ah, but he finds you pleasing enough," Arthur reassured me. "I am the one he disapproves of. He despairs of me, in fact."

"Surely not." How could any father despair of such a son, I wondered. A boy with such wit and charm, such good looks. A boy who would one day be king, but who had no arrogance, none of the thrusting, frowning self-importance that my father and King Henry had.

"He says I will never succeed in the tiltyard. I will never be a champion. I am a poor rider, and cannot wield a heavy lance."

He looked at me, all the usual amusement in his blue eyes suddenly gone.

"I am not like my brother," he added with a rueful smile. "He is only ten years old, and already he is stronger than I am. He rides farther and faster—"

"But I am told you have other gifts. You are a fine storyteller."

At once I saw the gleam in Arthur's eyes return.

"Yes, yes. I love stories. Tales of the Knights of the Round Table. The books of chivalry. Sir Gawain and Sir Lancelot. The quest for the Holy Grail."

"If you will write them, tell them anew, I would be eager to read them."

His smile broadened. "Dear Catherine," he said, and kissed me. My English name. Not Catalina, but Catherine. It sounded strange to my ears, but said in his gentle voice, it was beautiful.

I was welcomed to London by a great noise.

Cannons boomed from the Tower, so loudly and so unceasingly that I had to stop my ears. The clamorous welcome of the large crowds gathered along narrow streets cheered me—but nearly deafened me, especially when the heralds and their trumpeters added their shouts and fanfares.

I was quite accustomed to the sound of cannon fire, having spent most of my childhood in encampments of soldiers. But the Tower guns were by far the loudest I had ever heard, and the cries of the Londoners the most strident.

Bells rang out continually in celebration of my arrival, and choristers sang as my procession of horsemen and grandly robed attendants passed; at each of the city conduits, where wine flowed freely and where tables were laid with meats and bread, the eruptions of shouting and laughing made as great a din as I had ever heard.

But the smells! The stinks of London struck me with even

greater force than the noise. An awful stench rose from the river Thames, where the bloated bodies of dead animals bobbed in the eddies, and mounds of waste as high as haystacks awaited the arrival of the dung boats. Who could eat fish caught in that putrid river? Who could bathe in that water, or wash clothes in it? Yet Londoners did, and many of them got very sick and died, so I was told, as a result.

There were animals everywhere: sheep and goats being driven to market, fat pigs rooting among the entrails thrown into the road by butchers, stray dogs and lean, hungry-looking cats. The filth from the animals, the odors of the fish market combined with the unsavory stinks from the open drains to overwhelm me and force me to hold my spice-scented pomander under my nose.

Granada was not the sweetest-smelling of cities, I reminded myself (though the gardens of the Alhambra were full of the rich perfumes of jasmine and orange blossom), but it was cleaner and more orderly by far than this noisy, turbulent London, and far more pleasing to the nose.

I thought this—and then I chided myself. For I knew that I must now be loyal to my new land. I must put England first, not Spain. I am Catherine now, I told myself, not Catalina. Catherine, Princess of Wales, not Infanta Catalina.

I looked out at the cheering, waving Londoners and smiled.

On our wedding day the immense cathedral of St. Paul was crowded, and the spectacle and ceremony were very grand. But two things, and two things only, mattered to me. One made me joyful, and the other made me sad.

I was marrying my dear Arthur, the prince I loved. And my mother was not there to see me wed.

It was a brisk, cold November day and a chill wind blew through the high vaulted arches of the old church. Arthur and I shivered as we stood before the bishop, I in my white silken gown with its full hooped skirt, a white silk veil trimmed in gold and gems covering

my face, and Arthur, so handsome in his white silk doublet gleaming
with gold.

He looked every bit as happy as I felt, only I noticed that he was
limping slightly as he made his way along the raised walkway that
led to the altar. I had seen him limp before. He had told me that his
left leg was shorter and weaker than his right leg, and that sometimes
it hurt.

I tried to put out of my mind the memory of the afternoon,
months earlier, when I wore my wedding dress for my mother to
see and admire. It was bad luck to do that, so everyone said. Yet I
had not known then how delighted I would be with my bridegroom,
how fortunate I would feel on this day, when we were joined before
God and made husband and wife, with such a vast crowd of witnesses
looking on and wishing us well. There was no bad luck evident,
only blessings and good wishes, much splendor, and the heavenly
sound of singing.

No, there was nothing but good fortune on my wedding day. I
said as much that night to my dresser Maria de Caceres as she helped
me out of my wedding clothes and prepared me for bed.

"All has gone well today, has it not?"

"It has, my Infanta."

"You must call me princess now. I am the wife of the Prince
of Wales." I pronounced the words with pride. "I am the Princess of
Wales."

"But you will always be Infanta Catalina as well," was her stubborn
response, as she began removing my headdress and unpinning my hair.
I sat before the pier glass, watching my reflection as she removed the
pins and let the long thick ropes of hair fall in waves down my back.
They gleamed in the firelight as she brushed them, glints of russet
and gold shining out of the darker mass.

"My children will be half Spanish, half English," I mused,
partly to myself. "They will learn to speak Castilian, English,
Latin and French. I will take them to Spain to visit my mother and
father."

Maria brought my lace-trimmed nightdress and I put it on. I felt excited yet nervous. Soon Arthur would join me and we would become husband and wife in flesh as well as in spirit, bound by the sacrament of marriage. I hoped Arthur would find me pleasing.

The bishop came in, with three attendant priests, and blessed our marriage bed, sprinkling the embroidered velvet counterpane with holy water. When they had gone, Maria surprised me greatly by kissing me swiftly on the cheek.

Before I could punish her for her insolence she said, "Your mother Queen Isabella made me promise to kiss you for her, on your wedding night. You are lovely, little bride. May all go well for you."

And with a bow she left me.

After what seemed an hour I heard rude sounds outside the bedchamber door. The raucous singing, hooting, drunken cries and loud laughter of young men. I could make out a few words, most of them words that made me blush. The door flew open and Arthur, wearing nothing but his thin, short nightshirt, was pushed inside. Behind him I could see the laughing faces of a dozen or so companions, shoving and snickering. Then the door closed.

I trembled at the sight of my dear Arthur, coming toward me, staggering as he came, and holding out his arms. For the firelight revealed that he was shockingly, painfully frail: so frail, in fact, that I was afraid his bones could break at the slightest touch. He grinned at me, the silly grin of a boy who has drunk far too much wine. Then he swayed, and lurched to the bed, and without saying a word to me he collapsed onto the velvet counterpane.

3

WHAT WAS I TO DO?

Arthur was asleep. He was snoring. There was nothing I could do but climb up into the heavy oak bed with its four massive columns and lie under the warm fur coverings, listening to Arthur's ragged breathing.

I lay there all night. I couldn't sleep. I felt rejected, insulted, and very sad.

How could my Arthur, with his lightness of spirit and zest for amusement, turn into a drunken lout? How could he have abandoned me so cruelly, and on our wedding night? How could he have changed so much, so quickly?

Early in the morning he got up and left our bedchamber, without saying a word to me. When Doña Elvira, Maria de Caceres and my other ladies came in to attend me and found me alone, they were puzzled.

"Where has the bridegroom gone?" Doña Elvira teased. Instead of answering, I shook my head, trying very hard not to cry.

Doña Elvira hurried the others from the room—but not before Maria Juana had observed my troubled state. She looked at me fixedly through narrowed eyes, then left. Only Doña Elvira and my dresser remained. Maria drew a soft cloth from a pocket of her gown and held it out to me. I wiped my eyes.

"What's this, Catalina?" Doña Elvira said impatiently. "Where has he gone? To brag to his friends? To boast of his conquest?"

In an attempt to recover my dignity, I stood as tall as I could, and answered Doña Elvira, but my voice broke slightly as I did so. And I was aware of Maria's sympathetic glance. What I read in her eyes was, "Poor lamb."

"There was no conquest," I managed to say.

"You have not lain together, as man and wife?" was Maria's question.

I shook my head.

Doña Elvira threw up her hands in exasperation.

"But they are waiting to see the sheets! They are waiting now! The trumpeters have already come!"

I remembered my mother telling me how, on the morning after her wedding night, the bloodstained sheets from the bed she had shared with my father were displayed with pride to all the nobles of the court, as drums beat and trumpets blew a triumphant fanfare. Bloody bedclothes were a sure sign that the bride had been a virgin when she came to her husband for the first time—and that he had been manly and strong, and had taken his prize. It was something to be celebrated, especially when the bride and groom were royal, and their children would carry on the succession to the throne.

"There are no bloodstained sheets then," Maria said, adding, after a moment's thought, "unless we were to cut off the head of a chicken, and—"

But by then Arthur had come into the room, no longer the tottering, drunken boy who had collapsed on our bed the night before but a prince in full majesty, looking very handsome and fully sober. He was dressed in a blue velvet doublet braided with gold. On his head was a blue velvet cap with a white feather.

"What is this talk of bloodstains and beheaded chickens? Of trumpets and barbaric Spanish ceremonies? We'll have none of that here in my father's kingdom!"

And he ordered the guardsmen who had entered the room behind him to send the trumpeters away, along with anyone who had come to witness the evidence of our lovemaking.

At the sight of Arthur I brightened, and when he spoke, I began to feel greatly relieved. My Arthur, my husband, the boy I loved, had returned to me—and had intervened to solve the dilemma of our need to prove a physical union that had not yet happened. Surely it would happen, and soon. Arthur's drunkenness, and my dismay, were passing things; my anticipation and excitement began to return.

But after we had dined together, and the last of the servants had left us, we had a quiet talk that deflated my renewed hopes.

Arthur assured me of his love, then asked my forgiveness and understanding.

"I disappointed you last night," he said, "and I am so very sorry. But it was only because I was afraid."

"Afraid of what?" I asked him.

"Afraid that I would fail." He shook his head. "I regret my fear. My companions were taunting me, wagering with one another over how many times I could invade Spain, as they put it, on my wedding night.

"Their jokes and taunts made me uneasy. To calm my fears, I drank too much wine, and—" He shrugged. "By the time I reached our bedchamber, and saw you, looking so like an angel—"

He shook his head again.

I could not help pitying him.

That night we retired together in our bedchamber. Blazing logs high-piled in the hearth warmed the room, and our bed had been warmed with a heated iron, so that when we climbed into it and pulled the coverings over us, we were comfortable.

Arthur took me in his arms as we lay there, the only sound in the room the sharp crackling of the logs, the firelight playing on the walls. I could feel Arthur's heart beating. Lying against him as I was, I could also feel the bones of his chest, he was so thin.

He stroked my hair softly. I closed my eyes and sighed. After a time Arthur broke the silence between us.

"A prince is never supposed to fail at anything. Yet I fail at everything. In the tiltyard, in the forest when we hunt, at the gaming table when we play cards and cast dice. I cannot dance—my leg hurts too much."

"You are heir to the throne. Never forget that. That is your triumph over every failure."

He looked at me. "Thank you, Catherine," he murmured, and I cupped his face between my hands, his skin as soft and smooth as a child's, and kissed him full on the mouth.

I had never kissed a boy before. The kiss was sweet, so very sweet. I lost myself in its depths. I lost everything but sensation, feeling, an indescribable warmth. I was sure the same thing was happening to him.

When our kiss finally ended, we looked at each other for a long time.

"Loving is not a skill, like dancing," I whispered. "It is an urge, like hunger and thirst."

After that we gave ourselves to loving.

But no, I must not write that: the truth was, we tried to give ourselves to loving. Arthur struggled to perform as men do, and I did my best to help and encourage him. The more effort he made, the more the exertion exhausted him. He began to grow short of breath. His face grew very red. He coughed. He soon abandoned his efforts.

I remained a virgin.

The next morning I summoned my physician, Dr. Alcaraz, and told him what had happened. I confided everything to him, including my worst fear, which was that I would be sent back to my parents' court in disgrace.

Dr. Alcaraz said little, but listened closely to all that I told him, and pondered it. He was a thoughtful man, who had studied at the famed university at Salerno and had read the works of the most learned Arab physicians. I respected his knowledge and his skill.

"From what you have told me, Infanta Catalina, and from what I have seen of the prince your husband, it would seem that you are not in any way to blame for what has happened. You do not displease the prince. Should anyone say otherwise, I will dispute it."

I told the physician that Arthur was often short of breath. That this shortness of breath came over him whether he was walking or riding, or sitting, or even lying down. At this Dr. Alcaraz's thick black eyebrows knit together in a frown.

"The boy must rest," he said, looking worried. "He must not strain himself. It is possible he was too young to marry. Too young to couple with a lovely young wife. I will have my alchemist prepare a restorative medicine. One that will strengthen the prince and lift his spirits. Meanwhile you must be patient." He smiled slightly.

"Boys are like young whelps, or colts. When they are old enough, they mate. It is only a question of when."

I knew that the physician meant to reassure me, and I trusted his judgment and took his advice. Yet every time I saw Arthur my heart sank. Was he simply too young? And would the medicine be effective?

For weeks after our wedding the court celebrated with banqueting and pageants, jousts and special masses offered for our long life and my fruitfulness. Each day brought new festivities, including one feast given by Arthur's grandmother, Margaret Beaufort, who at the age of fifty-eight was still the reigning lady of the court, more honored than the queen though she held no royal title.

She gave me the privilege of sitting beside her, and told me stories from her own girlhood long past, when she had borne her son, Henry Tudor, at the age of thirteen or fourteen and had seen him crowned many years later as King Henry VII.

All the guilds and livery companies in their barges escorted our royal barge as we made our way along the river to Richmond, the king's favorite palace. The wintry air was full of music, for each barge held its own complement of lutenists, clarion players, drummers and performers on the sackbut and shalm. My feet itched to dance, but I held back, knowing that Arthur would not be able to join in and not wanting him to be left out.

It was in the elegant setting of Richmond, in the dancing chamber with its high windows and colorful tapestries, that I knew I must say my goodbyes to many in my household who had come with me from Spain. Not all were leaving; Doña Elvira and my dresser Maria de Caceres, my chamberlain and physician, Master Reveles my almoner, the Count de Cabra and a number of my women were staying on, more than fifty of them in all.

Unfortunately, Maria Juana was among those who were remaining with me in England. I did not dare dismiss her or send her away, since it had been my father's wish that she remain in my household. But I would have been glad to see her go, as she continued to be a thorn in my side.

It was not only that she blamed me for the death of her mother, and told everyone how I had deliberately failed to catch hold of her when I had the chance to save her from drowning. She spread other lies about me. She said that she had heard me insist that the king was mad and that all Englishmen were coarse in their habits and speech. She repeated as fact a gross invention: that she had overheard me telling Doña Elvira that I regretted having married Arthur, now that we lived as husband and wife, and that I wished I had married the prince of Portugal instead.

There was excited gossip about whether or not I might be carrying Arthur's child—and Maria Juana, I was told, dampened that excitement by hinting in whispers that I would never have Arthur's child, that I was not capable of conceiving a child at all, and that my barrenness was the reason no bloody bedclothes had been displayed on the morning after our wedding night.

Nothing would have satisfied me more than to punish Maria

Juana for saying these things, but I knew that if I did, she would tell my father, and would add her slander about my being to blame for her mother's death. I could only imagine what my father—whose rage could be terrifying—would do then.

So I endured her covert slanders, and her sly, furtive glances, her stifled laughter and the darkness that would come into her eyes and over her entire face whenever I summoned her (as I had to) or came into a room where she was.

I made certain that when the departing members of my household were given their gifts—silver goblets, gold aglets, scented pomanders, lengths of cloth—Maria Juana also received a gift, a purse of coins.

When I handed it to her she looked at me suspiciously, as if wondering whether it might be an inducement to join the others who would be on their way the following day.

I nodded to her and tried to smile. She hesitated, then made a shallow reverence and hurried away. For once I had managed to surprise her, I thought. Instead of punishing her I had done what the Scriptures advise: I had shown generosity to an enemy, and in doing so I had heaped coals of fire on her head.

Meanwhile Arthur was taking the medicine Dr. Alcaraz's apothecary gave him, and we were sleeping side by side every night—but not as husband and wife. The medicine did not strengthen Arthur as I hoped it would. After a month and more it was gently laid aside; Arthur said it gave him a headache.

His weakness was increasing and his cough growing worse.

"It is only the winter, the chill weather," Doña Elvira insisted. "He will recover when spring comes."

But long before spring came we had left Richmond and made the difficult, cold journey to Wales, and by the time we arrived at Ludlow Castle, high on its rocky peak, freezing winds and storms far more violent than any I had ever known in Spain were battering at the old gray stone walls and making my husband more ill than ever.

———

Arthur was Prince of Wales, Wales was governed from Ludlow. It was needful for him to be there, sitting on his princely throne, dispensing justice, settling disputes, overseeing the keeping of the peace, ruling in the name of his father the king.

And it was needful for me to be there with him, though there was little enough for me to do during the short, dark days of bleak weather and the long nights when we stayed near the fire, covered in furs and I read to Arthur from his favorite books of chivalry.

He no longer had the energy to write his own stories. Indeed he found the daily tasks of governing—most of which were carried out by others—quite wearisome.

He was becoming a wan specter before my eyes.

Thinner and thinner, more and more pale, he looked puzzled and confused. At times he forgot who I was—then suddenly remembered, only to forget again.

He limped. He stumbled. Before long he could only walk if a servant supported him, then two servants, one on each side, to prevent him from falling. During the Lenten season he tried to wash the feet of the poor folk who came to the castle for alms. But he soon gave up. The effort was too great. He had to ask Master Reveles to take his place. If he tried to speak he was overcome by coughing, so he ceased to try. Instead he smiled, his hauntingly sweet smile, and to see him smile so touched my heart that I had to look away.

I saw how those around him treated him in his sorry decline. His groom Thomas hardly left his side, and was most loyal and useful to him, even when poor Arthur reeked of piss and vomit, and the rushes on the floor were loathsome, they stank so badly. (Pardon me, I must write the truth.) But others, both servants and officers of his household, and especially the few nobles who were at Ludlow as Arthur's advisers, laughed at him. I wanted to order them whipped for their arrogance and lack of Christian feeling.

Some of the Welsh folk, frightened that they would be blamed if he did not recover, brought a wise woman, a renowned healer, to the castle. She put her hands on him as he lay in bed. With a great effort he was able to tell her that he felt better. All of us were relieved, and took heart, assuring each other that he would soon recover.

But Arthur, with one of his gentle smiles and a shake of his head, conveyed to me that the wise woman's visit had been for naught. He had only been pretending to feel better, so that she would not imagine that she had failed her prince.

One night he woke suddenly and cried out, a weak cry but loud enough to wake me, sleeping beside him as I continued to do throughout his illness. He waved away the guards and grooms and even Dr. Alcaraz. When the others had left, and only he and I were there together in the dimly lit room, he reached for my hand. His own hand was hot and moist, his cheeks flushed.

"Dear Catherine," he murmured, "my dear Catherine."

I forced myself to look at his pathetic face, his skin nearly translucent, his eyes sunk deeply into their hollows.

"I would not have made a good king," he whispered, then with a sudden shudder he was gone.

Poor Arthur was laid out, his innards removed, his body embalmed, filled with spices because he stank. He lay in the chapel at Ludlow, by torchlight. I went to stand beside his casket and said my prayers for his soul. I mourned him, and felt a grim sorrow for myself—and my future.

If only Arthur had died leaving me with a child, a son who would be heir to his grandfather's throne. Then I would be the honored mother of the next king. I would live at the royal court and my rank and standing would be assured.

I knew that was not to be. And I feared that once it became known that I was not carrying Arthur's child, I would be shunned and scorned. I would never marry a second time, even though I was the Infanta Catalina, daughter of King Ferdinand and Queen Isabella.

I stood in the rain, an icy wind whipping my woolen cloak,

watching as the carriage that held my husband's body passed slowly along the muddy road. He was being taken to Worcester, to be interred in the cathedral. He would have no monument there, no grand royal tomb. Before very long he would be forgotten. And I, his widow, his barren widow, would be best forgotten as well.

The rain fell harder, darkness was closing in. Though the wind was chill I suddenly felt hot, as if I had been standing too close to the fire. I swayed in the wind. I was unsteady on my feet.

Then the muddy ground rose up to meet me and I lost myself in its pungent depths.

I was burning. I was drenched in sweat. Cruel tormentors were pounding their mallets on my head. I clutched at my stomach. Sharp knives pierced my belly. Water! Oh, give me water!

I heard a woman's voice.

"She fainted."

I opened my eyes and saw Doña Elvira, bending over me. I felt straw underneath me. Wet straw. I was lying on a straw pallet. I had never been so sick.

"Is it—the plague?" Another woman's voice.

"It is the new plague. Sent to punish us for our sins."

I closed my eyes. Sometime later, the same woman's voice came again, this time so low it was almost a whisper.

"She will die, won't she."

"Hush! Say your prayers!" said Doña Elvira.

"But the others—they died—"

"Say nothing! The infanta will recover! The Lord will preserve her!"

Once again I closed my eyes. A woman's scream wakened me.

Men's voices reached me then, priests' voices, intoning Latin prayers. I tried to speak. I wanted to ask Doña Elvira whether the priests were praying for me, giving me the last rites. I tried to lift my arm, to feel my forehead. Was there holy oil on my forehead? Was I dying? But I was too weak even to raise my fingers. My arm was limp.

"Into Thy hands, O Lord—"

I could not even form the words.

Mother. Dear mother . . .

"If there is a babe within her," I heard Doña Elvira whisper, "it cannot live."

I thought that I would never recover.

Two of my women died, and seven of the grooms, and some of the Welsh gentlemen too, I never knew how many. All in those terrible days when the new plague, the one they called the sweating sickness, struck us at Ludlow in the weeks following Arthur's death.

I was sure I would die too.

Doña Elvira hovered near me, swabbing me with cool cloths, giving me sips of wine, talking to me reassuringly as she had when I was a small child.

Gradually the burning fever passed, and the throbbing in my head, and I was able to eat a little. I felt as though I was coming back to life. As though I had passed through a darkness—an infinite darkness—and returned into the light again. The joy I felt was beyond anything.

Doña Elvira smiled and nodded.

"The Lord will preserve her," was all she said, but I could tell that the strain on her face was gone, and when for the first time since I fainted on the muddy road, I heard her scold me, I knew that I would soon be well again.

My kind mother-in-law Queen Elizabeth sent for me as soon as I was well, and I was glad to leave Ludlow Castle with its unhappy memories and return to Richmond.

The queen embraced me lovingly and led me into her apartments. She wore a simple black mourning gown, and her ladies and maids of honor were all in mourning as well. I expected to find her in a state of inconsolable grief; instead she appeared subdued, but happy nonetheless and I soon found out why.

"I am expecting another child," she told me. "If the baby is a boy, we will name him Arthur."

"That is good news indeed. It must ease your sorrow—and the king's, of course."

I thought I saw the merest shadow cross her features at my mention of her husband, but I wasn't certain. At the time I thought little of it.

I knew that the queen had given birth to many children, and that only three of them were still living: Princess Margaret, the eldest, Prince Henry, who was now Prince of Wales and heir to the throne, and Princess Mary, still a little girl, and a very pretty one.

The queen told me that three skilled midwives were ready to attend her when the time came for the birth. She paused, then added, "They are the midwives I intended to send to you, Catherine, as soon as you conceived Arthur's child."

"I wish he had left me with a son," I said. "But it was not the Lord's will. I prayed that I would be able to give him many children. It was my dearest wish, next to the wish that he would recover, and once again be well and strong."

"So many were praying for that," she said softly, looking down at her hands, folded in her lap.

"May I tell you something about Arthur that I have not told anyone else, not even Doña Elvira?" I was moved to ask.

"Of course you may."

I swallowed. It was not easy to bring to mind what I was about to say.

"I was with him all the time during his last days," I began. "Sitting beside the bed, or on the bed. I listened to every sound he made. Every gurgle in his throat. Every cough. I watched him while he slept. He slept so poorly, his coughing woke him. Sometimes he woke very suddenly and cried out."

The queen nodded. She did not take her eyes from my face, and I saw much concern and compassion there. I saw in his mother the source of Arthur's depth of feeling, and I felt a fresh pang of grief and loss.

I took a breath and then went on.

"The very last thing he whispered was, 'I would not have made a very good king.'"

The queen hung her head and wept.

Arthur had died in April. The following winter, in an icy January, the queen's pains began. She prayed for another son, and the entire court prayed with her.

After many hours the three midwives she relied on so greatly were exhausted, and it was left to King Henry's physicians to bring her child into the world.

It was a daughter.

Within hours both the queen and her newborn baby were dead.

"I must write to mother, to tell her what has happened," I told Doña Elvira. "She will be very sorry. She knows how good Queen Elizabeth has been to me."

But Doña Elvira interrupted me by holding out a folded letter sealed with my mother's familiar seal.

"You need not write, Infanta Catalina. You will be able to tell her the news yourself when you see her."

I took the letter, broke the seal, and read it.

"Dearest Catalina," it began,

> I have dispatched the *Reina del Cielo* from La Coruña. May the Lord Our Savior and Protector grant her favorable winds, so that she will come into safe harbor before the Lenten season. Make haste to prepare, beloved daughter. We await your swift return to Castile.
>
> Given from our palace at Granada,
This second day of November, in the
Year of Our Lord fifteen hundred and two,
Isabella, Reina Catolica

4

THE ROPE STRETCHED BETWEEN A TALL WOODEN POLE AND A corner of the stable roof, where it was held down by a heavy stone. My acrobat, Sebastian, was practicing his tricks.

It was the first warm afternoon of spring, and I had insisted to Doña Elvira that no harm would come to me if I went for a walk in the gardens—alone.

"Not alone. Not unless I accompany you," was her gruff reply. Her mood was very sour just then, she said no to everything. Along with all the others in my household, she had not been paid her wages in over a year, and she was not at all inclined to indulge me.

"Not even if I promise to stay near the stables, where no one will see me? All the grooms and stable boys are sleeping at this hour."

She glowered at me, then relented and agreed. "But do not be gone longer than an hour. And whatever you do, stay away from the river stairs!"

We were living in the spacious but dilapidated palace known as

Durham House, which being beside the river Thames, attracted into its gardens the worst sort of dirty thieves and rogues who lived under the bridges. We often saw them creeping near the river stairs, where the barges unloaded provisions and messengers from the royal court brought news.

I assured Doña Elvira that I would stay far from the river, on the opposite side of the palace grounds where the stables were. Once there, I encountered Sebastian, walking along the rope, one careful step at a time, shifting a long pole he held to help him keep his balance. As I watched, he reached the roof and stepped lightly onto it.

I heard the sound of clapping, and saw Prince Henry striding toward the rope, looking upward and applauding Sebastian as he walked. It was hard to believe that the prince was not yet twelve years old at that time, he was so tall and strong-looking. He had none of a boy's clumsiness or shyness, he strode forward like a young guardsman, agile and quick. His round face was open and laughing, his blond hair lifted by the warm wind. He looked so much like Arthur that it pained me to see him, yet in vigor, size and strength he was as unlike his brother as it was possible to imagine. And his voice was twice as loud, and twice as rich and musical, as Arthur's had ever been.

"So ho, Spaniard!" he called out, smiling broadly. "I would see that trick again!"

Sebastian, with a bow, stepped out onto the rope once more and made his way back toward the other end. Before he reached it he suddenly swung himself into a new position, straddling the rope, and then, with one clean, swift movement, he was hanging from the rope by his toes.

The prince insisted that Sebastian show him how the tricks were done, and, throwing off his doublet, climbed up the pole until he reached the rope.

I watched while the prince tried in vain to find his balance, Sebastian patiently guiding him. But all Prince Henry could do was hang precariously from the rope by his knees, and after a short time he gave up, and slid back down the pole, ripping his hose and his linen shirt but grinning with pleasure. When he reached the ground he took a coin from his pocket and tossed it to Sebastian, who tucked the coin into his shirt and proceeded to hang from the rope by his teeth.

At this both Prince Henry and I clapped. I had seen Sebastian perform many times, at my parents' court and since coming to England. Yet he always amazed me.

I said as much to the prince, and added, "You are nearly as daring as he is."

He shrugged, but looked pleased.

"I will do better next time," he said. "I hope you will be there to watch me, and applaud me, as you did your acrobat."

Charmingly said, I thought to myself. The boy has a good wit as well as an agile body—and much daring.

"I would enjoy that," I told him, "but I am leaving very soon, to return to my home in Granada. My mother has sent a ship to fetch me."

The prince, who had been hopping on one foot, put both feet on the ground and appeared very surprised.

"But you can't. My father is going to marry you. I heard him say so."

I opened my mouth but no sound came out. I shook my head.

"No," I finally said, still shaking my head. "Whatever you thought you heard, it cannot be."

"My ears are keen," he insisted, reminding me once more of Arthur, who had made me laugh.

"Such a marriage would be a sin. The sin of incest."

"But I heard him. I know what I heard." He looked at me thoughtfully. Then, a moment later, he glanced up at Sebastian, and, spitting on his hands, began to climb the pole again.

As I walked back through the gardens and into the courtyard of the palace I wondered, could the prince have been right in what he told me? Could my royal father-in-law intend to make me his wife? It was unthinkable. My mother would never allow it. Was that why she was sending the *Reina del Cielo* to rescue me?

That night I could not get to sleep, not even when Doña Elvira brought me a soothing posset to drink and sang me a song that had comforted me when I was a child. I could not stop the worrisome imaginings that crowded into my mind. Why hadn't the ship come? Had it sunk? Had it been delayed by storms?

Or had King Henry, in secret, sent his own ships to capture the *Reina del Cielo* before it reached England, and was I, too, his captive, and soon to be his bride?

I worried over this, but not for very long. Toward the end of June of that year, the Year of Our Lord 1503, a new marriage treaty was signed. I was to marry, not King Henry, but Prince Henry.

We would not marry right away. Not for several years at least, until he reached the age of fourteen or fifteen, which seemed like a very long time in the future. And the Holy Father in Rome would need to grant us the favor of a document called a dispensation, which meant that he would dispense with the laws of the church that prevented a man from marrying his brother's widow.

Yet I trusted that all would go well, and that in two or three years I would be the wife of the prince. Until then I would continue to live in the riverside palace of Durham House, with my household of Spanish servants and under the vigilant eye of Doña Elvira.

And there was another great benefit of my betrothal: I was to receive the generous sum of one hundred pounds every month, to pay my servants and keep us all in royal state.

So this was the reason the *Reina del Cielo* had never arrived in England. It was because my mother and father, in their wisdom, had arranged a new marriage for me, one that would prevent the sin of a marriage to King Henry, who was an old man and who, I was certain, disliked me.

Now there would be no more long nights without sleep, no more threadbare gowns and worn-out chemises. No lack and no fear. Only full larders and storerooms, new gowns and new tapestries and furnishings for the old palace by the river. And in the fullness of time, when the old king died, I, Infanta Catalina, would become Queen of England.

With my betrothal to Prince Henry I was brought into the royal family more fully than before. The Lady Margaret, the king's aged mother, showed such benevolence toward me and was so considerate of me that Doña Elvira grew jealous, and made a sour face whenever she heard the venerated lady's name. She balked at accompanying me when I was invited to Richmond, saying that she knew no English (which was true) and could not converse with any of Lady Margaret's women, and adding testily that no one at the English court showed proper deference to her own rank and dignity.

Since I had grown tired of Doña Elvira's tartness and petulance, I did not insist that she accompany me. Instead I took along Maria de Rojas or one of my other ladies—which only deepened Doña Elvira's ill humor.

Lady Margaret could not have been kinder to me or more solicitous. She looked at me, not with an appraising or critical eye, but as if eager to find all that was best and most promising in me. I basked in her benevolent gaze, and heard her tell me how beautiful my long thick auburn hair was, falling in waves below my waist, how dainty my hands and feet were, how my gray eyes held intelligence and mirth, and how she thought I must sing well and with true pitch, my speaking voice was so resonant and low.

She flattered me—or was it possible that she saw something of her own younger self in me, a girl small in stature but pleasing enough to look at, and with a quickness of mind men thought rare in a girl or woman? Whichever it was, flattering or not, I could not help but feel that for the first time since Arthur's death, I looked forward to my future in England.

I saw little of King Henry, and when I was in his presence, always with many others nearby, he ignored me. He was said to be intent on finding a suitable wife. A wife young enough to give him more sons. Also Doña Elvira told me that she had heard he was not well, and in fact he appeared pale, and often frowned. Whether he was frowning in pain, or in bad temper, I could not tell. Whenever I saw him I could not put out of my mind the alarming thought that he had wanted to make me his wife.

My happiest days were spent hunting with Prince Henry, who was already a good horseman and a daring rider. One afternoon Doña Elvira announced to me that there was a man waiting for me in the stable yard.

"What man?"

"He says Prince Henry sent him."

"Then please tell him I will be glad to receive him."

"He says you must go where he is."

Taken aback, I thought for a moment, while Doña Elvira, her lips pursed in disapproval, stood before me, stolid and silent.

"Then I will do as he asks, since my lord and future husband sends him."

I went out to the stable yard, where a slim, smiling young man with sandy hair under a Flemish cap was waiting with a fine jennet and a small docile pony. Both horses had harnesses decorated with intricate designs worked in gold.

The young man bowed.

"You are sent by Prince Henry?"

He nodded. "I am Paul Van Vrelant, huntsman to the prince—and apprentice harness gilder," he added. "I am learning the craft from my father."

I moved toward the jennet, who shuffled her feet and twitched her long combed tail as I neared her. I have always loved horses. I was enchanted.

"Griselda. I will call you Griselda," I said to her, and reached out to pat her soft nose. She whickered and snuffled. She put me in mind of a beautiful mount my mother had ridden often when I was a child. A long-legged, spirited mare she called Esmeralda. Emerald. I asked mother many times to let me ride Esmeralda, but she said no.

"Esmeralda is a one-woman horse," she told me. "I ride her, and no one else."

I wanted Griselda to be my one-woman horse. I would ride her, and no one else.

"The pony is for Princess Mary," Paul told me. "The prince hopes that you and the princess will ride together."

I nodded, while continuing to pet and stroke my lovely new mount.

"I will send one of my grooms to care for them," Paul went on, but I barely heard him. I was preoccupied with Griselda.

Princess Mary soon made her new pony her favorite. At seven years old she was a daring and spirited rider, like her brother Henry, and her new pony was capable of trotting very briskly beside my much larger Griselda, if I kept Griselda to a walking pace.

Prince Henry's older sister Princess Margaret had just left their father's court for Scotland, where she was to marry the Scottish King James. Mary missed her, and as I too missed my older sisters, we were happy to spend time together in a newfound sisterly bond. Mary was a very pretty child, as I have said, and good-tempered and lighthearted. She chattered endlessly, asking me one question after another as we rode.

I told her about my sisters.

"Juana is lovely to look at and full of passion, Maria is quieter, and steadier. My oldest sister, Isabella, died when I was very near your brother Henry's age. And I had a brother, Juan, who only lived to be nineteen years old."

She grew quiet. "I will have to go away one day just as Margaret has, won't I." She looked up at me, as if wanting me to agree.

"Yes, Mary. I imagine so."

"Will it be far?"

"I don't know. I hope it won't be too far. But I know you will be an obedient girl, and will go wherever you are sent."

After a long silence I heard her say, "But I want to stay here, with you. And my brother." There was a stubbornness in her voice.

"Daughters of kings and queens cannot do whatever they choose. We must do as we are told."

She did not answer, but spurred her pony forward. I heard her call out, as she passed me, "Must we indeed!"

On the day I learned that my beloved mother had died, I felt as though my very soul had been torn out of me.

Of that day, that saddest of all days, I cannot write. I can only remember an old song she sang to me.

> *Ayee ayee! My heart is wrung*
> *I am a lifeless thing*
> *She I loved most, she is gone*
> *I am a stone*
>
> *Only the crying of the wind*
> *Only the tears of the moon*
> *I am alone*

In the midst of my grieving, feeling cold and ill and comfortless, Prince Henry came to me.

He seemed much altered. Not only taller and stronger-looking, but apprehensive. I could see fear in his light blue eyes.

"I must be quick. My father has set a watch on me—the guardsmen—I cannot stay long." He looked around and behind him, then went on.

"Catherine, he orders me to sign a new paper saying I will no longer be betrothed to you. You must know this is not of my choosing. It is being forced upon me."

"But why?" was all I could say, in my bewilderment.

He shook his head, and reached for my hands.

"He no longer needs the might of Spain. And since your mother's death—"

"There is no might left," I said, interrupting him. "Yes. I understand."

He pressed my small hands in his much larger ones.

"I must go, or—"

"Go then," I told him. "And may the Lord protect us both."

After he had gone, I pondered what had happened. I had been expecting to marry Prince Henry when he reached his fourteenth birthday, or soon afterward. That birthday was at hand. Yet with my mother's passing, all had changed. Now the prince would marry someone else—and all because royal marriages were, as everyone understood, marriages between thrones and realms, not men and women. And my mother's throne, and the force and power of her kingdom of Castile, had been inherited by my sister Juana.

"It is said that Prince Henry will marry one of Queen Juana's daughters," I was told by an envoy from my father's court. "Most likely he will choose Princess Eleanor. And your father King Ferdinand is contemplating marriage to a French princess."

I, Catherine, was still Princess Dowager of England, yet I was no longer of any importance—and never would be of any importance, unless my father arranged another marriage for me. And though I wrote him long, pleading letters, telling him how wretched I was, and how I could no longer pay my household servants or officers or even (this saddened me terribly) manage to pay my purveyor to buy oats for Griselda—King Henry having stopped sending me my much-needed hundred pounds every month—he did not reply.

Months went by. I prayed. I fasted, hoping for divine aid. I grew thin and often felt ill. When I was strong enough, I rode Griselda, who was also thin and seemed to lack her usual speed and stamina. Princess Mary was no longer allowed to go riding with me. So I rode alone, even when it rained and the wind was cold.

How I longed, in those bitter hours, for the sun and heat of Spain! Even for the dry, parched Estremadura, where every drop of water was precious and no crops or flowers would grow.

My servants were leaving me, complaining that Doña Elvira shouted at them and bullied them, and that they had too little to eat.

In desperation I went to moneylenders, who demanded that I pawn my jewels. But my jewels, alas! were not truly mine. They were part of my dowry, and my dowry was in dispute.

One evening, after I had retired for the night, my stomach growling and my head aching, I heard a shriek coming from the chamber next to mine. My maid of honor Maria de Rojas, sleeping on a pallet bed beside me, heard it too.

We hurried into the next room. There was Doña Elvira by the hearth, a pile of letters on a table in front of her, crying out and beating at the skirt of her gown, which had caught fire. Maria snatched up a blanket and smothered the flames, making us all cough from the smoke.

Doña Elvira had been burning the letters. Scraps of charred paper were scattered at the edges of the fire, among the ashes.

I snatched up two of the letters from the pile in front of Doña Elvira and quickly realized that they were letters I had written to my father. Letters I believed had been sent months earlier by courier or with ship captains bound for Spanish ports. She had assured me again and again that every word I wrote to my father had been delivered.

She had been deceiving me! Betraying me! Now I knew why he had never responded, or sent me money, or even acknowledged my distress!

"Liar!" I shouted. "Deceiver!" And I slapped Doña Elvira as hard as I could, until her sagging cheeks were red.

"How dare you betray me, when you knew I loved you and trusted you!"

In my fury I felt dizzy, but only for a moment.

"I hope you burn in hell for what you have done!" I shouted, but my voice was not as loud as it had been, and I felt the sting of tears.

Hoping to steady me, Maria de Rojas took my thin arm, but I angrily yanked it away.

"Whip the traitor! Torture her!" I cried again and again. "Do you hear me?"

I looked around, expecting to see Count de Cabra and my guardsmen, or at least the nearest of my grooms and valets, come rushing into the room. Then I remembered: Count de Cabra had left my service, to join the household of my sister Juana, and a number of the soldiers had gone with him. Who was there to protect me?

I shivered, suddenly afraid. Almost in the same moment, I recovered, and straightened my spine and lifted my head. I was the daughter of the great Queen Isabella. I was in no danger.

But Doña Elvira had seen my weakness—and the tears that I tried to keep from falling. She did not cower, or submit. Instead she squared her shoulders and glared at me.

"You foolish, foolish girl! You stupid fool! No one will obey you. Shout all you like! Look around you. How many servants do you see? Ten? Twenty? Once there were sixty. Soon there will be only a handful."

"Because you drove them away, with your demands and threats!"

"No! Because your mother died, and no one wants you anymore." She paused for breath. "You are nothing, less than nothing. You belong to King Henry. He can do what he likes with you. But even he won't marry you now!"

Her face had turned a vivid purplish red. I thought she might collapse. Instead she reached for a goblet and, at a single gulp, drank what was in it.

I was aware that Maria de Rojas had slipped out of the room and into the corridor beyond. I felt my anger rising once more.

"How dare you say such things to me! I will have you hanged by your heels and flogged, like a dog, until you cry for mercy!"

But Doña Elvira only laughed.

"Then you will have to have Don Fuensalida flogged as well, and Dr. de Puebla, and every other Spaniard at King Henry's court. For they all say the same thing! That you are nothing. A worm, a spot of dust. A gob of spit in the rushes!"

"Leave me," I said in quiet fury. "Leave this place."

And just then, as if in answer to my command, my steward

entered the room, with half a dozen others, among them my aged doorkeeper, two kitchen boys and several sturdy gardeners, all of them out of breath. Maria de Rojas was with them, she had evidently called for help and they were the first to arrive.

The men rushed to seize Doña Elvira, who swore and struggled. I did not look at her as she was dragged from the room, but I could still hear her shouting as she was taken down the corridor.

"You are cursed! You killed Doña Aldonza, you killed Prince Arthur! You killed the queen's baby! You were cursed the day your mother saw you in your wedding dress!"

The sounds of her outburst thinned until they became one long wail, and I, trembling and weeping, sank into Maria de Rojas's waiting arms.

I had lost my mother, my promised future husband, and my duenna, all within a very short space of time. My household was in chaos now that Doña Elvira was no longer there to keep order. I had sold two gold bracelets to buy provisions for my remaining servants, but thieves had broken into the storerooms and larders of Durham House and much had been taken.

I wrote to my father, begging him to send me at least a small allowance, and asking that he would pay the unpaid portion of my dowry—since I knew that King Henry resented the debt. I entrusted my letter to my almoner Master Reveles, feeling certain that he would not deceive me as Doña Elvira had. He was soon to leave on a journey to my father's kingdom of Aragon, and he promised me that he would return with a response as soon as he could. In the meantime, there was little I could do to improve my situation.

Then I had what I thought was a stroke of good fortune. Good fortune for me, that is. My favorite sister Juana and her husband Philip, Duke of Burgundy, had been caught in a violent storm and their ship had been wrecked, along with many others in their flotilla, on the English coast. They were on their way to King Henry's court.

My hopes rose. Juana would surely rescue me from my needy, friendless state. She had always been the most active and energetic of my sisters, quick to do whatever she could when needed, agile of mind and tongue. I could hardly wait to see her.

But when we met, at Durham House, I was shocked to see the change in her. When I had last seen her, nine years earlier, she had been saying goodbye, leaving Granada to travel to Flanders, to begin her new married life. She had been full of excitement and hope, for her future husband Philip was said to be exceptionally good-looking and strong, highborn and wealthy, his bloodline lofty and worthy of our own as daughters of King Ferdinand and Queen Isabella. I remembered how spirited she had been on the day she left, promising to return as soon as she could, promising to keep us all in her prayers.

Yet as I looked at her on that raw January morning at Durham House, she seemed shattered, fragile, as though unable to recover from some mighty blow or shock. It was not easy to believe that my sister was now Juana, Queen of Castile, our mother's heir. Though as we talked, I thought I glimpsed in her, from time to time, something of our mother's regal dignity.

Juana had her young son Charles with her, a hefty blond square-faced boy who regarded me gravely when I smiled down at him. Juana told me that he was not yet seven years old.

"Do you like to ride?" I asked him. He nodded. "If only Princess Mary were here, the two of you could ride her pony."

"I have my own horses," the boy told me. He seemed self-possessed, his gaze unflinching.

"Of course you do. But it is always a pleasure to ride with a companion, and the princess is good company."

To this the young prince said nothing, but merely looked up at his mother.

"He has heard it said that the princess may become his wife one day," Juana told me when Charles was taken away by one of his nursemaids.

"Is he always so solemn?"

She nodded, then suddenly burst into tears. Tears that soon turned to sobs, then to a violent shaking that racked her whole body.

I watched in alarm, not knowing what to do or say.

I called her name. I asked her if I ought to send for my physician. But she shook her head, with such vehemence that I hesitated, once again feeling alarmed.

Finally her spasms seemed to grow less, and she shrank into herself, exhausted. I called for wine, and when it was brought, Juana drank thirstily. After a time she spoke.

"I smelled it, you see," I heard her say, her voice low, as if coming from a long distance away. "I smelled the storm. It was night, only there were no stars, no wind. Only the storm-scent, and then the horses were whinnying and stamping. The waves began to rise, and the ship rocked, and then we heard it, the roaring of the wind."

Her eyes widened, and her face grew pale at the memory of what she was describing. She seemed to have forgotten I was there with her.

"There were so many of us, you see. Dozens of ships, thousands of soldiers. And the great guns, so terrifying, the noise of the great guns."

She paused, then went on.

"But the guns could do nothing against the wind, and the huge crashing waves. All that night it went on, and the next day and the next night. We couldn't sleep, we knew we were going to die. We did die—"

"No, Juana, no. You are here, and alive. You did not die."

"Oh yes! We did. So many did. So many bodies—"

Horrified by what I was hearing, I thought she would begin to cry and shake once again. Instead she calmly folded her hands in her lap and began repeating a prayer. Then the words of the prayer turned to a groaning noise, and I thought, what has become of my sister?

"It was the ship. It was in pain. I heard it moan, calling out in pain. I knew it would die, just like the rest of us." She lifted her face, and looked at me. Suddenly she smiled.

"I wanted him to die, Catalina. He is cruel to me. The Lord is punishing him, I thought." Once again she began to quiver. She got up and paced around the room.

"Please, Juana, let me summon my physician."

She glared at me. I was frightened. She was my older sister. She had to be obeyed. I hesitated.

"Listen! Watch! The torches are out. The sea devours them—" She ran into a corner of the room and sank down onto the floor, making herself as small as possible. "The mast—watch out for the mast—the fire—the rocks—" She made gulping sounds.

She is lost, I thought. Not to the sea, but to the fancies in her mind. The realization made me weep.

I went over to where she cowered against the wall and tried to help her to her feet. She laughed. She was jubilant.

"I loved it all, you see. All the noise, all the dying—"

Then, all at once, she was quiet. The look on her face changed. She blinked rapidly, as if regaining her bearings. I backed away. She stood up, walked gracefully to the hearth, then turned toward me, composed and serene.

"My daughter Eleanor will not be betrothed to Prince Henry, whatever you may have heard," she told me. "I have a better match in mind for her, with the King of Portugal's oldest son. Catalina! Why do you weep, Catalina? If Eleanor is matched to Prince Manuel, then you can become betrothed to Prince Henry once again, do you not understand that? Just as our mother meant you to be."

It was as if she had become someone else entirely. As if she had been possessed, then returned to herself once more. Only this self was not a Juana I recognized.

I had hoped that Juana would be the loving sister I remembered, who would bring me back from the desolation I felt. Instead, having seen the troubling woman she had become, I felt more lost and alone than ever.

Not long afterward I was told that my sister and her husband had quarreled, loudly and bitterly, and in the presence of King Henry and his courtiers, and that she had left London, taking her son with her.

I did not see her again.

But I did see Duke Philip. I was summoned to Richmond, and watched with many others of the court as the duke invested Prince Henry with the Order of the Golden Fleece. He did not have the look of a man who had just survived a harrowing storm at sea. He looked like a man freed of a vexatious burden. And he was surrounded by a cluster of young girls, among them my half-sister Maria Juana.

5

I WAS BEGINNING TO THINK THAT KING HENRY WOULD NEVER LET me leave England.

He kept me shut away at Durham House, year after year, while I grew older and (I felt certain) less desirable. When I looked in my pier glass I saw an unhappy girl who should already have been married and given her husband three or four children. A sad, wistful girl. I tried not to think about what Doña Elvira had told me in anger: that I was cursed.

My new maid of honor Maria de Salinas, as loyal and encouraging as Doña Elvira had been domineering and critical, told me that I was far from being old and that when I smiled, I was lovely to look at. She was a beauty herself, and only a year younger than I was. She did not regard herself as undesirable, and she expected to be married before long, just as soon as her sister Inez found the right husband for her.

My new young confessor, Fray Diego Fernandez, told me I must not look at myself in the pier glass at all.

"Vanity, vanity, all is vanity!" he cried when he heard me admit that I had been looking at my reflection. "Smash the glass, mortify the flesh! Keep vigil against your own self-praise, Infanta Catalina! Else your heavenly Father will reject you, and you will be damned for eternity!"

Fray Diego reprimanded me, but he also praised me for my learning. I had been tutored in Latin and could read the writings of St. Jerome and St. Augustine and Pope Gregory, as well as the Roman historians and the least impure of the poets. I had pleased my mother by reading to her from the lives of the saints—in Latin. She prided herself on being able to understand at least some of what I read, having made an effort to learn, as an adult, the language of the church and the mass.

She was envious of my learning, never having been tutored herself as a child. Yet envious or not, she was very proud of me, and encouraged me to compose verses myself, though I did not imagine that they had value. I knew that they were only the raw and stumbling efforts of a novice. Still, I was pleased when she praised and encouraged me, and with her encouragement, wrote more.

I needed such heartening just then, and was fortunate in that Maria de Salinas and Fray Diego helped to raise my low spirits. But it was Prince Henry who did the most to keep me from despair.

Oddly enough, he did this by sharing with me his own anger and his conviction that his father the king was losing his wits.

"He's mad, I tell you, Catherine! Utterly mad!" The prince paced up and down on the grass beside his own private tiltyard at Richmond, the only place King Henry allowed him to go for exercise. As he paced he ran his large hands through his curling reddish-blond hair in exasperation. He was rosy-cheeked and sweating, he had triumphed over every challenger he faced in the lists. At sixteen he was already the tallest man at his father's court, and the strongest.

"He keeps me caged like a dog, he won't let me out. I sleep under guard, in a room next to his bedchamber. He listens through the wall. I can hear him coughing. He spies on me day and night.

The only exercise I am allowed is to come to this park, through a secret palace door. He keeps the key to the door. He thinks he has the only one."

"Is there another key?" I asked.

"Paul has one. That is how he brought you here, by means of that second key. It opens the door and also a gate—a gate my father does not know exists."

Prince Henry's huntsman and harness gilder, Paul Van Vrelant, had come to me earlier that afternoon to ask me courteously to accompany him. I did not hesitate. He brought me along quiet, seldom-used paths to the prince's small hunting park, with its woods and tiltyard, and led me in through a gate concealed by a screen of trees.

"He keeps me locked away here at Richmond, and you, Catherine, are imprisoned at Durham House," Prince Henry was saying.

I nodded. "I am not allowed much liberty. If only he would let me return to my father's court!" As I spoke the prince was shaking his head in exasperation. "Perhaps in another year or two—"

"No!" he shouted. "Another year or two makes no difference at all to a madman! Don't you see, Catherine, we are both being made to suffer, because he has taken leave of his senses! Can you not send word to your sister Queen Juana, and her husband, and ask for their help?"

His words startled me.

"Then you have not heard—" I began.

"Heard what?"

"What has happened to poor Juana."

The prince stopped pacing, and came nearer to me. "I am not allowed to know anything of what is going on outside the palace."

I sighed and squared my shoulders. "Juana is living at my father's court. She is—an invalid. She is not capable of caring for herself."

His small eyes grew wide with astonishment.

"Why not?"

"Because she is no longer in possession of herself. She is as simple, as confused, as a child. A dangerous child. She is the victim of strange fancies."

"She is possessed by a demon, you mean," said the prince, and I saw a shudder pass through his strong young frame.

I told him what I had seen and heard from others about my sister. How she became violently angry at her husband, and at my maid of honor Maria Juana, who had become his mistress, and tried to stab Maria Juana with a pair of sharp scissors. How her husband Philip had died—some said by poison—and how, after his death, my sister had refused to attend his funeral mass and continued to treat him as though he were alive—even though he was lying in his coffin.

Prince Henry listened, horrified yet fascinated, as I relayed what my father's envoy Don Gutierre Gomez de Fuensalida had confided to me.

"He said that Juana believed that she had poisoned Philip. She told her confessor that she was already in hell, but that if she nursed Philip back to health, she might be released from her torment."

"So she refused to let him be buried," was Prince Henry's astonished comment. "By all that's holy, what sacrilege!"

"Sacrilege or not, she kept his coffin with her, everywhere she and her unfortunate son Charles went. She kept watch beside the body. She never slept at all. She brought the dead Philip his favorite food, and imagined that he ate it. She covered him with blankets when it was cold, and fanned his lifeless face when the sun was hot.

"When she arrived in Granada, our father was already there, waiting. Don Fuensalida says that Juana now lives in her own apartments in the palace, and never leaves them. She is queen, but he rules in her place."

Prince Henry was thoughtful for a time.

"If your sister cannot help us, and your father will not—then we must endure," he said at last.

The smile we exchanged then established a bond between us.

"Whatever lies I am told, however badly I am treated—" I began.

"Whatever he may do to me—" the prince interrupted.

"We will hold fast."

The harness gilder brought Prince Henry his horse, and he mounted and returned to the tiltyard, riding up and down the lists until rain started to fall, and both horse and rider were mud-splattered and tired, and Paul Van Vrelant accompanied me back to Durham House.

We held fast, Prince Henry and I, through another year and more of the king's harsh treatment. It grew worse. Cruel words and shouted accusations gave way to fierce rages and, before long, to blows. When the king imagined that Princess Mary—who was not yet twelve years old—was in bed with a serving boy he beat her and kicked her until she bled. And when Prince Henry tried to defend his sister, the king attacked him with a knife—and would have killed him, as the prince told me, were it not for his own greater strength and agility.

"He hates me. He wants me dead," the prince insisted. "He imagines that I am raising a rebellion against him. He is so frightened of me—and my imaginary army of rebels—that he keeps his crown on a pillow right next to his bed, and his jewels and treasure in heavy chests underneath the bed. His servants say he never sleeps at all, but watches over his crown and his treasure chests, all night long.

"He has given orders to his physicians that when he dies, his death is to be kept secret. He made every member of his household swear to keep silent about it. He knows that once the truth becomes known, everything he owns will be stolen."

The prince threw up his hands. "I tell you, Catherine, I cannot endure this madhouse much longer!"

Nor did he need to endure it. At last, in the spring of the Year of Our Lord 1509, King Henry quietly expired—so quietly that for several days no one but his most trusted servants knew it.

We knew that he was ill, there were reports that his physicians were going into his bedchamber and coming out again. We did not doubt that he was alive, however, as food was taken in to him and empty platters brought out. But there was no disguising the stench that seeped from the royal bedchamber: it was the stench of the death-rot. And so it was that, in the end, the announcement was made.

His Majesty King Henry the Seventh was dead. His Majesty King Henry the Eighth was king. May the Lord preserve him!

Amid the shouts of rejoicing and well wishes another announcement was made. That the new king, of his goodness, was graciously pleased to take unto himself as his bride the Lady Catherine, Dowager Princess of Wales, England's next queen.

Oh to breathe again the sweet, fragrant air of those heady days, the days of our freedom—and of our wedding!

All that spring, as the lilies and roses bloomed in the royal gardens and the flowering trees sent down showers of pink and white blossoms, we rejoiced. Outwardly, to be sure, we wore for a time the black vestments of mourning. But beneath those somber garments our hearts beat with excitement, and we all gave vent to our inner joy.

No one celebrated our deliverance with greater energy and zest than the new king, who was soon to be my husband.

Like a young bull suddenly released into a wide pasture, with no restraints and nothing to impede his rampaging vitality, King Henry charged headlong into his new reign.

The corridors of Greenwich palace rang with boisterous shouts and running feet. Everywhere the king went, it seemed, he left cheerful disorderliness behind. Surrounded by a dozen of his favorite companions, he visited me in my new apartments, interrupting me in the midst of whatever I was doing and calling for his musicians to play us a lively tune. To my delight, he would sweep me up and lead me in a dance, all but lifting me off the ground, perspiring heavily as he capered and jumped and shouting to the others to dance with my maids of honor. Then as swiftly and suddenly as he had arrived, he was gone, taking his companions with him, the sounds of the sackbuts and viols and drums still lingering on the air.

I was caught up in his noisy frolics. He insisted that I come along when he went plunging and crashing through the hunting park, or riding in the royal barge—often taking a turn at the oars himself—or picnicking in the open air, throwing scraps to his dogs and grinning broadly to watch them leap up yelping to catch them.

I was glad to see him as he was then, exuberant and full of vigor. Yet he seemed unable to stop, to rest. He danced until his muscles ached. He sang with his chamber gentlemen until his voice was raw. And though some said he was tireless, I saw how, after many strenuous hours in the tiltyard, he would all at once become pale and start to pant, and then, just as suddenly, empty his stomach into the nearest hedge.

His spasms of illness soon passed, and before long he would be capering vigorously once again, and showing no signs of numbness or pallor. I reminded myself that he was still very young, only seventeen years old in that spring when he became king, and that all his boisterousness and clamor was the natural behavior of a royal boy—a boy who had been kept too long in unnatural restraint.

Yet there were times when I wished I did not feel so much older, so much more a mistress of my impulses and my emotions. I reminded myself that I was indeed older than Henry by five years and more. I made an attempt to join him in his exuberant pastimes. Henry was an excellent lutenist, and I was a passable one; we were able to enjoy playing duets. When he and his chamber gentlemen dressed in Lincoln green and declared themselves to be Robin Hood and his band of outlaws, I put on my Moorish waistcoat and silken pantaloons and velvet slippers with turned-up toes and played at being an Arab slave girl.

Yet even when I felt best able to subdue my will and desires to his, as I had always been taught to do, for a wife must subordinate her will to her husband's, I had the constant feeling that I was indulging him, and that he was aware of it. And as the day of our wedding drew closer, this feeling did not decrease.

———

My wedding to Henry was nothing like my wedding to Arthur had been, so many years earlier. There was no grand cathedral, no trumpets to play a fanfare, no great crowd to witness our union and hear us repeat our vows.

It was Henry's wish that we marry quietly, in a small chapel at Greenwich, and I was more than content with his choice.

Many of the women in my new, greatly enlarged royal household were discontented when they heard there was to be no magnificent ceremony. But one among them was not only understanding, but warmly sympathetic: my lady-in-waiting Elizabeth Boleyn.

She was slender and graceful, with an attractive face that was just beginning to show the lines of age. Her brown hair was lightly streaked with gray, but her expression was youthful, and—this I found most remarkable—she had no hint of hauteur, though she belonged to the highest nobility, the Howard family. She was respectful to me, as indeed she should have been, yet she seemed to sense when I was unsure of myself in my new role as King Henry's future wife and was quick to offer whatever help I appeared to need.

I was at a loss to decide what gown to wear for my wedding, and asked her for her opinion.

She was thoughtful, and took her time replying.

"Has the king not said what he would like you to wear, Your Majesty?"

I shook my head. "He is concerned only about the coronation ceremony, and what we will wear when we are crowned. To him, our wedding matters far less."

Henry had decreed that his coronation would take place only a few days after our wedding, and that I too would be crowned on that day.

"And Your Majesty would not wish to wear the gown you wore when you were married to Prince Arthur, even if it could be altered. The silk was of very fine quality, as I remember," she added. "And the beautiful veil—"

"I had that gown burned," I said bluntly. "It brought me bad luck."

"Then it is to be hoped that a new gown will alter your fortunes, and that Your Majesty's wedding to King Henry will be enduring and fruitful. Now, as to the shape and stuffs of the new gown—"

"It must be of Bruges satin, white, with an underskirt of gold," I told her. "That much I have decided."

"With a wide, round skirt or a more narrow one, that drapes like a waterfall?"

"More narrow, I think."

"And the sleeves? What of the sleeves?"

We went on, back and forth, discussing the cut of the sleeves, the shape of the bodice, even the weight of the satin and which jewels I should wear, from among those Henry had given me. (He had been lavish with his gifts; since his father's death he reveled in dispensing the late king's abundant treasure.) Soon we had made together the decision I had found it so difficult to make on my own. I summoned my dressmaker and the work of cutting and stitching and fitting began.

Over the following weeks, while both my wedding gown and my coronation garments were prepared, I often asked Elizabeth Boleyn to keep me company. She told me of her family, and of her own wedding years earlier to Thomas Boleyn, who though he was not of noble birth did come from a wealthy merchant family with lands in Norfolk and Kent.

I asked her to tell me more about him, less out of genuine interest than because I was tired of standing where I was, surrounded by seamstresses who were slowly and painstakingly marking the hem of my gold underskirt.

"Thomas is an exceptional man," she began. "He seems to do twice as much in a day as anyone else. He has a quick mind and never seems to tire, or even to need to sleep."

She paused as the seamstresses shifted their positions.

"He took pride in his studies when he was a boy. His father sent him to study at Oxford, where we will send our son George when he is older. He is able to converse in Latin with officials and clerics from other realms, which fits him well to serve as a royal envoy.

And he speaks the French tongue—the tongue of the north of France, that is. The speech of the south, the Languedoc, he says is not worth learning."

This made me smile, though I said nothing. I was well aware that the English both feared and hated the French, and that the Languedoc was looked on as an unimportant, backward region, quaint and odd.

"And what of our Castilian tongue? Is he master of that also?"

"I shall have to ask him. I have never heard him speak it."

"Is he courtly?" I asked. "Does he dance well?"

"He does his best, Your Majesty," she answered, and I detected both loyalty to her husband and fondness in her tone. "My daughters are very good dancers," she hastened to add, "especially my younger one, little Nan. Her dancing master says she is very quick to learn and graceful."

She showed me miniatures of her children.

"This is Mary, my older daughter. She is not yet nine." There was pride in her voice as she handed me one of the miniatures, and I could see why. With her delicate, pleasing features and engaging smile, Mary showed promise of becoming a beauty.

"This is Nan," she went on, handing me another miniature with a noticeable scratch across it. The portrait showed an unsmiling girl quite unlike her sister, with dark hair and eyes and sallow skin.

"This one is the graceful dancer," I said. Elizabeth nodded.

I studied the miniature, unsure what more to say. "How unfortunate that the portrait has been marred."

I heard my lady-in-waiting sigh. "She can be obdurate," she began. "Quite defiant, in fact. The likeness displeased her. She took a sharp pin and tried to destroy it."

Hearing this I was reminded of my beautiful sister Juana, who was never satisfied with her portraits and who, according to Doña Elvira, had once thrown a goblet of wine at an Italian painter as he was sketching her.

Yet I did not say this to Elizabeth Boleyn.

"My confessor would say that defiant girls not only disobey their parents, they disobey their Maker," I remarked instead.

"And this is George."

"Your son who will study well, like his father." The miniature revealed a round-cheeked, bright-eyed young boy who resembled his sister Nan.

"A fine family," I said, and handed the last of the portraits back, adding, "I trust that your daughters will join my household when they are older."

But Elizabeth was quick to contradict me.

"Oh, we intend to send them to Terveuren, to join the household of the Archduchess Margaret."

At this I merely nodded and made some approving comment. The archduchess was known for welcoming the children of noble families to her court, and providing an exceptionally cultivated environment in which they could refine their manners and learn to be at ease among their peers from a variety of lands. I knew that she was building a new palace at Mechelen, said to be in a style that was a departure from tradition and was causing much comment—and no little criticism.

I wondered whether my lady-in-waiting was aware that the Archduchess Margaret had been my sister-in-law, married to my brother Juan. Married for only a few months, to be sure, then widowed when my brother died. Hearing of her reminded me of my own brief marriage to Prince Arthur. And of my nephew Charles, Juana's son, the solemn, stocky little boy who had been so silent during my sister's visit to England three years earlier. I knew that Charles was living at Terveuren, as Archduchess Margaret had been made regent for his lands. It was her responsibility to administer his territories until he came of age.

As the day of my wedding came closer, I became less and less able to think or talk of such matters and gave all my thought and attention to the momentous change I was about to undergo. I was about to marry King Henry, and to become England's queen.

It was all over so quickly, it seemed almost furtive. We repeated our vows, we were blessed, my gold wedding band was put on my finger, prayers were said—and then, in far less time than it had taken for me to be dressed in my gown of Bruges satin with its lovely gold underskirt, we were married.

We were married early in the morning, with only a few witnesses present. And in the afternoon, my husband went hunting.

That night he came to our bed, gleeful and affectionate and full of energy, flung off his clothes and bore down on me again and again with the full weight of his huge athlete's body—a body that felt three times my size. I suffered under the crushing, choking weight of him and endured the pain between my legs for as long as I could without crying out. We Spanish women bear pain well, or so I had always believed. But in the end the sharp, unendurable pain overcame me, and I could not help myself. I screamed.

"No more! Have mercy, no more!" I heard myself shout.

Henry immediately heaved his body off mine, looking very surprised and puzzled.

I lay where I was, panting, trying to catch my breath, close to tears from hurting so much. All I wanted, all I could think of, was how much I needed the pain to stop. Gradually I began to recover my breath, and the hurt began to grow less.

"Paul told me it might be like this," my new husband said as he put on the nightshirt that had been laid out for him. "That you might complain. None of the others ever have."

"What others?"

"The girls of the Maidens' Bower. The ones I take my pleasure with, when we are at Greenwich. The ones Paul sends there."

"Your huntsman, your harness gilder, Paul Van Vrelant?"

Henry sat down on the bed, grinning. "The same. I have made him a gentleman of my bedchamber. I may appoint him lord of misrule, if he agrees."

My body hurt, my mind reeled with unwanted thoughts, unwanted images. That kings had mistresses I knew only too well. But Henry, who had told me so often how he had been kept caged, confined, spied on by his father—had he been far more worldly than I realized?

I thought of my mother, who had endured my father's infidelities for years. What would she tell me now? I needed her answer. I closed my eyes, and imagined her, the last time I saw her, in the Court of Myrtles, in the gardens of the Alhambra. I heard the fountains, I smelled the sweet perfume of the jasmine. I saw her smile. And then I knew what she would say. She would tell me to remember that I was her brave daughter, Infanta Catalina, and to do my duty. Leave the transgressions of others to God and their confessors, she would say. Forgive them, and forgive their companions in wickedness.

The image faded. I opened my eyes. I looked over at my husband, my friend with whom I had once, amid great difficulties, exchanged a pledge of enduring trust. My king. The man who would be the father of my children. I wanted to tell him all that was in my thoughts as I lay there, aching and in need of comfort.

But he had fallen asleep, still grinning, his breath coming and going with a whistling sound. So I prayed for forgiveness—though what I had to be forgiven for, I could not have said. And so all passed in silence and sleep.

6

I SET ABOUT TO LEARN WHAT I COULD ABOUT BEING A WIFE. ABOUT the pain of joining with my husband in hopes of conceiving a child, and what unguents and salves could ease that pain. I needed to know what I imagined the girls of the Maidens' Bower must surely know: how to give my husband pleasure yet spare myself the agony I had endured on my wedding night.

I looked on this as a challenge, and I was determined to meet the challenge and overcome it.

Yet I felt certain that if I asked either my physician, or his apothecary, or my confessor for help they would all tell me the same thing—that pain is the lot of all women, that it is Eve's curse. I must expect to conceive children in misery, they would say, and bear them with much suffering. Yet surely a merciful God would not allow this, I told myself. Not if the suffering was so great that there might be no children at all, or that the woman might suffocate, as I feared could happen to me.

I decided to ask Lady Margaret for her advice, as she had shown me much attention and concern in the past. Had my mother been alive, she and Lady Margaret would not have been far apart in age.

As I hoped, she received me graciously and with a bow that reminded me I was now queen. She had grown thin, her face more deeply wrinkled than when I had seen her last. Strands of white hair spilled out from under her black headdress. But her eyes seemed undimmed, and her wits as sharp as ever, and when she spoke her words were carefully chosen. I asked her to send her serving women away, then explained why I had come to see her.

She did not answer me right away, but reached out to pat my hand. It was such a motherly gesture that all my dignity crumpled, and tears came into my eyes. I wiped them away at once, and turned my face away as well—but I did not move my hand.

"Poor girl," she murmured. "Poor girl. You have no one to help you through all this great change in your life. There is no Doña Elvira to help you and defend you anymore."

I nodded.

"And I assume that you never had this pain, or felt this crushing weight on top of you, when you were married to Prince Arthur."

"No," was all I said—and all I needed to say.

"Dear Arthur was such a frail boy," she began. "So very unfit to be a king—or a husband. But then, you have not come to me to talk about Arthur, but about your urgent need at this moment.

"First, as to the lot of Eve, the lot of all women because of Eve's sin. We women must endure sorrow and pain, yes—but the Scriptures say nothing about how much sorrow, or how much pain. Nowhere is it written, I believe, that we must allow our very lives to be in peril. That is not pain, that is sacrifice, which is another sort of curse altogether.

"Besides," she went on, "from what you tell me I suspect it is my grandson your husband who needs the help, not you. He needs to be made to realize that he has married a small and delicate woman, and that if he smothers her, there will be no heir to his throne!"

She laughed then, her laughter joyous, not a cackle of age but a youthful peal of merriment that made me think of Arthur. I felt a surge of hope. I smiled.

"I will speak to Henry," she assured me. "And until I do—" She left me to go into an antechamber. In a moment she returned, carrying a small earthenware pot, which she handed to me.

"This balm has eased many a pain of my own," she told me. "I hope it will ease yours."

And it did.

Much heartened by the Lady Margaret's assurances and advice, I set about once again to learn what I needed to know. How to join our bodies in ways that did not leave me gasping and hurting.

It astonishes me now to look back on that time, and to admit to myself how little I knew of love and lovemaking, how I had been kept in a state of protected innocence, sheltered from the ways of the world and in particular, the ways of love. At my parents' court, men and women were kept separate from one another, they did not even eat together at the great court feasts. Men expected women to serve their needs and desires, not to understand or question them.

As Doña Elvira had once explained to me, men could not allow themselves to love their wives, for as everyone knew, a great many wives died from the rigors of giving birth, or from the fevers that attacked them soon afterward. To survive childbearing was a feat of endurance. Men expected to lose their wives and to remarry, often three or four times. And with that expectation, they withheld their love—although the best of them, she assured me, showed a knightly courtesy toward all wellborn women. They reserved the pleasures of love for their mistresses.

As I have said, I sought to find out what I needed to know, confident that I had Lady Margaret's support and help.

I read the Roman poet Ovid who wrote on the art of love (a book Fray Diego would have condemned as perilous to my salvation) and also the bawdy stories of the Spaniard who called himself the archpriest. I saw it as my duty to read these works, not because I sought to inflame my lust, lust being one of the seven deadly sins, but because I knew it to be my duty to bear sons. My one and only duty, as my father had once told me. And before I had read very far, I found an answer to my dilemma.

There were many ways of making love, I learned. Gentler and less wounding ways than I had experienced with Henry. I am happy to write that my husband was not too proud to learn them, especially since he discovered that his pleasure was increased. And that he was not too proud to heed the advice of Lady Margaret as well. By the time we set out on our summer progress that August, I was feeling ill each morning and the seamstresses had to alter my gowns, as I was putting on weight. I was all but certain that I was carrying Henry's child. Our first son. England's future king.

I learned many things that summer and fall, as I waited for our son to be born. I deepened what knowledge I had of the English countryside—of its forests, of which trees are best suited for lighting fires, and which winds are most likely to bring rain. I was too ill, most mornings, to hunt with my falcons, but by afternoon I was often able to walk in the fields, or watch the others fill their game bags or gather mushrooms. I remember an old man cautioning me that I must never eat any mushrooms that have grown beneath an oak, and I took this to heart. I was eager to protect not only myself but my child from every harm.

Everything that harvest season gave me pleasure, as all that I did reflected the joy of my condition. Yes, joy—for even though my stomach was often in distress, and I could feel my body growing heavy, my spirits were high and I lived in a daze of happy expectation. Henry too seemed content, not only with the success of each day's hunt but with the pleasure he took in riding or tramping through the yellowing grass, whistling as he went. He loved the birdsong. His fine ear for music helped him to tell by their songs alone which birds were in the higher, hidden branches of the trees, and from time to time he tried to teach me this art as well.

I must admit that one reason I enjoyed our progress that autumn was that it kept Henry away from Greenwich, and the Maidens'

Bower. To be sure, Paul Van Vrelant was with us, both as my husband's chamber gentleman and as a valued adviser on the hunt. (He had put aside the craft of harness gilding.) I hoped that he had no other role, though I could not be certain of that. It would have been easy enough for Paul to bring into our large traveling party a brace of maidens, kept in a special tent or housed in a nearby country inn, waiting for the king to visit them. I had no wish to discover that this might be true, and so I told myself that during our progress, Henry's attentions were devoted to me—and to each day's sport.

When we returned to Richmond at the end of our two months in the country, I summoned midwives who felt my belly and confirmed what I was certain of: that I was carrying a living child, a child that had quickened in my womb. The entire court was informed, and the royal nursery prepared.

The elaborately carved and gilded cradle that had held first Arthur, then Henry when they were babies was brought from where it had been stored and lined with crimson cloth of gold. Down-filled counterpanes embroidered with the royal arms were swiftly sewn to enhance the cradle, along with swaddling bands which would enfold the infant prince. The birth chamber where I would be delivered was cleaned and put in order, the bed made up with fresh linen sheets and bearing panes, and beside the bed a heavy chair was put in place—the dread groaning chair where I would sit, legs spread, gripping the armrests, while I endured the pains of my labor and the midwives did their work.

The sight of the groaning chair made me tremble with fear. Beneath it was a wide copper bowl, waiting to catch my blood, and beside it, piled high, were thick towels to wipe my son clean when he emerged from my womb. I shuddered at the thought of the ordeal I would face, and prayed to St. Margaret that my delivery would be an easy one.

My newly appointed lady mistress of the nursery, Lady Denton, stood by, watching me as I surveyed the room. I knew that my husband had chosen her, as he had our son's cradle, because she had belonged to the royal nursery when he was born.

"I trust Your Highness is satisfied with all that has been prepared," she said crisply. "I have ordered the furnishings laid out as they were when the late queen was delivered."

The chill in her tone, and the mention of my mother-in-law Queen Elizabeth who had died giving birth in that very room, along with her child, made me bristle.

"I have not yet decided," I said. "I shall have to speak to the midwives, and choose my rockers and wetnurse—"

"If Your Highness please, they have already been chosen."

"The choice shall be mine," I said firmly, without looking at the lady mistress, adding "Leave me," as I had seen my mother do when any of the household servants dared to oppose her or attempt to argue with her.

When the angry Lady Denton had gone, I called for my chamberlain and ordered him to dismiss her from my household, and to send my lady-in-waiting Elizabeth Boleyn to me. With her efficient help I chose a healthy-looking wetnurse who had served in the noble Courteney household and two plump, kindly women to be my rockers.

"I shall need a new lady mistress of the nursery," I told Elizabeth. "I would like to appoint you."

"You honor me, Your Highness, but I cannot accept. The king has ordered me to accompany my husband to France. We are to leave very soon." She seemed genuinely sorry. I thanked her for her help and sent her off to prepare for her journey. After she left I took one last look around the birth chamber. The golden cradle shone, the bed with its spotless linen looked inviting, and even the groaning chair had lost a little of its terrors. Confident that I would find a new lady mistress who would be more to my liking, I left the room and went in search of my husband.

My belly was growing quite round, and I was no longer ill in the mornings. Indeed I felt exceptionally well. I was urged to rest, not to become excited or to let anything agitate or upset me. I did my best to follow this advice as winter closed in, spending my time in reading or sewing, sitting quietly by the hearth when the weather was stormy or a cold wind made me call for a thick shawl.

It was not yet time for me to withdraw into the seclusion of the birth chamber as royal women always do when their time is near. I told Henry that I found the waiting tedious, and that I wished I had some amusement beyond the companionship of my women and my books. I was certain that he heard me, but did not expect him to take my words so much to heart.

Late one wintry afternoon he burst into my apartments, full of high spirits and dressed as a Turk in a wide short gray cloak, tightly fitting hose and trunks, slippers with turned-up toes and a gray velvet cap that covered his abundant red-blond hair. Six or seven of his usual companions were with him, all similarly disguised, capering and shouting and laughing, acting more like boys than men. Yet one among them, I noticed, was smaller and more slim than the others, and the black hair that was beginning to escape from under his cap as he leaped about was far too long to be the hair of a man.

Then the cap fell off—and I saw that it was Maria Juana! A smirk of triumph crossed her seductive features as she paused, facing me, before reaching down to snatch up her cap and put it on again.

What was Maria Juana doing among my husband's companions in amusement? Had she always been one of them, in disguise as they inevitably were? Or was her presence there something new? She had not been a member of my household for a long time, though she still followed the court when we moved from palace to palace, and had been the mistress—so it was said—of more than one wealthy nobleman. My father no longer concerned himself about her, or insisted that I keep her among my maids of honor. He had become more wary of demanding my obedience on any matter, now that I was queen—and not only queen, but soon to be mother of the heir to the throne.

The king and his disorderly Turks were soon gone, but I had been startled by what I had seen, and as the evening came on I became more and more unnerved. That night I felt a pain in my knee that kept me from sleeping, and the pain continued, and worsened on the following nights. I had hoped to be able to make a pilgrimage to a nearby shrine to pray for a safe delivery. But my throbbing knee and a heavy rainstorm that went on for days on end prevented me from traveling even a short distance, and for a week and more I was shut indoors, brooding, more and more convinced that Maria Juana was my husband's mistress.

One night my back ached, and the ache worsened despite the massaging hands of the midwives. Maria de Salinas and Maria de Rojas kept the other servants and my chamber women away, though I wanted Fray Diego nearby, and he stayed near at hand.

"Do not worry," the oldest of the midwives assured me as she moved her hands over my belly. "I feel him kicking, he is a lusty one, a strong one." I saw the concern in her wrinkled face. "I have brought a thousand babes into the world. I know when they are weak, and when they are strong."

"But it is too soon," I protested. "You told me he was not due to be born yet. Not until spring."

"He may be in a hurry," another of the midwives said. "Or it may be that Your Highness has nothing more than a pain in your back."

Poultices were applied, and hot cloths that reeked of oil of lavender. Physicians came and went. I saw worried faces, and overheard whispered conversations. Meanwhile my pain grew worse until, after many hours, I was lifted up and put into the groaning chair.

In my fear and confusion I cried out, and struggled against the restraining hands that clutched at me. No one heeded me. I heard women's voices, some soothing, some insistent. Then all was a blur, a delirium of pain and anguish. Then all sound ceased, all feeling ebbed away.

I am told that hours passed, many hours, and that messengers were sent to find the king, to tell him that I did not have long to live. That the physicians despaired of me, and left it to the midwives to give me what succor they could. That in the end they delivered my child, a small, frail baby girl who had no life in her and could not even take her first breath.

Fray Diego assured me later that he had baptized her, before she was taken away, in secret, her body kept hidden and her very existence never announced to the court.

I was told all this, but not until long afterward. At the time, when I began to return to my senses, I was told nothing at all—except that I must never speak of having been in any pain, or having suffered any difficulties whatever.

It was as if nothing at all had happened, as if I still had a babe in my womb. I believed that I was still carrying the king's son, and would be delivered in the spring. I took my chamber, isolating myself with my women, and everyone at court—everyone but my husband, and Fray Diego, and the midwives, who were too frightened to reveal the truth—waited in hope and expectation that before long I would give birth.

My belly grew and grew, just as if the terrible episode of pain and oblivion had been nothing more than a bad dream. I wondered why I no longer felt the babe quickening within me, when I had felt the inner pummeling of his small feet so strongly before. But the swelling mound beneath my gown and the awkward way I walked seemed assurance enough that I would soon be a mother.

But after a month, something very mysterious happened. Something that still haunts me, still mystifies me. My swelling suddenly went down. My vast belly simply disappeared.

I had no need of the groaning chair, for there were no birth pains. No flow of water, as I had been told to expect. No blood. Nothing at all. What had been inside my swollen flesh? Nothing but empty air.

The midwives were frightened, and crossed themselves whenever they came near me. I heard them murmuring that something had inhabited my body. Something that was not human.

"I've never seen anything like this," the oldest of them said, her voice quavering as she approached me. "Who are you, that your belly should rise up like new bread and then—and then—collapse again so swiftly? The king will surely blame us for this demonic thing!"

But I felt certain that he would blame me, whatever the midwives might do or say, and I was very apprehensive, especially when a message arrived from my father, who was growing more and more impatient for news of my delivery. Had I not yet given birth? he wanted to know. Or if I had, why had he not been told?

I waited, nervously, not knowing what to do or say, how to answer his urgent message—or how to answer the second, even more urgent message that followed the first, this one conveyed by a personal envoy. Besides, there were other messages, other envoys—from France and Portugal, from the Archduchess Margaret and even from far-off Sweden, all wanting an answer to the same inquiry, and a special ambassador from His Holiness the Bishop of Rome. All wanted to be informed about my condition. Had I or had I not borne the heir to the English throne?

It was then, after I had come out of my isolation and the birth chamber was being dismantled, that Fray Diego quietly revealed to me what I had not known—that during my time of pain and unconsciousness I had given birth to a very weak, undersized baby girl. Far too small and too fragile to live. And that everything that happened after that sad birth, especially my mysterious swelling and deflating, was impossible to explain.

"Yet we must believe that all is for the best," my confessor reassured me. "The Lord governs all, He orders every event in His world. Good fortune and bad, healthy babies and sickly ones."

"And dead ones," I added bluntly, suddenly angry that the truth had been kept from me for so long. I sent Fray Diego away, I was feeling too tired to listen to his pious reassurances. And I dreaded my husband's recriminations and blame. He too could be blunt.

"You have not only disappointed me, Catherine," he told me, "by giving me a weak useless daughter instead of a strong son. You have made a fool of me. I am laughed at. Do you know what they are saying about you, not only here but at other courts? They call you a prodigy of nature, a freak. I am no longer the king who married the great Queen Isabella's daughter, but the king who married a freak."

"I see that the midwives have been eager to escape any blame by revealing to the world what should have been kept within the walls of the birth chamber."

"It is no use trying to prevent talebearing," was Henry's sharp retort. "The monstrous puffing and flattening of your belly is making all of Christendom laugh. The best anyone can do is to make certain the tales are told in the most favorable way. One of my almoners, Thomas Wolsey, has been bold enough to undertake this. He is spreading the story that your womb is blessed, that its changing size and shape are a rare sign from the divine. A sign that my reign is a blessed one, and that a male heir of my body will soon be born."

"I must thank this almoner, for his inventive mind." I heard the scorn in my tone, and wondered at it, for in actuality I was very tired.

"You would do well to thank him," was the last thing Henry said to me. "If only you were as productive as he is!"

Although I was much affected by all that I have described, my sorrow and bewilderment did not make me despair. I was young, and strong, I told myself. I had already endured many things that would have broken the hearts and spirits of a weaker woman. I was proud of who I was, and of my royal blood. My faith was stronger than my pride, and I prayed to be given even greater faith as I faced the days ahead.

I was well aware of the blame and ridicule that surrounded me, but I steeled myself to overcome its worst effects. I told myself that what I was facing was a time of trial, such as all Christian souls must endure. But that my time of trial, of testing, would not last forever. I would be freed. I awaited my freedom in hope.

All this was true—but I must also record that there were many nights when I struggled to overcome my darkest thoughts and fears, above all the fear that Doña Aldonza's curse was hard upon me, and inescapable. I feared the nighttime dark as I never had before, and insisted that my chamberers light twice as many candles as in the past. Fearsome dreams terrified me, and when they did, I cried out—and reached for my duenna, just as I had as a child. I had no duenna, but I did have Maria de Salinas, and Maria de Rojas, who slept beside my bed each night and gave me comfort when I needed it.

My husband too came to my bed, not every night but often, though his visits did not last the night through but only an hour or two at most. We had a task to perform, after all; we had to provide the realm with an heir.

And before long, we did.

It was with great relief that I heard my chamberlain announce to the court that I was once again with child.

I saw the smiles and nods of satisfaction on the faces of the courtiers, and especially of my officers and the servants in my household. My husband's joy was noisy and unrestrained. The royal secretaries, whose task it was to compose letters to be sent to other courts, went efficiently about their task. Thomas Wolsey could not restrain his grin of satisfaction. He had seen in my body a rare sign of divine favor; now that favor was coming to full fruition.

As for me, I hoped fervently that this time, with this child, there would be no confusing symptoms or mysterious events. No embarrassment or ridicule—or fear. This time, with good fortune, I would give birth to a living, breathing prince.

7

ALL THE BELLS OF LONDON RANG OUT THEIR JOYOUS CLAMOR ON the first morning of the new year, the Year of Our Lord 1511, to welcome my newborn son.

The Tower guns boomed again and again, making the ground shake underfoot. It was a cold, dark morning with snow falling and a thin margin of ice along the river's edge. As soon as the clanging and thundering began, bonfires were lit in the narrow streets and alleys, and Londoners crowded near the warmth of the crackling flames, shouting and singing in celebration.

Even before the heralds announced the good news that I had been delivered of a son, and that his name was Henry, the more raucous rejoicing had begun. Londoners knew that whenever a king's son was born, the king's wine flowed freely from the conduits, and there was food in abundance laid out for them to share.

I envied them their revelry, for I was very tired that morning, and all the noise was keeping me from sleeping. My little son slept soundly despite the excitement and all the booming of the guns and jangling of the bells, at peace in his gilded cradle near my bed, his wetnurse and his rockers standing by to care for him when they were needed.

My labor had been swift and without danger or drama. I had felt the pains begin at twilight the previous night, and by midnight the four new midwives who attended me (I did not want to be surrounded by any of those who had been present at the birth of my daughter, and had been alarmed by the frightening appearance of my belly) were encouraging me and telling me that my son would soon be born. Long before dawn I heard him cry and watched as the wet ropy cord of flesh that bound him to me was severed.

It was impossible to sleep amid the surge of sound outside the palace so I lay where I was, content to rest, for a time, with the holy relic that had aided my labor, the Girdle of Our Lady, still clutched in my hand. By evening I was able to sit up and eat and drink a little, and afterward the prince was laid in my arms.

His sweet-smelling body was warm, his round face and blue eyes expressionless. The small hands that clenched and unclenched seemed to me perfect in every detail, the small red mouth well shaped and healthy-looking. He resembled his father the king, I thought, more than he did his Trastamara ancestry. He had King Henry's square face and a few wisps of fair hair. His firm, compact body seemed to me, as I held him, robust and strong. He will be a warrior king one day, I thought. A valiant king, who will lead his knights and footsoldiers into battle, just as my mother had done, and who will defeat his enemies.

Warmaking was in the air that winter, my husband was impatient to follow the example of his heroic forbear King Henry V and attack the French. He talked at length of his plans, how he would soon set sail with thousands of knights and bowmen, cross to the French coast and then, in battle after valorous battle, overwhelm the enemy and seize the French throne.

Master Reveles, who had helped me to learn English and had also taught me much about England's past, had told me the story of the great battle of Agincourt, in which the young King Henry V had not only led his men but fought among them himself, with the utmost courage, urging them on to triumph against a much larger force of French. That battle had been won a hundred years earlier. Now my husband was eager not only to repeat what the earlier Henry had done but to surpass it.

"I vow, Catherine, that I will fight the whoreson dogs of Frenchmen just as King Hal did, and win, no matter how many men he brings against us. I will win," he repeated again and again. "I will win an even greater victory than his at Agincourt!" It was a pleasure to see his excitement, and the grin on his handsome young face as he spoke, rubbing his hands together and pacing in agitation.

"Did you know that when he defeated the enemy, King Hal married the French princess Catherine, and their son became the heir to both England and France? Did you?"

I assured him warmly that I did know that.

"Do you see? You and I and our son are about to restore England's glory by once again defeating the enemy and uniting the two realms of France and England under a single king. Our son, the ninth Henry, will be that king."

Messengers were sent to carry the good news of the prince's birth to all the foreign courts, and I sent a letter to my father telling him all about his grandson, and about the magnificent tournament soon to be held in celebration. I described the pony Henry had bought for the baby prince, with its ornate gilded saddle and harness, and the small suit of gleaming silver armor he had ordered from an armorer in Brabant for young Henry to wear once he reached his second birthday. I told him about the prince's christening, and about the costly gifts of gold that his godparents, Archduchess Margaret and King Louis of France, had sent him.

I hoped that my letter would assuage my father's disapproval of me and restore me in his good graces. I had, after all, done my duty and given my husband and the realm a prince.

And I was much honored at the splendid tournament held at Westminster, where for several days I sat under a canopy of cloth of gold, with my women around me, receiving the loud cheers and good wishes of the onlookers while the king challenged all comers in the lists and wore my colors as my champion, calling himself Coeur Loyal, Sir Loyal Heart, and shattering lance after lance until he had won the prize.

In his usual zest to surpass himself and all others, he outdid all the competing jousters—and overdid. He rode far more courses than any of the others. He went beyond the limits of endurance. It was a feat of prowess such as I had never witnessed.

And it left him faint and ill, panting and retching, though he hid his weakness skillfully, so that only his groom was aware of it.

He surpassed himself—and I wanted to believe that he did it out of love, his ardor inspired by his soaring hopes. At that tournament, for those few days, I believe that he rose above himself as heroes do, as his idol Henry V had done, impelled by his happiness at the fulfillment of our union in the birth of our son.

I could not bring myself to tell him that on the second day of the tourney, while I was being dressed in my robe of crimson velvet, one of the prince's rockers, Margery Garnett, came to me, red-faced and out of breath, and insisting that she had to speak to me at once.

She had made the journey from Richmond to Westminster to see me. Her cap was awry, her plain blue gown and white apron wrinkled and smudged. Though my dresser tried to restrain her I saw at once that her errand must be important.

"Let her come," I said to my women, and listened while the rocker, too distressed to remember to make a low bow, inclined her head rapidly and then poured out her message in a voice trembling with fear.

"If you please, Your Highness, the wetnurse says he will not take the teat. He cries and frets. He will not suck. She soaks her finger in sugar water, but he will not suck it."

For weeks the little prince had been a lusty eater, growing fat on the wetnurse's milk. What could have happened to make him refuse it?

"Why hasn't my lady mistress of the nursery come to tell me this?"

Margery hung her head. "She would not, though we pressed her. She forbade us to tell you."

"She forbade you?"

Nodding vigorously, Margery assured me that she and all the others in the nursery were forbidden to reveal anything about the prince.

"But we could not keep silent," she went on. "We were all agreed. One of us had to tell you. We drew lots. I was the one chosen." She looked at me, pleadingly, as if to say, please understand.

"I will see that you are rewarded, Margery—" I started to say, but she interrupted me.

"Oh no, Your Highness. I do not want anything for myself. I would so much rather there was nothing at all to tell you." The quaver in her voice widened.

"You see, we all know you are a good and loving mother. You would want us to tell you if your son—when your son—" She could not go on.

"Of course, Margery. You did well. I will see that the lady mistress does not punish you for your disobedience to her."

"Thank you, Your Highness."

"Go now, do your best and say your prayers. Take care of my son. With the Lord's favor he will start to suck once again."

All that day, as I watched Henry ride up and down the lists again and again, making his powerful mount cavort and leap and pound on the wooden walls of the tiltyard with his hooves, delighting the crowd of onlookers and making them shriek and cheer, I felt increasingly worried and unwell.

Princess Mary, who at fourteen was among the beauties of our court, and had been a close and loving sister to me ever since she was a young child, sensed my dismay and reached for my hand. I was well aware that she had been watching her own hero, the broad-shouldered, handsome Sir Charles Brandon, as he ran his courses and took part in the parades and pageantry of the tournament. Yet she was sensitive to my unease as well.

She started to whisper to me, but I shook my head. We could not talk just then, not only because of all the loud clamor but because we were being observed by those nearest us. We needed to appear entirely absorbed in the spectacle before us, overjoyed at every triumph of the king, my champion.

When the last of the contests had ended I handed out the prizes, with the greatest number awarded to the king. I was hesitant to tell him what the rocker Margery had said, but during the evening feast I decided to be bold.

"I must go to Richmond," I said quietly, as Henry sat savoring his meat and wine. "The prince is in need of a new wetnurse."

Henry frowned, then looked alarmed.

"Why must you go? Why not send someone?"

"I need to select the woman myself. And to assure myself that he is eating well."

He regarded me, weighing what I said. "Go then," he muttered in an undertone. "And send me word at once how he does."

I left the great hall quickly, stopping only briefly to tell Princess Mary why I was leaving so suddenly. She offered to go with me, but I said no. I told her that if we both were seen to leave at the same time, there would be a buzz of questions, and the mood of revelry would be disturbed.

"Are you certain?" she asked.

I nodded, and told her that if anyone asked why I had gone, she was to say only that I was feeling unwell, and hoped to rejoin the others once I felt better.

The night was very cold, the stars bright in the winter sky when I rode, escorted by my chamberlain and a dozen trusted guardsmen, along the river to Richmond. When we reached the palace I made my way at once to the royal nursery, where the fretful baby lay in Margery's arms. As she rocked him she was doing her best to soothe him. The lady mistress of the nursery was not there. I asked where she had gone.

"She left as soon as she found out I had been to see you at Westminster," Margery told me.

The others nodded.

"And we have another wetnurse now," one of the other rockers said, "but still the prince will not suck."

I could see that he was thinner than the last time I held him, his cheeks less full and his face more pale. I had promised Henry that I would send him word right away. Calling for writing materials, I wrote a few words as quickly as I could and sealed the written message, handing it to my chamberlain.

"Take this to the king. Let no one else see it, and let nothing impede you. Haste!"

He left at once, and I went to sit beside the hearth fire, holding out my arms to receive my child.

"There now, hush now," I crooned to him, and before long my voice and the slow movement of my body began to lull him. Margery and the others, eased to have me among them and to see that the baby was growing quiet, were beginning to smile. I sang him my mother's cradle song. His eyes closed. He went to sleep.

What kept me awake were the few words I had sent to the king: "The prince is ill. Come quickly! Your loving wife Catherine."

My husband did come to the royal nursery, but he did not arrive for two days. Instead he sent my physician Dr. Alcaraz, who could do little but scold the midwives and shake his head over the prince as he lay in his cradle, and my confessor Fray Diego, whose breath smelt of wine and who was unsteady on his feet. I was impatient with them both.

"The king has no stomach for pain, or illness," Dr. Alcaraz told me bluntly when I asked why he hadn't come at once. "He shuns the sight of death."

"Our son is not dead!" I insisted. "He is weak. He needs his father's blessing!"

"As Your Highness wishes," was all the physician would say, with a deferential sweep of his cloak.

Fray Diego, who as I well knew always turned to wine for

comfort whenever he feared bad fortune, could do little to restore
my spirits. He looked at me with sad, red-rimmed eyes and, laying
his hand on my head, murmured a prayer.

When at last the king came to the royal nursery, he did not stay
long. One glance at our boy was all he needed. He crossed himself,
swore a profane oath and turned away. Before he left he gave me
such a look as I had never before seen, and hope never to see again.
It was a glare of rage—yet I could see the hurt in his eyes as well.
For an instant he seemed bewildered. Then I heard him say, "Why
did I ever marry you?" as he pushed past me, half stumbling in his
hurry to get away.

I will not attempt to describe how we held prayer vigils for
Prince Henry, how I knelt before the shrine in the nursery, praying
for his recovery, or how many masses I told Fray Diego to say to
Our Lady for his return to health. I could not eat or sleep, I could
only give him what comfort I could and watch as he grew weaker
and more quiet.

Then, on a freezing cold morning in February, while I sat
beside his cradle, he grew still. He was gone.

> *Ayee ayee! My heart is wrung*
> *I am a lifeless thing*
> *He I loved most, he is gone*
> *I am a stone*
>
> *Only the crying of the wind*
> *Only the tears of the moon*
> *I am alone*

It was in October of that year, the year we lost our son, that I went
down to the London docks with Henry to watch the Twelve
Apostles come ashore.

It took thirty men, sweating and straining, to push and pull each
of the twelve immense cannons along on its wheeled cart as it came

up onto the pier, the wooden planks beneath the cart wheels sinking and groaning under the weight.

The twelve great bronze guns had been cast in Flanders, and as I stood watching them, their long metal snouts gleaming wet from the rain that had been falling all that day, I looked over at my husband and thought to myself that I had rarely seen him in better spirits.

"Pull then! Pull together men!" he shouted to the gunners as they tugged and hauled at their task. In his exuberance he tore off his cap and doublet and threw them to Thomas Wolsey, then joined the line of laboring men, grasping the thick ropes that bound the guns to their carts and pulling for all he was worth.

He was in high spirits every time we went to the docks, shouting encouragement to the fitters and joiners at work building his ships, admiring the stamping horses—strong plowhorses, bought from farmers in Kent and Suffolk—as they drew heavy carts loaded with barrels and chests, shaking their large heads and swishing their tails.

"How he does love a challenge," I remarked to Thomas, who was standing nearby, holding the king's red velvet doublet and jeweled cap, watching intently everything that was going on and intervening as often as he thought it necessary. "My other pair of hands," Henry called him laughingly, or "the other head on my shoulders."

It seemed to me that Thomas Wolsey's strong weatherworn hands were always ready to serve my husband in those days, and that his shrewd eager eyes missed nothing. As for his head, it was put to use writing letters or preparing documents in the royal chancery—indeed to any purpose required. Though he was a man of mature years and a tonsured cleric, and had been appointed royal almoner, he was swift to undertake any task, even the most menial. He would not only hold the king's doublet and cap, he would sweep up the rushes and make up the fires, even turn the spit in the palace kitchens if my husband required it.

Not that I had ever seen him do these things, to be sure. Yet I had seen his diligence, and was aware of his constant presence, and

I had no doubt he would undertake any duty, so long as it would increase his value in the king's estimation.

Instead of answering me, Thomas called for a page and handed him the doublet and cap, at almost the same moment reaching out to steady a barrow that was leaning badly to one side and threatening to overturn.

"I only wish he would attend to the challenge of his chancery," was Thomas's low reply. "He reads none of the letters sent to him," he added, frowning. "He leaves them unanswered for weeks, while he amuses himself with whatever else takes his fancy, whether it is hunting or hawking or warmaking."

"He has you to read them and answer them for him, so that he can prepare his army for battle."

Everything Henry did, it seemed, was for the sole purpose of invading France. Nothing mattered more to him than the victory he believed would soon be his.

The Holy Father, Pope Julius, had declared King Louis of France deposed. Henry was now the rightful king. And as such, he had not only the right but the duty to invade the realm that the Holy Father had declared to be his.

It was a crusade, a holy cause. Just as he was a renowned champion in the lists, Henry would now become the champion of the Bishop of Rome. He was determined to lead the holy war against the wicked Louis, who dared to claim a crown not his own. That this same wicked Louis had been godfather to our son was forgotten, a stray inconvenience that warmaking would soon put right.

I watched as another of the twelve heavy guns rumbled slowly past, and caught my breath as one of the gunners lost his footing on the slick wet planks of the dock and fell with a cry. Just then a grain sack fell from one of the provision wagons, bursting open and spilling its contents of damp oats. With an oath Thomas ordered two serving boys to sweep up the oats, meanwhile helping the injured gunner to hobble under a tent, so that the cannons could roll on unhindered.

"War!" Thomas muttered when he returned to my side. "He

knows nothing of war! He toys with the pikes and bills and armaments as if they were playthings, brought out for his amusement."

The almoner did not look at me as he spoke, but kept his eyes on the stream of horses and men, goods and weaponry being unloaded from the ships. I knew that his mutterings were about Henry, who was striding down the length of the dock, calling out to the workmen, urging them on in their exertions, rubbing his hands together, eager as ever to join in the common effort.

"My father was a pikeman. He went to war!" As he spoke Thomas allowed himself a swift glance at me. "He fought for King Richard. I was only a lad at the time, or I would have gone as well." He grimaced. "He fought—and he came home bloody. He came home with a leg half gone, and pain that never left him, not for the rest of his life."

He paused, his expression sullen, darkening at the memory, then went on. "He knew war."

"As did my mother, Master Almoner. As do I. Did you know that I was born in a fortress? In the midst of a war against the heathen Moors?"

But Thomas did not hear me. He had darted away to assist the king, who was shouting, "Cord! Stout cord for the bowstrings!" And we did not speak again that day.

If Henry was impatient to go to war, I too looked forward to it, for the sight of the Twelve Apostles and the other guns and equipment brought ashore from the German lands and Flanders, the splendid tents and pavilions, the suits of armor and swords and banners all quickened my vivid memories of my mother and our soldiers, of victories won and alarms and prayers sent heavenward when victory seemed remote.

Despite the danger we had known, I loved those childhood days, and missed the exhilaration they had brought me. I could not help thinking how my mother would have rejoiced at the might of the cannons, the soldiers, the creaking, jostling carts and the shouting men and neighing horses. She was at home among men of war, and so, I felt, was I.

All that winter and into the spring, as the numbers of soldiers increased and the bulk of their arms and equipment grew ever larger, I began to realize that Henry would do well to look to his ships. He had ordered his shipwrights to build two dozen new warships, one of them to be named for me, the *Catherine Fortileza*. And he had hired several dozen others. Yet I was sure that many more would be needed.

I had often heard my mother speak of the vast Arsenal where the ships and naval stores of the Venetian Republic were held. I took it upon myself to summon the Venetian envoy Sebastiano Giustiniani to the palace and asked him whether the Republic of Venice would be willing to donate twenty-five ships to my husband's crusade. I reminded him that the Holy Father Pope Julius had granted the throne of France to Henry, and that the conquest of France was a holy cause.

"Most assuredly, Your Highness," was the Venetian's immediate reply. "The galleys of the Republic are always at the service of the King of England—for a price. We would be able to provide, let me see, perhaps ten vessels from our Arsenal very soon, and more could be built by our shipwrights should the king choose to order them." He spoke ingratiatingly, though his response was not all that I had hoped for. Still, I was pleased. I was certain that the royal treasury was full, and that Henry could afford to buy the ships. After all, I reasoned, if Henry could spend hundreds of pounds (as I knew he had) on magnificent suits of armor for himself and gold and silver trappings for his horses, he could pay the Venetian Republic for its ships.

I waited for a day when we were once again at the docks, and Henry was happily engrossed in the fitting out of one of his newest ships, the *Peter Pomegranat*. The pomegranate was my emblem, and thus the emblem of Spain, and the ship paid honor to the close ties and promised alliance of the two realms.

Suddenly we were startled by the sound of a huge explosion. One of the wooden storage sheds near us burst into flame, and men began running in all directions, some calling for help, others doing their best to drag carts and horses away from the fire, still others drawing up river water in buckets and throwing the water on the flames.

Without so much as a glance at me Henry ran off at once in the direction of the dockside taverns and warehouses and did not stop until he reached the safety of a brick stable some distance from where we had been standing. Once there, he did not look back.

"Your Highness!" I heard a voice at my side, and felt a strong hand grip my arm. "You must come away!"

It was Thomas Wolsey, who led me protectively through the maze of running feet and flailing arms while I looked in vain for our guardsmen.

"Where are the guards? What happened to the guards?" I kept asking, panting as I was short of breath.

"With the king," Thomas told me brusquely. "With the brave and valiant crusader."

Startled to hear such sarcasm from the almoner, but too out of breath to chastise him, it was all I could do to hurry along at his side, frightened by a second explosion that led to more outcries and more chaos. After what seemed like an eternity Thomas left me in the care of a cordon of pikemen and laborers who had taken refuge from the fires. I wanted to be with Henry, and described the brick stable where I had seen the king go.

Promising to return as soon as he could, Thomas hurried away in the direction of the stable. Before long he was back, with a cart pulled by a strong plowhorse.

"Take Her Highness to the palace at once," he ordered the pikemen. "Entrust her to the palace guard. I must stay to ensure that the traitor who has done this villainous thing is punished."

"What traitor?" I demanded as I was helped into the cart. "Is the king safe? Where is the king?"

"The king has gone to the palace. As to the traitor—" He

lowered his voice, and I bent down so that I could hear what he said. "One of the gunners was seen setting fire to the gunpowder stores. A Frenchman. A spy for the wicked Louis of France!"

Then with a jerk of the cart the huge plowhorse moved away from the docks and the clamorous tumult beside the river, the smoke from the burning storehouses thick in the darkening air.

8

At last the long-awaited day came, the day the royal army sailed for France.

Wind gusts swept the harbor, lifting the water into peaks and troughs and making the flags and pennons that flew from the ships' masts snap and curl in the mild summer air. The smallest boats bobbed up and down, the galleys and store ships pitched and tossed, lurching from side to side until late in the afternoon, when a calm settled over all and the fleet weighed anchor, prepared to sail with the outgoing tide.

It was an auspicious departure, on that June afternoon in the Year of Our Lord 1513, for I knew that I was once again carrying a child and I hoped that this prince—how could he not be a prince?—would one day wear the crowns of both England and France. I expected him to be born in December, or perhaps early in the new year. Until then, or until my husband returned victorious, I would rule England in his name and as his regent, and all royal powers would be mine.

As the fleet sailed I exercised those powers for the first time. One of the carpenters, a rogue in the pay of the French called Antoine Bedell, had been caught boring holes in the hull of the *Catherine Fortileza*. I ordered the wretch hanged.

I knew that I would have many responsibilities as the king's regent, and I looked forward to carrying them out. I would settle disputes and oversee the royal justices, I would receive messages from foreign courts and send messages of my own in return. All the wealth of the royal treasury would be mine to dispense. My husband's subjects would come to me for aid, and I would preside, I hoped graciously, over the feasts and ceremonies that called for a royal presence.

My one regret was that Thomas Wolsey would not be there for me to rely on, as he was sailing to France with the king. Nor would Master Reveles be at my service for he too was aboard the king's flagship.

I knew that I would need a secretary, and competent clerks, and experienced men to assist me with any matters new to me or requiring knowledge I did not possess. I felt proud and exhilarated at the prospect of reigning in Henry's absence, but humbled by it as well. I trusted that I would not attempt, from mere pride, to undertake anything that I was not capable of doing well.

And I did not forget that, even as regent, I was still a wife and soon to be a mother; before Master Reveles left I required of him that he send me frequent news from France, especially news of the king's health and diet, of his daily habits, and especially of his exertions in leading his men and doing battle. I admitted to him my fear that warmaking would tax my husband's judgment and lead him to drive himself to do too much, for too long.

Hearing this, my almoner nodded. "I have seen it, just as you have, Your Highness. He makes mighty efforts, but does not rest himself."

"You must make him rest. Tell him you speak for me. Otherwise he will go on and on until he pants and clutches his chest and makes himself ill. No warrior should let his men see him in that state of weakness."

Master Reveles promised to do all that I asked of him, and I was satisfied. But no one, however trustworthy, could help me prepare for my most pressing task as regent: that of ordering and commanding the guard and soldiery.

"The Scots are sure to sweep down into the northern borderlands as soon as I leave the kingdom," Henry cautioned me just before he sailed. "You must send our soldiers to meet them and stop them. They will have arms and money from the treacherous French. They must not believe that you are weak, that you fear to confront them, just because you are a mere woman."

That he called me a mere woman made me bristle. I reminded him that I was the daughter of the great Queen Isabella, and also of King Ferdinand, whose soldiers were at that moment marching northward from Aragon to aid in the crusade against the French.

Henry dismissed my argument with a shake of his head.

"You must prove yourself brave. Otherwise they will scoff at you, and your commanders, and any men they lead."

"None will fault me for lacking courage. And as for my commanders, I will rely on the earl marshall." The aged Earl of Surrey, whom Henry had appointed earl marshall, had proven himself able and resolute despite his years. I only hoped he would not scoff at me, or show me any lack of respect or obedience, just because I was a woman.

With Henry's words in mind I ordered a metal helmet brought to me from the Tower armory, and had it embellished with gold so that it glittered in the sunlight. And to ensure that I wore it bravely, unencumbered by any womanly vanity, I ordered Maria de Salinas to cut my long thick auburn hair, so that it no longer fell to my waist but only to the midpoint of my back. She wept as she cut it.

"My mother did not allow her hair to grow any longer than this," I said as she brushed out the shortened strands. "The soldiers respected her not only because she was brave but because she was not vain. She knew her valor lay in her courage, not in her beauty."

In truth I was aware, in that year of warmaking, that my own beauty, such as it had been, was long past. My complexion, once bright and fair, was becoming dull and sallow. My gray eyes had lost much of their youthful luster. Childbearing had thickened my waist, and I was no longer as nimble or agile as I had been as a girl. I did not rue these changes, but I could not fail to acknowledge them. I was a small woman, no longer young, without uncommon beauty such as Henry's sister Mary possessed in such abundance. But I was Queen of England, and the king's regent.

When Maria had cut my hair, I put on my helmet. I stood before the pier glass, and studied my reflection. I found it very satisfying indeed.

I was no beauty, as my mother had been. Yet I had the look of a warrior queen all the same. I remembered my mother's confessor reading to her the passage from the Scriptures about putting on the helmet of salvation, and the breastplate of righteousness. About fighting the wicked wearing the armor of the Lord.

The recollection thrilled and inspired me, yet at the same time it made me sorrowful. I went to the cupboard where I kept, out of sight, the small suit of armor Henry had ordered for our son, the New Year's Boy. I took it out and laid it on my bed. The Lord had seen fit to take unto himself that son I had loved. Now he had granted me another to carry under my heart. I vowed that the prince I would bear at the end of the year would wear this armor, and be strong and vital. He would not succumb to illness as his brother had.

This in turn led me in my musing to think of Prince Arthur, whom I had married so long before, when I was an affectionate, trusting girl. Prince Arthur who had been born to be king of England. I had loved him, with a love as strong as that I had for the New Year's Boy. How different Arthur had been from Henry! He was no warrior, yet he had won my heart and my sympathy, and my memories of him were sweet.

I took the little suit of armor and put it away in the cupboard. I would keep it safe for our new son.

I had reminded Henry with pride that my father King Ferdinand was his staunch ally, whose soldiers were on their way to aid in his crusade. But within days of Henry's embarkation for France I learned that my father had not done as he promised. He had not kept faith, either with Henry or with me. Instead of sending his soldiers northward from Aragon to join our English soldiery he had made a truce with the French, abandoning his allegiance and proving himself not only untrustworthy but dishonorable.

He had betrayed those who trusted him, just as he had betrayed my mother with Doña Aldonza. I was ashamed of him, and felt that my own honor had been stained by his betrayal.

This in turn made me worry that, added to the scoffing and contempt that might well be shown to me because I was a mere woman, I would now be regarded as the daughter of a faithless, deceitful father who was unworthy to be named as a champion of the Holy Father or to join in any crusade.

Dreading this, I suffered, as I had always struggled to keep my own honor pure. I could not imagine giving my word, and then breaking it.

Yet I had little leisure for brooding on my father's faithlessness. A messenger arrived with a letter from Master Reveles, written from a camp near the French town of Thérouanne, in the midst of a rainstorm, as the stains on the document clearly showed. True to his promise, Master Reveles was sending me word of what was being said and done in France.

What his letter told me was that news had reached Henry and his commanders that King James of Scotland was coming southward with a large force of men at arms, and that they were well equipped for battle.

"The French have sent much treasure to pay the Scots," Master Reveles wrote. "And not to buy arms and provisions only, but to hire spies and troublemakers."

I could well believe what he wrote, when I brought to mind the explosions on the docks, the treachery of Antoine Bedell, and other things done in secret intended to thwart our crusade. Spies and troublemakers were indeed at work, and in our midst.

"The French are devious," Master Reveles wrote. "They are adept at acts of cunning and crime. It is because they are cowards at heart. The English, however, are stout of heart and fear nothing.

"King Henry has the stoutest heart of all," the letter went on.

"He rides through our camp all day and half the night, changing his mount every few hours, shouting orders to the men and urging them on until he is hoarse. He boasts that when we begin the siege of Thérouanne, he will throw off his armor and walk up to the walls and dare the French bowmen who defend it to shoot him."

It was as I feared. Henry was doing too much, overtiring himself and putting himself in danger needlessly. He was abandoning good judgment. I hoped he was not ill.

I sent word at once to the earl marshall to fortify the borderlands, and set about raising the shire levies of men and arms and horses. My summons were obeyed, for the most part, and within a week the first of many hundreds of men were arriving in the capital, to be sent north by sea. I was glad then for the Venetian galleys, with their large holds and wide decks. They held not only fighting men but tents and provisions, and seven heavy cannons, nearly as large as the Twelve Apostles, that became known as the Seven Sisters.

By the time I was ready to lead my own men—a chosen force of some five thousand—toward the border to support the much larger army of the earl marshall, several more letters had arrived from Master Reveles. Not only had Thérouanne been taken by our English soldiers, but there had been another triumph—hundreds of mounted English knights had met and overwhelmed a much larger contingent of the French and put them to flight.

"It was a triumph," the almoner wrote, "but I must tell you that the king was not in the forefront of the horsemen, leading them on against the enemy. He was not among the English knights at all. His delight is not in fighting, but in feasting and dancing. We have had much revelry among the ladies."

Much revelry indeed! I could imagine Henry amusing himself as he loved to do, indulging himself and performing at the things he did best while being praised and flattered by those around him.

I did my best to banish such disloyal thoughts from my mind, but when another letter was brought to me, telling me of my husband's weeks of tilting and masquing, of how he entertained the Archduchess

Margaret and her women by playing his lute and piping and singing, I grew angry and cut the letter to pieces with my knife.

How dare he waste weeks dancing and piping while I was heavily burdened with so many duties, so heavily burdened, some days, that it was all I could do to find time to drink and sup and even to rest! I had not written to him to complain of this, nor had I told him that my swelling belly was a hindrance to all that I did. My letters to Henry were full of praise and encouragement. And did he send letters to me of the same sort? No. He sent no letters at all.

Then arrived the most vexing news I had received since the day Henry left for France. News so disturbing that it could not be written down (lest it be read by others) but only delivered by a trusted servant, who told me in confidence what I least wanted to hear.

My informant, my almoner's laundress, arrived in a boatload of French prisoners. One of my more onerous tasks as regent was to receive captured French knights and see that they were placed under guard in the Tower. The laundress had been instructed to wash the prisoners' shirts and mend them as necessary. But I soon discovered that she had come on a different errand: to pass on to me the secret that Master Reveles was certain I needed to know.

The laundress was shy and unsure of herself at first, but when I gave her a coin and reassured her that I wanted to hear her news, she became more confident.

"Your Highness's almoner wishes me to say," she began, "that there is a girl who has become King Henry's favorite companion. She is the daughter of Sir John Blount, who serves His Majesty as captain of the guard."

"Yes," I nodded. "Her cousin is my chamberlain, William Blount, Lord Mountjoy."

The laundress licked her lips, her uncertainty returning. "They sing and dance together. She is such a lively dancer, and sings so sweetly. They—are together day and night."

My heart sank. "Is she his mistress?"

The woman began to answer, then hesitated.

"I must know. Is she his mistress? And is she young and beautiful?"

"She is—a very charming girl. Always smiling and laughing. And very pretty—as Your Highness is—"

"Hush! No false flattery! Save that for my husband, who appears to crave it! Her age. What is her age?"

"I am told by Master Reveles that she is not yet fifteen."

"Very well then. You have told me. Now you may go."

I felt my entire body stiffen. My heart was beating too quickly. I was beginning to feel faint. The laundress stayed where she was.

"Yes? What is it? I have said you may go," I repeated, more harshly than I meant to.

"If you please, Your Highness, there is more to tell."

I felt, then, as if I had turned to stone, to marble as cold as the pillars in the gardens in the Alhambra.

"Yes?" I asked, this time my voice was weak.

"It is said that she is with child by the king."

The men were beginning to sing about me.

Their songs were no poetic odes or melodic airs, but plain soldiers' rhymes, set to the rhythm of tramping boots. "The warrior Catherine in helmet of gold, the warrior Catherine so brave and so bold," they sang. "The Scots went a-running, she put them to flight. They ran from her presence by day and by night." On and on the verses went, until a ballad of sorts was fitted together and written down.

I had not put the Scots to flight, but my men were confident that I would.

We had marched north out of London, intent on joining the Earl of Surrey and his far larger army in the borderlands as swiftly as our cumbersome train of men and carts and horses would permit. We traveled under a banner with the combined arms of England and Spain, and also the banner of the Virgin Mary and of Saint

George who had killed the dragon. My puirsuivants bore their own coats of arms, and my trumpeters also.

I was bent on war, I let nothing hinder me. Not the damp weather or the lowering clouds, nor the thought of the enemy, in full battle array, or the Scots King James and his guns and soldiery. Not even the dread thought of Bessie Blount and the king, together day and night. Day and night. For was I not wearing the golden helmet, and was not ours the Lord's cause?

We had been traveling for nearly a week when a messenger came from the earl marshall, bringing us word of a great victory. The earl and his men had held firm against King James and his thousands, with their French guns and their knights and pikemen, on a sere meadow known as Flodden Field. The Seven Sisters had boomed a strident answer to the cannons of the enemy, and it had not taken long—a single afternoon—for the Scots cause to be ruined leaving many men, even King James himself, lying dead on the field.

We could hardly believe the wondrous news. This was no skirmish such as had taken place between King Henry's knights and the French after the capture of Thérouanne, but a full-out contest of arms, a defeat far more final than any battle fought against the Scots for hundreds of years.

The armed might of the Scots lay in ruins.

I could not rest until I had seen for myself the scene of battle, the field of death. Though hindered by pain in my rounded, bulging belly I rode on north at once, taking only an escort of a hundred of my guard and a dozen bowmen. We traveled in the greatest haste, over rough terrain soaked by the autumn rains and full of broken ground and much stubble. Here and there trees had fallen across the roadway, and streams overflowed their banks to flood the low-lying valleys.

We smelled the battlefield before we reached it, the overpowering stench of death was like an assault. I felt my stomach heave, and saw that others in my company sickened at the odor and purged their stomachs. When we came to the bloody ground itself, with its mounds of corpses, its litter of dead horses, covered with flies and vermin, and its abandoned weaponry, flung away as if in hasty flight, I had to force myself to look at what lay before me.

For it was, as we had been told, a scene of utter ruin. And the very symbol of that ruin was the scarred, mutilated body of King James. A body so rent by sword cuts and wounds that no one, not even my sister-in-law Margaret, could have recognized it as that of her husband. What if this had been Henry, I wondered. What if Henry had fallen dead on a battlefield in France? It could happen yet. It could happen at any time.

The bloody coat armor that covered the body of the Scots king, with its royal crest, proved his identity. I made the decision to send it, rent and stained as it was, to Henry in France, as the prime trophy of our victory. I would send the king's corpse entire, as my mother would surely have done had she been in my place.

But my mother's victories were against the heathen Moors. Not her Christian relatives. And as I had good reason to know, Henry shunned all reminders of death. He had barely spared a glance for our New Year's Boy in his last hours. He would be glad to receive the Scots king's stained surcoat, but to receive his flesh—I was certain that would horrify him.

No—I would have King James's embalmed body taken to Stirling Castle for burial. I would bear in mind that for the moment, the late king's baby son, who was not yet two years old, was not only King of Scotland as James V but heir to the English throne as well. I wondered whether Margaret was thinking these same thoughts.

I had no wish to linger at Flodden Field, especially as bad weather threatened, but there was provisioning to see to, and lookouts to post along the border, before I gave the order for our armies to return southward. I did what I could, as quickly as I could, doing my best to ignore the strong twinges of pain in my belly.

I took heart from the singing of the men, the truest sign of their honor and respect. They are proud of me, I told myself. They are so proud of me.

The warrior Catherine her story is told
The warrior Catherine in her helmet of gold
Her heart was for England, her zeal was for Spain
We never shall witness her equal again

The Scotsmen atremble, they scatter like down
She raises her sword nigh to Edinburgh town
Let all men remember for many a year
How Catherine defeated the enemy here

The warrior Catherine in her helmet of gold
The proudest and bravest of warriors bold
Her mother's true daughter, her father's true heir
Our queen and our lady most true and most fair

I heard them singing, and knew that they were full of the joy of battle, the joy of victory. But the ghastly sight of the battlefield, and my exertions there, had made my pain much worse. I huddled, shivering, near the camp fire, my clothing soaked in sweat. When a midwife was found in Branxton village and brought to our camp she made me lie on a straw pallet, under a mound of blankets. There was little else she could do. There in the damp and cold of a long night, I suffered my own defeat.

England had won a great victory, but I had lost my child.

9

Henry rejoiced to hear of our triumph over the Scots at Flodden, and ordered feasts prepared and bonfires lit in celebration. He even pretended to be pleased to receive King James's bloody, battlestained surcoat—though I am certain his pleasure was all for show—and held it high and waved it while his admirers cheered.

When the news and the grisly trophy reached him he was at the court of the Archduchess Margaret, at Lille, enjoying more weeks of revelry and masquing, tourneying and—I had been warned—the companionship of Bessie Blount. He had reason to be gratified by his own attainments, having seized both Thérouanne and Tournai, but he had enjoyed no hard-won personal glory from either conquest, and in fact, as Master Reveles wrote me, his soldiers joked to one another that he was a better dancer than a fighter. And that I, a woman with a babe in my womb, had won a far greater victory than he ever would.

"He seldom speaks to me," my almoner wrote, "since he heard

some of the men singing a ballad about you. I believe he envies you your renown, and resents you."

And indeed I saw this resentment for myself when Henry returned to England at the end of October. His manner toward me was brusque and dismissive whenever I tried to talk to him, his very posture was different and his tone scathing.

When I congratulated him on his success, he barely acknowledged my congratulations, or thanked me.

"And I have heard echoes of your own acclaim," he snapped, "from among my men at arms. As I have heard it said that you lost the child you were carrying, there at Flodden."

At this I hung my head, more in sorrow than in shame, though his words were meant to shame me. If he felt any regret over the death, or over my own suffering, he did not show it—which made me resentful in my turn.

"It is also being said that your mistress, young Bessie Blount, will bear your child before long."

He dismissed my words with a slight wave of one large hand.

"Mere rumor. And she is soon to become *your* maid of honor."

"Not of my choosing, as you know."

With a shrug, Henry turned aside and shifted his attention to a document brought to him by one of the chancery clerks.

"At your chamberlain's urging, I believe," was Henry's low response.

There was no point in arguing with him, though I was well aware that it had been Henry himself who told my chamberlain William Blount to come to me and inform me that his cousin Bessie was being appointed to my household. Such things were always done indirectly; my mother had told me that Doña Aldonza, when she was a young unmarried girl, and my father's mistress, had been appointed to be one of her maids of honor. But the appointment was made to seem as though it came from the steward of mother's household, and not from my father.

In truth I found cheerful, innocent-looking young Bessie, with her thick cloud of tight light brown curls and her trusting blue eyes, more endearing than odious. Had Arthur and I been able to have a daughter, she might well have been like Bessie.

Arthur! How he crept into my thoughts. So often, so very often . . .

But Henry was saying something to me, breaking my train of thought.

"There is a troublemaker at the French court, spreading false rumors," he was saying. "A Spaniard. Thomas tells me she is the mistress of the French prince, that long-nosed jackanapes who imagines he can joust and wrestle and run against the strongest men in his father's kingdom. He has no idea how much less formidable he is than an older, stronger opponent—such as myself."

The long-nosed French prince was Francis, heir to his father's cousin King Louis XII and married to the king's daughter Claude. But who was the Spanish troublemaker? I was soon to find out.

"Catherine! My sweet sister! Is there nothing you can do to help me?"

It was Mary, in tears, imploring my aid. I wanted very much to help her, but for the moment at least there was nothing to be done but listen to her despairing plea.

"But he promised me that I could choose for myself!" she was saying. "He swore to me, on the very day he returned from France, that I would be free! And he knew very well who I would choose! I have never loved anyone but my dearest Charles!" Her lovely face was flushed. I had never seen her in such distress.

Henry had indeed given his word to his favorite sister Mary that he would not in future put her under any obligation to marry, as I and all my sisters had and as her own widowed sister Margaret had, in order to seal a bargain between kingdoms. I knew this to be true. Yet I also knew that in the year since his return, Henry had changed.

He had never relished the work of governing, or of making decisions about how to conduct the business of dealing with foreign monarchs. What he enjoyed was pageantry and show, renown and admiration. Most of all he savored pleasure, courtly pastimes, being surrounded by music and laughter and in the company of charming young women—young women such as Bessie Blount.

"I'm sure he meant to keep his promise—" I began.

"Then why has he ordered me to go to France and marry that hideous wrinkled old man! He's so feeble he can barely walk, and his face is full of ugly pockmarks, and he must be at least sixty years old!" Her voice rose and became a thin wail.

"Because, Mary, he now relies on the archbishop to advise him, and nothing is as it was."

Hearing myself refer to Thomas Wolsey as the archbishop still sounded odd, I continued to think of him as the king's almoner. Yet during the past year he had risen not only to being Archbishop of York but to being Henry's foremost adviser, the dominant voice on the royal council.

It seemed to me, and to most others, that Thomas Wolsey had taken over the burdensome task of making most of the important decisions in the realm. He had taken over—and Henry relied heavily on him to continue to do so.

Mary was at first puzzled, then crestfallen at my words. Then her tearstained face grew set and determined.

"I will not have my future ruined by some lowborn clerk who imagines himself worthy to be an archbishop!"

I saw then how useless it would be to reason with my sister-in-law in her present state of mind and heart. How little good it would do to explain that Thomas had decided—with Henry adopting his decision—that it would be best to ally with the French rather than fight them, and that Mary's betrothal to the aged French King Louis was to be among the prizes awarded to bind that alliance.

Mary was set on marrying her beloved Charles Brandon, and it would do no good to try to tell her what I believed to be true: that her loved and trusted brother was choosing to rely on the stronger will and more focused intelligence of the newly appointed Archbishop of York, Thomas Wolsey, to determine her future.

Still, it pained me to see her suffer, and it hurt all the more the day I watched her leave for her new home. On her wedding day she would become Queen of France, an honor she had never sought. But she would despise Thomas Wolsey for the rest of her life—and she would never trust her brother again.

Meanwhile I had my own inner battle to wage, also over questions of marriage and trust. For Thomas had cautioned me that the king was looking into the possibility of putting me aside.

"If you had a son it would be quite a different thing," he said in his usual blunt-spoken way, "but since there is no heir, and not likely to be one, after so many failures—"

"Hush! Never speak of the Lord's will in terms of failure. If I have not yet brought my husband a son who lived, it is in accordance with His divine purpose."

"To be sure, Your Highness, to be sure. And we must acknowledge that His purpose may be to replace you with a different wife for King Henry. One who will be fertile, one whose father will keep his word instead of breaking it. One whose valor in war will be less like her mother Queen Isabella and more like, perhaps, the Archduchess Margaret, who did not attempt to lead armies and whose deeds did not threaten to surpass those of her husband."

I was accustomed to Thomas's adroit logic—he had after all been an outstanding scholar at his Oxford college—though I admit that on this occasion he took me by surprise. For the moment I was silent.

"I wonder if you know what this is," he said after a time, drawing a document from an inner pocket of his robe and starting to peruse it.

I shook my head.

"The king asked me to study it, to see whether it might suggest a path for him to follow, in finding his way to a new wife."

"Only the Lord can determine that," I insisted stubbornly. But Thomas did not argue with me. He went on reading.

I became impatient. Finally my curiosity got the better of me.

"What is this document, and where did it come from?"

"From Sir Charles Brandon," was the astonishing reply. The strong, vigorous master of the joust and my husband's staunch friend. The man my sister-in-law had hoped in vain to wed. Not, I would have thought, a man of keen mind, or given to composing lengthy writings. But then, perhaps the document had come from one of his clerks or men of law.

"Did you know, Your Highness, that Sir Charles has been married three times?"

"I did not." The thought was unsettling. Did Mary know this about him?

Thomas was shaking his head, apparently in wonderment, as he went on reading.

"Brandon is as cunning at marriage, it would seem, as he is skillful at the joust." He gave a rare low chuckle. My worry grew.

"First he married a girl named Anne who brought him a bit of land, and gave him sons, but then he had his marriage declared no marriage at all—he had it nullified, as the canon lawyers would say—because he had a clever plan. He went about it all very carefully, you understand. I have to admire his cleverness!"

Thomas cleared his throat, then proceeded.

"It all had to do with the mingling of blood and flesh. I have heard it said by those learned in the law of the church that any marriage can be nullified if only there has been mingling of blood or flesh. Which is to say, if there are ties of blood or uniting of bodies."

"Go on."

"Sir Charles found out that his young wife had an aunt named Margaret who was much older and very much richer. He wanted her fortune. So he had his clerks argue that he had never really been married to Anne, and once he was free of her, he married Margaret—and as her husband, he was entitled to her treasure.

"Then he pretended that his conscience would not allow him to go on being Margaret's husband once he realized that this marriage too was null, because Margaret and Anne were aunt and niece. So he went back to Anne and remarried her—taking all Margaret's money with him!"

Thomas burst into laughter. "And now, it is said, he wishes to marry yet again. This time his wife will be his young ward—but she won't have him!"

Hearing this tale of calculating greed appalled me. How much had Brandon told Mary about his past? Or was it possible she knew it all, and cared only that she loved him?

I had known Mary for most of her eighteen years and she had always been a reckless, impulsive girl, inclined to take risks and follow sudden whims. Only her love for Brandon was no whim, it had lasted too long and meant too much to her.

But what of his true feelings for her? She was after all the king's beautiful sister, a rare prize. If he married her Brandon would not only be far more wealthy than ever, he would become a dominant figure at court, at least as dominant as Thomas and with far greater power—always provided Henry trusted and favored him.

For though the realization was a dreadful one, I had to admit that there was a chance that if Mary was to marry her beloved, and not King Louis, it was possible that Brandon might be the father of the next king of England. Was that his hope and intent?

I wondered whether I ought to warn Mary. But she was already gone, embarked for France and her elderly wrinkled bridegroom with his pockmarked face and his unsteady legs. And I, if I wasn't careful, was on my way to being put aside.

As it turned out, my charming sister-in-law was not only beautiful, she was fortunate.

Less than two months after she married King Louis, he died. She became Mary, Queen of France and a widow. She was free to marry again—and she did not hesitate.

She married her beloved Charles Brandon in a swiftly arranged, private ceremony in Paris. And then, on a sunny May morning with much of our English court in attendance, she married him again, this time at Greenwich.

I am happy to say that my misgivings about my jovial, good-tempered new brother-in-law Charles turned out to be groundless. Mary herself reassured me when I asked her about her husband's past.

"Ah, dear Catherine, but all that was long ago! Who can say why he chose to act as he did! His children love him, I love him. And I assure you most heartily that he loves me, and no one but me!"

Her radiantly happy face, the laughing way she dismissed my few rejoinders, above all her reminder that Thomas Wolsey was no friend of Charles Brandon's but rather his rival, all combined to lessen my worries, and in the end, dissolve them.

"You should have heard the way my brother tried to persuade Charles to marry that dragon Archduchess Margaret!" she told me with a smile. "He had a grand plan, one I now know was not his, but Thomas Wolsey's. I was to wed King Louis, and Charles would become Archduke of Savoy and lord of the lowlands. How he would have hated that!"

Mary was eager to tell me what I had wanted most to find out: who the troublemaker was that was spreading false rumors at the French court. It was Maria Juana.

"I might have known she would be the one," I said as soon as I heard Mary say my half-sister's name. "She hates me and begrudges me every happiness, every success."

"She tells the most vile lies about you," Mary said.

"Does she say that my maid of honor Bessie Blount has borne the king a bastard child?" Mary nodded. "And that I caused her mother's death?" At this she nodded even more vigorously.

"I assure you, none of what she says is true."

"She will say or do anything to injure you. To become your equal, to surpass you even. She is not content merely to be the mistress of King Francis. Her aim is to become his queen!"

"But he is already married to Queen Claude," I put in. The young king's wife, I had been told, was a feeble, stunted creature with twisted limbs, yet she had given her husband several children. And she had a kind heart and a generous nature.

"There are those at the royal court who fear that Maria Juana will contrive to poison her, so that she can take her place. Maria Juana is not only a liar, she is an intriguer. I wonder you don't send her back to Spain where she belongs."

"I cannot. My father protects her. He has ordered me never to thwart her or oppose her, no matter what she does or says. I must obey him."

Mary shook her head. "I shall ask my brother to command her to return to Spain, before she does even more harm."

"If only he would," I murmured, more to myself than to Mary. But I knew that Henry was dissatisfied with me, and that, if Thomas Wolsey was to be believed, he was even pondering how to rid himself of me. This was not the time for Mary to ask anything of him on my behalf.

"Not now," I said. "Please, not now."

Unsure of what I ought to do, I decided to make a pilgrimage to the shrine of Our Lady at Walsingham to pray for guidance. Women had been visiting the holy place for many centuries, especially those who, like me, hoped to bear sturdy sons.

Once there, I knelt before the golden altar in the dim chapel. I soon discovered that I had much more to pray for than the grace to bear a strong, vital heir to the throne.

"Please Lord," I prayed, "don't let my earthly pilgrimage be for naught! Don't let me disgrace my mother's memory, or let it be tarnished by the lies of my envious half-sister! Don't let my husband put me aside!"

I prayed, most earnestly, for a very long time.

And my prayers were answered. For like my lovely sister-in-law Mary, I too was fortunate in that year, the Year of Our Lord 1515. Not long after her marriage to Charles Brandon at Greenwich, I knew that I was once again carrying the king's child. And I felt certain that we would be blessed at last with a strong, healthy son.

Rain pelted down on the palace rooftops on the winter night my child was born, and a cold wind brought in the dawn. My labor was long and painful, and through it all I shivered with the cold. Yet no mother had ever been happier than I was to hear my baby's first loud cries, and when the midwife put her into my arms she warmed me at once.

For I saw at first glance that she was a true daughter of Castile.

"Isabella," I whispered to her. "I shall call you Isabella, for you have the look of your grandmother, and I know you will have her strength."

Thinking back to that happy dawn, I wonder even now why I felt no disappointment that my baby was not the son I had been sure would be born to us. Why I felt such immediate and complete contentment in my daughter.

All I know is that my happiness was full, and nothing, not even Henry's sharp words, could lessen it.

"What name, sire? What name shall I give to the herald?"

My chamberlain William Blount, Lord Mountjoy, was respectful, but insistent. The baby had to be proclaimed, her name and title announced.

"Mary, I suppose," I heard Henry respond irritably, his voice hoarse, his eyes dull and red-rimmed. He had been spending the long winter nights at the Maidens' Bower, I was told. Or by the fireside among his favorite male companions, where they drank and laughed and pummeled one another like boys. He was always restless in winter, he needed to be active, riding or hunting or just tramping along in the open air, fending off boredom and anxious thoughts. Henry had never been one to take his ease.

"But my lord—" I began.

"Her name is Mary," he snapped. To the chamberlain he said, "Have the christening as soon as you can. With as little show or fuss as possible. Thomas will arrange it."

He glanced down into the gilded cradle with its royal crest and drape of purple velvet. Our tiny daughter slept quietly, undisturbed by his loud voice and the sudden stir of activity in the room.

"From the look of her, he'd better do it quickly, before she— while she still lives."

"Ah, but she is strong, my little Isabella," I spoke up, more passionately than I meant to. "She has a lusty loud cry, she eats well, see how pink and plump her cheeks are—"

"Did you say Isabella?" Henry asked irritably.

I nodded, smiling.

"Her name is Mary." He spoke slowly, giving each word emphasis and leaving me and the others in the room in no doubt that his decision was final.

"Could she not be called Mary Isabella?" I asked, nothing daunted. After all, royal and highborn children were always given a long list of names.

"She could not. I want no more reminders of Spain! No sneering or jibes about my Spanish wife who can fight like a man but cannot breed sons!"

His voice shook, he trembled with anger. The baby woke, and began to cry.

I let Henry sputter on, without contradicting him, until I heard him say, in a gruff tone, "At least your traitor father can't complain any longer."

"Why not?"

"Because you no longer have a father."

Stunned, and not certain I had heard him correctly—baby Isabella did indeed possess a loud and lusty wailing cry—I hesitated.

"But he sent me his most skilled physician, and a midwife from Granada, only last month. They were with me throughout my long hours of pain!"

My protest went unheard. Henry was not listening to anything I said, he was moving toward the doorway, hands over his ears, pausing only to glance into the gilded cradle with a grimace of distaste. All but ignoring our daughter who so resembled her grandmother Isabella, and deserved to be given her name.

"The traitor Ferdinand is dead!" he snarled. "And a good thing too!"

It was true. My father had died, and no one had told me of his death for fear of upsetting me. For fear that the shock would so alarm me that I would lose my child.

Yet now that she had arrived, she continued to be my chief

source of contentment, despite all. I persisted in vain to persuade Henry to add Isabella to her long row of names. He continued to insist that she be called Princess Mary, and that no one allude to her Spanish grandparents.

He blamed my father and his failure to serve as a loyal ally in war for weakening the crusade against the French, and spread a grotesque story (which may have been true) about his death. A story he told and retold, much to my discomfort.

"The old lecher began to go wobbly at the knees," Henry began, with a laugh, "and then he shook all over, like a lame horse with a quinsy, and then he screamed like a madman until his grooms had to tie him to the bed."

The others in the room, especially his fireside companions, laughed with him, the men heartily, the women uneasily, and some of them gave me fleeting looks of sympathy. I remained calm as Henry went on.

"The priests all said he was possessed by a demon. The physicians shook their heads and murmured, 'It is a quartan ague.' But the apothecaries"—here Henry was overcome and could not stop laughing, as I struggled to keep my composure—"the apothecaries took one whiff of his piss and shouted, 'It's a love potion! He's dying from a love potion!'"

At this a roar of laughter burst forth, loud and long, and even I had to smile. Yet it was a forced smile. For though I had not seen my father in many years, and had never loved him, it was evident to me that Henry was telling this cruel story in order to wound me, to avenge himself for my failure as a wife. And, I felt, he was dishonoring our daughter, who was even then becoming the one person I loved most, my dearest treasure.

I might not be able to breed sons, as Henry said—but I had given the realm a daughter worthy of her valiant grandmother, a daughter I would always think of as Isabella, no matter what other names she bore.

Her christening was worthy of her high birth and valor. The church blazed with the light of hundreds of wax tapers, the silver christening font shining and the red and blue and green tapestries hanging along the walls glinting with jewels. Four knights held a golden canopy above her while she was brought to the altar, and she was accorded every honor as heir to the throne. At Henry's order, Thomas Wolsey had arranged it all, and was the princess's godfather. He had undergone yet another elevation in rank and honor; he had become a member of the College of Cardinals in Rome, and there were those who predicted that Cardinal Wolsey would one day be chosen to serve as the Holy Father.

Only one thing marred the princess's christening: the presence of Maria Juana, dressed in a costly silken gown and with ropes of fine pearls at her neck and wrists. King Francis had sent her to represent him as little Mary's godmother, and her smile of satisfaction and air of superiority were evident to all—and exceedingly galling to me.

"I suppose it amused him to send his whore to his rival's court," was Elizabeth Boleyn's sour comment after the ceremony ended and I was sitting among my women, embroidering a coverlet with the arms of Castile for the princess's cradle. "King Francis imagines himself superior to King Henry in every way," she went on. "He delights in mocking his adversaries. That way he does not have to fight them, to prove his own superiority. I have often heard my husband say so."

Lady Boleyn, newly returned from France, was once again among my ladies-in-waiting, and I was very pleased to have her back. Her husband Thomas Boleyn had been among those who carried the golden canopy over the princess at her christening. Like Cardinal Wolsey, Thomas Boleyn was rising in responsibility and prominence.

"I know what my mother would have said about him," I remarked without looking up from the needlework in my lap. "She would have called him a coward."

Laughter rippled through the room.

"Is it not true then, Your Highness, that Princess Mary will soon be betrothed to the coward's son?"

It was my young maid of honor Bessie Blount who asked, her low sweet voice like liquid honey. Bessie had the most beautiful singing voice of any woman then at court, and her speaking voice too was very pleasing. But her words were unwelcome. Instead of answering her, I merely sighed and went on with my embroidery. After a moment Elizabeth Boleyn answered for me.

"Indeed it is true. My husband spent many hours with the French king's secretaries drawing up the marriage contract. Princess Mary is pledged to wed King Francis's son."

I had hoped that my daughter would become the wife of my nephew Charles, the stolid, silent boy I had met many years earlier when my sister Juana came to England. According to Master Reveles, who had seen Charles at the court of the Archduchess Margaret, the quiet boy had grown into a subdued, slow-witted young man. And now this young man had inherited the crown of Spain, for he was my father's heir.

What could be more fitting, I thought, than a union between my daughter and my royal nephew, who was King of Spain? But I was not to be allowed to make that decision. The princess would marry the coward's son, and become, in time, Queen of France.

I had no wish to be reminded of that, and was grateful to hear Maria de Salinas ask Lady Boleyn about her own daughters, and whether they were yet betrothed.

I thought I saw a flicker of uncertainty cross Elizabeth Boleyn's attractive features before she answered. Then she brightened.

"Mary, our eldest, is not yet betrothed," she said, "though I have good reason to believe she soon will be. She is of high birth and fair to look upon, and her charm and good temper are very pleasing."

Many nods of agreement met Elizabeth Boleyn's words. Although her husband's Boleyn ancestry was not noble, Elizabeth herself was a Howard, of very high birth indeed, as I have said.

"Our son George is appointed to the privy chamber as the king's page," she added.

"And your younger daughter Anne, is she yet promised to a nobleman?" Maria de Salinas asked.

I paused in my embroidery to wait for the answer. I remembered the miniature portrait of Anne that Elizabeth Boleyn had shown me, with its deep scratch, and her account of how Anne had defaced it because it displeased her.

"Of that we are not certain as yet. There was talk of a Flemish nobleman, the Seigneur de Courbaron—" she began, then broke off abruptly, as if uncertain how to go on.

"She is young yet, is she not?" I asked.

"She is nearly fourteen." Elizabeth paused again, then went on in a much lower tone. "In truth, we are at a loss to know what is best for her. Thomas and I are very nearly at our wits' end."

10

THE SULLEN, DISHEVELED GIRL WHO STOOD AT HER MOTHER'S SIDE in my apartments was taller than I was, and much more slender. Her nose was too large, her thin-lipped mouth too small, and I could see that she disliked being there.

She is a wayward girl, I thought. She will never be brought to obedience. There is far too much pride and defiance in her dark brown eyes, though they are quite lovely eyes, and no doubt alluring to men. Why then had no husband been found for her?

Lady Boleyn had asked if she could bring Anne with her when she spoke to me privately, and I agreed.

"She is willful," Elizabeth began. "She has been sent away from the archduchess's court in disgrace."

"What manner of disgrace?"

"For—the sin of lust, Your Highness."

"It's a foul lie!" Anne burst out. "I am much envied by other girls. They tell lies about me, so that they can have me sent away. So that they can have all the men to themselves!"

"No more! Or I will have you whipped." At her mother's exasperated command, Anne grew silent.

"Whenever she is accused," Lady Boleyn said to me, "she blames others. She will never admit that she has done anything wrong! She refuses to be repentant."

"Do you confess your sins?" I asked Anne, "As all Christians are taught to do?"

A slight nod from Anne.

"Would you confess your sins to a cardinal of the church, if I asked him to hear your confession?" She blanched.

"Not if he is a sinner, who has a wife in Ipswich and three children!"

Anne was repeating what was often said about Thomas Wolsey, that like many among those in holy orders, including my own confessor Fray Diego, he was unchaste and had a family. Fray Diego had been dismissed from my household and sent back to Spain as punishment for his own tavern sins, sins of the flesh displayed once too often and too flagrantly.

"I see that you have been unable to teach your daughter to curb her tongue or guard her purity," I went on, as Anne glared at me, her dark eyes full of suspicion, saying nothing. "If she is to be brought into a noble or royal household, she must be trained in courtly manners. She must learn how to make herself agreeable, how not to give offense by anything she says or does. Otherwise, Anne," I added, turning once again to the girl, "I am very much afraid that you will not marry."

A brief silence fell. I could see that instead of taking my ominous warning to heart, Anne was finding everything I said tedious.

"We had thought that a union between the young Ormond heir, James Butler, and Anne could be quietly arranged," Elizabeth Boleyn offered, "as it would have settled an old quarrel over the title of earl."

Anne snorted. "A squealing piglet, a short-sighted blinking boy chorister too fragile to do anything but sing like a girl!"

Ignoring Anne's outburst, Lady Boleyn went on.

"But even when the boy's father was assured that Anne's dowry would be doubled and that he himself would be promised a place in the king's privy chamber, he refused. He knew of her banishment, and what was being said about her at the archduchess's court."

Suddenly Anne pushed up one lace-edged sleeve of her gown, to reveal deep red scars that ran from above her elbow nearly to her wrist.

"This is my marriage portion. My dowry."

"Thomas whipped her for her transgressions, and for staining our family's honor, but she would not be cowed," Elizabeth explained.

I thought it stark punishment indeed. Even when at his most angry, when sputtering with rage, my father had not dared to inflict such a punishment on any of his children. I had heard it said that the English were brutal to their sons and daughters. Now I saw why.

"If Butler will not have her for his son, we fear that no one will," Elizabeth Boleyn was saying.

"There is always the convent," I put in after a time. "It is no disgrace to live among the holy sisters, and the daughters of noble houses who do not marry often find contentment there."

Anne's eyes blazed at this suggestion. "Such a sorry life might satisfy you, Your Highness, but I—"

"You will do as you are told!" Elizabeth would have slapped her daughter had I not intervened.

"I have heard enough!" I said to them both. "I shall not insist that you make your confession to Cardinal Wolsey, Anne, but you must ask forgiveness of your own confessor."

"She will, I assure you," Lady Boleyn said as she grasped Anne's scarred arm, making her daughter wince. "And if she does not, she will be whipped until she does."

Mother and daughter bowed to me and were about to leave the chamber.

"There is one thing more," I said. "True repentance cannot be forced, it must come from the heart." I knew, even as I spoke, how pompous—even sententious—I must sound. Had I not known, the scornful look in Anne's eyes would have told me. Yet I went on.

"Repentance is a spiritual gift, as is truthfulness itself. Anne, I insist that you answer two questions truthfully."

I led her to the prie-dieu and told her to kneel. She hesitated, looking from her mother to me, unsure what to do. Then with a defiant swish of the satin skirt of her gown, she knelt on the embroidered cushion.

"Anne, do you avow that all that is being said about you and the Seigneur de Courbaron is untrue?"

She nodded.

"And do you avow, to your mother and to me, that you are a virgin?"

She nodded once again, though less readily and with less conviction.

"Then we will accept your word and your vow, and not let this matter trouble us further. You may get up now."

I felt a wave of relief, Elizabeth Boleyn squared her shoulders and settled into calm, and even Anne appeared to be subdued as she got up slowly from where she knelt and stood beside her mother, looking down at the floor. She seemed to be trembling, but whether from fear or anger I could not have said.

All was quiet for a time.

"Now then," I remarked at length to Anne, "what is to be done with you?"

I scrutinized her, taking in once again her scrawny, emaciated body and unappealing face with its overly large nose and thin-lipped small mouth. Then I looked again, doubting my own eyes. For it seemed to me that she had become even less appealing, more an awkward overgrown child than the unruly, wayward girl with the lovely dark eyes who had challenged me.

Her carapace of defiance had crumbled.

"I am told that Queen Claude welcomes nobly born girls to her household, girls who may—how shall I put it?—girls who may lack polish and self-assurance." I smiled. "She molds these awkward young girls into marriageable young ladies, who know how to dress with elegance, how to present themselves pleasingly, how to dance—"

"Oh, I am already an excellent dancer, Your Highness," Anne interrupted me.

"She is indeed," Elizabeth Boleyn put in, smiling for the first time that afternoon.

"Why not send her to France then?" I said, relieved that the interview was at an end. "It would seem the wisest thing to do."

What pride I felt on the day my fair, blond daughter Mary was betrothed! She was not yet three years old in that October of the Year of Our Lord 1518. A small, fragile girl in her regal gown of cloth of gold, agreeable and poised and much admired.

The Great Chamber at Greenwich was so overcrowded and so full of smoke from the hearth fires and cressets that I was afraid she would find it hard to breathe, especially in the tightly fitting golden gown she was wearing with its jeweled stomacher and with many heavy gold chains around her delicate neck.

But Mary was stronger and more resilient than she appeared. She had survived the dread scourge of the sweat, that plague that had killed so many babies during the previous year. She was energetic and clever, quick to learn and eager to please. When her godfather Cardinal Wolsey reached for her hand and placed a ring on her finger in token of her betrothal, she smiled—and my own sense of pride and satisfaction grew.

I had done all I could to make certain that Mary would be seen as the undoubted heir to her father's throne. Her gown, her mantle furred with ermine, even her feathered cap so like the one her father wore were all reminders to those who were watching her that she was indeed the only rightful heir—or so I hoped.

For she had a rival. Bessie Blount was once again said to be carrying my husband's child, and this time it was no idle tale spread by the spiteful Maria Juana—a tale that turned out to be nothing more than a rumor. This time I feared that the gossip was true. And if Bessie's unborn child was a boy, then Mary's rights might be ignored.

A loud wailing cry from the little dauphin broke into the silence of the immense room, startling me. He was not yet a year old, squirming and crying in his nurse's arms. How much more satisfying the ceremony would be if Mary's fiancé was my nephew Charles, I thought. How my mother would have rejoiced to know that the two royal cousins were to become husband and wife.

The more I tried to banish these vain musings, the more they plagued me. Yet I knew that there was nothing I could do to change what was—only what was yet to be, if I had the courage.

It was at the Christmas masquing of that same year, the year of Mary's betrothal to the dauphin, that I knew for certain of Bessie's condition. For months Bessie's round, smiling face had been growing fuller, her cheeks more plump and her generous breasts more ripe and raised. When Henry chose another of my maids instead of Bessie— always his favorite partner—in the masque of "Ladies of Castile," and Bessie, cheerful and blushing, did not join in the dancing at all and left the banqueting chamber after only a few hours, there could be no doubt: she was indeed pregnant.

And when, the following spring, she was delivered of a son— the king's son—and he was given the name Henry Fitzroy, I wept.

I wept, in secret, night after night, while doing my best to appear unperturbed when others were near during the day. I confess that, to my everlasting shame, when my grief and anger were at their worst, I not only wept, I prayed that Bessie's son would not survive.

I confess it—and I regret it.

Yet I understood it. I understood this sinful, uncharitable urge I felt to destroy the boy who stood between my dearly loved daughter and her inheritance, her destiny. I did not want Mary (who I still thought of quite often as Isabella) to be thrust aside, her worth and royal lineage disregarded, merely because she was a princess and not a prince.

That Henry Fitzroy was my husband's natural son was of no importance. What mattered, if he survived, was that he was a son, and would be called prince and regarded as heir to his father's throne. Mary would be forgotten.

If Henry Fitzroy survived.

How I wrestled with my conscience that spring! Each time I saw Bessie Blount, or overheard a whispered conversation about Henry Fitzroy, or saw him given an honor or a title (he received many), I clenched my fists and wished him out of the way. Many a night I wished him dead, as my own babies had died, all but Mary. It was Mary who deserved every honor and title, not the wriggling little runt of a boy who had no right to the throne of England. He was a bastard, conceived in lust, Mary was the true daughter of a king and queen, conceived honorably and already betrothed to the dauphin of France.

Surely it was Mary, not Henry Fitzroy, who bore the favor of the Lord. And I would defend Mary and protect her rights, at whatever cost, even if it meant—what? Could I really bring myself to do harm to an innocent child in his cradle?

It had happened before. I remembered what my old duenna Doña Elvira had once confided to me about my mother.

"The great Queen Isabella," she said in low tones on that long-ago afternoon, "was far from scrupulous in all she did. It was rumored—and I believed the rumors, and still believe them—that she hounded her niece, who was the rightful heir to the throne of Castile, into exile. That she bribed and threatened the grandees of Castile to make them support her and not the rightful heir. Any woman who wins the throne of a realm such as Castile must fight and lie, threaten and even bribe those who oppose her. 'Women are thought to be weak,' I heard her say more than once. 'We must make ourselves appear strong, indeed invincible, in order to crush our enemies.'"

Doña Elvira had had a gleam in her eye when she told me these astonishing things, a gleam of triumph, as if she had played some small part in my mother's transgressions and ultimate triumph.

I thought often about what my duenna had told me years earlier. It troubled me, for whatever her faults, Doña Elvira was not generally given to lying and I too had heard the rumors about my mother's forcing her niece aside and using any and every means to fight off her opponents. I had never wanted to believe the rumors. I wanted to continue to believe, as I had when I was a child, that my dear, revered mother was blameless, a great and heroic queen, entirely without sin or fault.

I also remembered Doña Elvira's having said that my mother truly believed that she had been born to do the Lord's bidding, to carry out his work. If doing his bidding meant setting aside his teachings and committing sins, that was none of her concern. She was merely the Lord's instrument, and because she was, everything she did was done in his name, for his good purposes.

I wondered where in the Scriptures it was written that evil could be done in the name of good, and how often such reasoning was followed. I remembered the story of how all the young boys in Bethlehem were killed on the orders of King Herod, so that the newborn King of the Jews would not survive. Surely those children were innocent victims—yet they had to be sacrificed. It was all part of a divine plan.

Puzzling, troubling thoughts gnawed at me every time I saw the helpless little Henry Fitzroy, carried proudly in my husband's arms. Was I meant to be the Hand of Vengeance of the Lord to strike down Henry Fitzroy? And even if I succeeded, wouldn't Bessie have another of the king's sons to take his place?

As I turned these thoughts over in my mind, I felt chastened, reproved by my own conscience. I had insisted that Elizabeth Boleyn's wayward daughter Anne confess her sins. How much more, I thought, ought I to confess mine. I had far greater sins to confess, with my thoughts of harm.

I sought out my own confessor and poured out my heart, was shriven, and felt somewhat better.

———

My nephew Charles was coming to visit me.

He would be traveling from Spain to his new realms far to the north, and on his way would land at Dover, and we would commune together there.

I hurried to prepare for our meeting, eager to see him and talk with him, now that he had taken on new powers and titles no one in my family had ever imagined he might one day acquire. For Charles had become not only King of Spain when my father Ferdinand died but Emperor of the German-speaking lands as well. He bore the exalted title Holy Roman Emperor, and what was even more important, as ruler of Spain and the empire, he not only commanded thousands of skilled fighting men but was exceedingly wealthy, his treasury enlarged each year by newfound riches from the Americas. I had heard my husband say that my nephew Charles had the fattest treasury of any monarch, certainly far fatter than his own.

The last time I had seen Charles was when he was a solemn, taciturn little boy of six or seven, traveling with his mother, my beautiful sister Juana. I remembered his reserve, and that he did not smile. What would he be like now, I wondered. Would he remember me, and be glad to see me?

I rose at dawn on the day he was due to arrive, and watched from the castle parapet for a ship bearing the arms and pennons of Spain. The port was windy on that winter's day, and full of ships, among them the immense four-masted *Great Harry,* my husband's magnificent flagship. Henry was once again bound for France, not to make war this time but to meet with King Francis in grand tourneying, amid much splendor and display.

The feats of arms, it was said, would be less impressive than the gorgeous pageantry surrounding them. Henry and Francis would compete in the lists, and would wrestle with one another, and vie for the honor of most skilled horseman, and their knights and chief gentlemen would compete against one another in the same fashion. But there was another, more significant purpose in the event; it was to be a celebration of unity. Our daughter Mary was betrothed to

Francis's son, and the expectation was that England and France were to be allied, putting an end to the warfare that had drained England's treasury and led to much grumbling in Parliament and among the people of both realms. It was only fitting, Henry thought, that a magnificent tournament should be held to celebrate the peaceable union.

I waited, there on the parapet, for nearly an hour, watching for my nephew Charles to arrive. At last the large imperial ship was sighted on the horizon, and her guns fired a greeting. I continued to watch while the pilot brought the vessel into port and dropped anchor. My nephew, his hound, and a dozen of his attendants were rowed ashore and before long made their way to the castle.

No sooner were Charles and I settled in comfort in a warm, firelit upper room, food and drink spread before us and our servants sent away, than he began to speak plainly of his suspicions about the French.

"Warn King Henry," he said, his voice thick and hoarse and marred by a lisp, "that the French are fortifying Ardres. At least four thousand fighting men are concealed there and in nearby villages. They are not there for tourneying, but to invade England."

He came closer, leaning toward me so that he did not need to raise his voice above a whisper. "King Francis means to seize the English realm within the year and make it his own. My scouts are keeping watch at all the ports. French ships disguised as Hansa freight vessels are waiting for the signal to make the crossing, while King Henry disports himself at Guines."

The announcement took me by surprise, but I lost no time in sending word on to the captain of the *Great Harry,* confident that he would in turn make certain that my husband received this news.

It sounded dire. The tourneying was to be held in the Val Doré, between the towns of Guines and Ardres. If the French should indeed invade England in force while King Henry and his most skilled knights were in France, unable to mount a defense, and if Henry himself were to be captured—I could only imagine what harm would result. Clearly my nephew had become an astute observer, watchful and wary of armed might, whatever its source, despite his youth and inexperience in war.

I looked at him with new interest, even respect. His body was still stout, his face square, though a dark beard circled his chin and his once blond hair had darkened to a rich brown. When he moved he lacked my husband's grace and agility, and his speech was thick, his jaw unnaturally slack. He resembled more his late father Philip than my sister Juana. But there was an unmistakable air of majesty, even of command, about him—or did I imagine it, knowing the titles he bore and the powers he held? Either way he impressed me, and I thought for a moment how proud Juana would be if she could see him now, wearing his authority with ease, his hound crouched beside him with its head on his knee.

I hesitated to ask the question that was uppermost in my own mind, then decided to go ahead.

"What news of your mother?"

He frowned, then sighed as if resigned to telling me what he knew I was anxious to hear, though it was both sad and distasteful.

"She lives in comfort, in the Alhambra, with physicians and priests to attend her," he began, speaking slowly and thoughtfully, "but she is hardly aware of where she is or who is watching over her. She imagines that my father is still alive, asleep in his coffin—"

"His coffin?" I interrupted. "But he has been entombed for years."

Charles nodded. "She refuses to believe that. When she first moved into her apartments in the palace, she demanded that he be brought to her, to share her dwelling. So a coffin was brought—an empty coffin."

He paused before going on. "She is in distress unless she is allowed to care for him. She orders food and wine brought to her, and imagines that she feeds him. She has medicines brought by the apothecaries when she says he is ill, and blankets thrown into the empty coffin when she insists he is cold. She ministers to him as if he were a helpless child. It soothes her to do this. Otherwise she screams and cries without ceasing."

"Does she know you?" I asked after a moment. "Would she know me if I went to visit her?"

He shook his head.

"Can nothing be done?"

"A companion was found for her who seems to soothe her. A healer from Ghent who is known as the Great Woman of Flanders. They talk to one another, after a fashion, and when the healer is there, mother is able to sleep. Before the woman was found and sent to our court, mother never slept at all. Instead she spent every hour pacing and ranting, and had to be kept from running out to the verandah and jumping to her death."

We continued our meal in silence for a time, though after hearing about poor Juana I had no appetite and simply sat, trying not to imagine my sister in her private torment, throwing herself down from the heights of the Alhambra onto the sharp rocks below and ending her life. Now and then I took a sip of wine, while Charles consumed three courses and afterward belched loudly in satisfaction, throwing the scraps to his hound.

We strolled together in the private garden, braving the wind as Charles talked further about what he had seen on his recent journey, and what his informers had told him about the treachery of King Francis. Our talk left me with much to ponder.

The following morning Charles surprised me once again by asking to see a portrait of Princess Mary.

I showed him the portrait miniature I always kept with me.

"I only wish she were here with us," I said as he looked at the likeness, his features softening, a slight smile on his lips.

"So this is the little Queen of France, that is to be," he murmured.

"Henry calls her his prize possession. He is fond of carrying her in his arms and showing her off to everyone at court."

"As he does with his other child, so I am told. The one he calls Henry Fitzroy."

I nodded.

"His mistress's son," he added. He did not spare me, but looked me squarely in the eye, as if to say, "The son you should have had."

What he did and said was disrespectful, but it was no more than the truth. It was I, Catalina, who should have borne the son who would inherit the throne of the Tudors.

"Your nursery is still full of empty cradles, then," my nephew remarked, handing me back the miniature portrait of Mary. "Uncle Ferdinand was beside himself with anger when you failed to bring sons into the world, year after year—"

"I continue to pray that the Lord will send me sons," was my curt reply. I surprised myself by the bitterness in my tone.

"You are thirty-four years old, are you not?

I nodded.

"You cannot expect to conceive many more times. Sons born to aged women are small and weak. Or if they are strong, the mothers die. As the midwives say, boys are much harder on their mothers than girls, from labor onwards."

Charles paced the floor, his brow wrinkled, whether in thought or worry I could not tell. The hound kept pace with him, looking up at him from time to time.

"Does the king continue to come to your bed?" Charles asked after a moment.

"He does," I insisted. "And I have twice felt babes leap in my womb, since Mary was born. But both times they were lost." I hung my head. "I could not carry either of them for more than a few months."

"Perhaps it is as well. At least you have your daughter. She will reign in good time." He slapped his thigh, making the hound yelp and jump, putting its great paws on the wide golden panels of Charles's brocade coat. "Yes, she will reign. All the more reason to make certain she does not marry the French dauphin."

"But the grand celebration of unity, the tourneying—" I began, thinking of all the months of preparation, all the costly arrangements, that had gone into the meeting of the two kings, Henry and Francis. The meeting that would soon take place, unless . . .

"As to that, leave everything to Cardinal Wolsey and his minions. And to the diplomats and secretaries who even now are meeting, aboard my ship, to undo all the agreements and renounce them. The real celebration will come after the tournament is over, on the day the world is told that Princess Mary is betrothed, not to the French prince, but to me."

11

THE EIGHTH WONDER OF THE WORLD! THAT'S WHAT IT IS."

"There's never been another tourney to match it. And never will be again!"

"They say it is costing eight thousand ducats a day, and more, to pay all those men."

"The king swears he won't cut his beard until the day the tourney begins."

In windswept Picardy, on a plain called the Golden Valley, a wonderment was indeed in the making. Day after day, hundreds of carpenters and joiners, plasterers and bricklayers worked in wearisome shifts to build the king's imposing palace and rig the tents, paint the walls and hang the tapestries to adorn them. Our court was always full of mutterings and predictions, but that spring the talk was louder than ever and the expectations high indeed.

While we watched, from our hastily erected tents, a splendid gatehouse took form, turrets and battlements arose, choristers were heard singing in the palace chapel and the smells of spices and roasting flesh and freshly baked loaves began to reach us from the kitchens and bakehouse. Stables were built, horses exercised and groomed, and raised stands, sheltered from the sun and wind, constructed for the crowds expected to watch the jousters as they couched their lances and lowered their visors and thundered down the lists.

As my nephew Charles had predicted, Cardinal Wolsey ordered all, with the sergeant painter and the chief designer of pageants—an impatient Italian—as his deputies. The cardinal let it be known that the workmen must build the entire tourneying site in twenty-two days, whatever delays might arise from storms or plagues or quarreling between the English and French craftsmen. Unless this deadline was met, no one would be paid.

For twenty days and more the hammering, sawing and pounding continued, amid shouts of encouragement and threats from those in charge. Then, on the twenty-third day, we awoke to find that the noise had stopped. All the structures appeared to be complete, each one decorated with carved ornaments and painted blazons and pennons waving in the Tudor colors of green and white.

A large winged statue of Cupid symbolized the enduring love between the English and French. Not far away a statue of fat, smiling Bacchus symbolized enduring drunkenness—and offered conduits of free-flowing red and white wine below the inscription "Let all who will, make good cheer."

Cheer indeed there was—and not a few jibes. For the hastily erected palace was quickly given the name "Palace of Illusion" by those who mocked its flimsy construction, the walls painted to look as though they were made of bricks, the timbers too weak and insubstantial to withstand even the mildest of winter winds. Some of the Flemish artisans were overheard to mutter that the amity between England and France was also illusory, for had King Henry not ordered his builders to construct a secret passageway through which he could escape should the French attack while the tournament was under way?

Escape seemed the farthest thing from my husband's mind as he rose each morning before dawn to hunt, returning in time to have his new armor fitted—proud of the lithe slender figure he made when wearing it—and then sat at his desk, open books spread around him, composing his treatise to refute the teachings of the heretic monk Martin Luther. He met with his lutenists and organist and shawm-players and had them write out a song he had composed about friendship, "Let me then rest, among those I love best." And not until he had done all this did he take time to talk with the cardinal and his secretaries and attend to the letters and papers that required his signature.

I was less and less a part of his daily concerns in those weeks, though he did sometimes boast to me about the number of birds his falcons killed and the dozens of hares he had supplied to the kitchens after he returned from the hunt. I rode my cherished jennet Griselda, taking care not to tire her as she was no longer in her prime and easily winded, and sometimes I dismounted and walked, Griselda trailing obediently along behind me, enjoying the fitful sunshine in the low hills and the spring green and early flowers along the riverbank.

Then one afternoon my dresser Maria de Caceres brought me a large, finely wrought basket and said that it was a gift from the king.

I could tell from her delighted expression that the basket must contain something extremely pleasing. Maria could never keep a secret for long. Inside the basket, wrapped in a length of fine soft yellow silk, was a swansdown gown, so light it seemed all but weightless. The bodice was of white velvet, the sleeves and wide skirt were entirely covered in soft feathers.

"Ah! How lovely!" I cried, and let Maria fasten the delicate gown over my kirtle, pinning back my hair with a swansdown-trimmed comb. I looked in the pier glass and smiled with satisfaction. For despite the tufts of gray at my temples and the lines at the corners of my eyes, in the pristine gown I felt like a girl again, aglow with happiness, and when the king unexpectedly entered my apartments and saw me wearing his gift, I could tell that he was more than pleased.

In fact he was vaguely mystified. He waved the servants away and took both my hands in his.

"Catalina," he said, in a voice I had not heard him use in a long time. "You look—like another woman entirely."

Our embrace lasted until evensong, and beyond, and when we finally sat down to supper the swansdown gown had been laid aside, to be kept for another tryst.

I was to treasure that long and pleasurable afternoon, for after the grand tourney in the Golden Valley ended and the prizes had gone to the victors, I had a prize of my own: I was once again carrying the king's child, and my hopes rose as I imagined that this time I would give my husband a son.

It was about this time, when I was sure that I was once again with child, that my half-sister Maria Juana came back to our court.

She arrived at the palace drawn in a golden litter, borne by eight handsome Aragonese youths in coats of cloth of gold and black velvet, the gilded spurs on their red leather boots polished to a high shine.

"The Lady Maria Juana Ruiz de Iborre y Alemany!" her attendants cried, drawing back the spangled curtains of the litter to reveal my slender, veiled half-sister who looked, I must admit, far younger than her thirty-five years.

From the gleaming circlet on her abundant curling brown hair to the rubies at her throat to her jewel-encrusted belt and beringed fingers, Maria Juana wore a fortune in gems. Her gown too was costly and sparkled with silver trim. It was clear from her slight smile and the proud tilt of her head that she was very pleased with the stir she was creating.

Maria Juana had been the cause of much talk and speculation at our court for years. It was said that she had been the mistress of King Francis himself, and before that the betrothed of the Seigneur de Courbaron and several others. She let it be known that her lovers had been lavishly generous to her and that their many gifts had made her wealthy, yet she still awaited a husband. A husband of high enough breeding to marry the daughter of the late King Ferdinand of Aragon. King Ferdinand who was, of course, my father as well.

I urged Henry to send Maria Juana away, back to Spain—away anywhere, in fact. I told him she was causing me worry and that I must not be troubled in my condition. But in truth he was not much concerned with Maria Juana just then, or even with Bessie Blount (heaven be thanked!), nor was he more than mildly hopeful about my being able to present him with a prince by springtime. I had, after all, disappointed him often in the past, and besides, it was being said that he needed, not one, but two or three strong sons. And that I, at my age, could not be expected to provide them.

No, just then my husband was preoccupied with something more vital: he was attempting to rid the realm of its highest-ranking nobleman, the redoubtable Edward Stafford, Duke of Buckingham. The nobleman most likely to lead a rebellion, should Henry's throne become even weaker than it already was.

Why was he doing this? Because, as he told me curtly, our daughter Mary could not possibly defend England as long as such a strong nobleman as Buckingham, with his Plantagenet descent, was there to remind all Henry's subjects that a king, not a frail girl, was what they needed.

"You know as well as I do that no mere woman can rule this realm," Henry insisted, as he had often before, "or defend it against the armies of the French." He was more than ever convinced of this after the tournament in the Golden Valley, in which there was much display but little actual force or power.

I had to agree. Henry, splendid, dashing and strong as he was, a brilliant showman and horseman, had won the prize of the tourney, but in doing so had driven himself far past the limit of his strength. He had been sick after every joust, and in allowing himself to ride too hard, for too long, he had shown himself weak in judgment. This weakness was noticed. And the suave, handsome King Francis had commented on it. As had Buckingham and many of the other nobles who had taken part.

No, Buckingham had to go. Henry was convinced of it. So the

duke was accused of plotting the king's death, and judged and condemned by his peers—who dared not make any other judgment, lest they go against the king's wishes. The wretched duke was imprisoned in the Tower to await his execution.

It was soon done. On a bright May morning in the Year of Our Lord 1521, Edward Stafford, Duke of Buckingham, was executed, and soon afterward the betrothal of Princess Mary to the French dauphin was broken, and a treaty with my nephew Charles was signed.

"Mary will wed the emperor," Henry announced, and though I felt sorrow at the thought that my lovely daughter would be sent far away to live at the imperial court, I realized that my husband was right. Mary needed a mighty husband, one who commanded armies of mercenaries, one possessed of immense wealth.

Which was why, when Maria Juana made her appearance at our court, I felt a frisson of worry. Why had she chosen to come to England at all? Why not return to Spain, or seek her fortune in Italy, where there was so much turmoil and disarray, with warring armies contending for princely riches? The Medici of Florence were reputed to be wealthy beyond imagining; that family had spread its tentacles very wide, from the secular courts to the papal court of Rome. Maria Juana de Medici: that name had a welcome ring to it. Could she not find a husband in Florence, and leave England forever?

Yet she stayed, and continued to inspire gossip and curiosity, and despite my urging, Henry did not remove her, not even when I took my chamber to await the birth of my child.

He was late in arriving, and so large, so heavy and active inside me, that for the last week before he burst out of my womb, I could not sleep at all.

He exhausted me with his kicking and thumping, preventing me from resting, from gathering the strength I knew I would need to bring him into the world. My midwives did their best for me, giving me drinks to induce the sweat trance and pushing down on my swollen belly for hours on end. But the baby seemed unable to break free until after a last long, painful night he emerged, bloody and writhing, into the chief midwife's waiting arms.

I could hear him choking. I could see, by the firelight and the flickering light of the many candles around my groaning chair, that his face was red and his lips thick with mucus. Again and again the chief midwife slapped his plump buttocks, his back, even his red cheeks in an effort to get him to breathe. At last, in her desperation, she opened his mouth and reached down into his throat with one finger.

"Breathe, little prince!" she commanded. But the baby's eyes were closed and his tiny fists, which had been clenched with the effort he made to catch his breath, had gone limp.

"Give him to me!" My voice was hoarse, my own throat tight as the helpless baby was handed to me, half naked, half wrapped in a swathe of stained linen. I opened his mouth and blew into it as forcefully as I could, as I remembered doing when Princess Mary was born. He choked, then coughed, and began to breathe. In a moment I put him to my breast and he suckled, strongly and evenly. Before long he opened his eyes and clenched his fists once again.

All that day he appeared to thrive, suckling, whimpering, crying—though not very loudly—and sleeping. He lived for six days, then fainted, and did not recover. My husband, his own fists clenched and his face purple and contorted with anger, ordered five hundred masses to be offered for his soul.

I cried as I had never cried before, not even when my beloved mother died. The little prince had been my last child, I was in no doubt of that. I would never be able to have another.

Now I was certain that I was not destined to bear a son to rule England. I was a failure, of no use to anyone. And indeed it was the death of the prince, the death of my last child, that brought everything to a head: our marriage, the succession to the throne, and England's future.

Even as I was recovering from my own physical ordeal—for the long, painful hours of labor had left me weak and spent—my husband was taking counsel with his astrologers and alchemists, and with the cardinal, who guided all our fates just then, and with his commanders.

Henry's plans had been disrupted. He had been determined to conquer France, then lead a grand army of crusading knights far to the east, to recapture the Holy City of Jerusalem. He had hinted at these ambitions when talking to me, but I had looked on them as nothing more than fancies, vain imaginings.

"Men want more of everything, it is their nature," I remembered hearing my old duenna Doña Elvira say. "The weak ones cringe and connive, but the strong ones dream great dreams of conquest and dominion. Of overcoming all odds. When their world is broken, they use all their might to restore it again."

Her words seemed to me very apt just at that time, for King Francis was struggling to recapture his conquests in Italy and my nephew Charles, with his stronger army and overflowing treasure chests, was pushing deeper and deeper into the lands once dominated by the church. In battle after battle the soldiers of the emperor were winning, and it was being said that England could not survive long in the churning cauldron of war.

I saw clearly, or thought I did, how all that was happening was likely to affect me. I had become an encumbrance to Henry. I had given him a daughter, my dear Mary, but our daughter could not be expected to rule effectively on her own, no matter how capable she might be. Even little Henry Fitzroy, once my husband's hope for the future, was a weak and sickly child, thin and small for his age.

What England needed was a strong, energetic heir to the throne. What Henry needed was a young and fertile wife who could provide such a prince. I was incapable, and I knew it. I mourned, and in my mourning, I prayed. And by the following Advent season, when I had turned these thoughts over in my mind again and again, and resigned myself as best I could to whatever future lay in store for me, I decided it was time I had yet another serious talk with my nephew Charles.

Once again we met at Dover Castle, in the midst of a storm, the skies dark with rain and the sea flecked with gray-white foam. I had thought of taking Mary with me, then changed my mind. She was nearly six years old, quick-witted and sensitive. Her health was delicate, especially in autumn and winter, and I was not at all sure that I wanted her to be disturbed by what Charles and I needed to talk about. In the end I left her with her nursemaids, and came on alone.

Alone, that is, with my gentleman usher Griffith Richards and three of my ladies-in-waiting, who sat quietly by as I waited for my nephew the emperor to arrive.

But when Charles arrived, he was not alone. He had with him not only his attendants and his faithful hound, but Maria Juana! Maria Juana, demurely dressed, seemly in her manner, outwardly obedient, the image of a pious young virgin—which she certainly was not.

I had been told that she had gone on a pilgrimage to the shrine of St. Walafrid, patron saint of unmarried women praying for husbands. But I had not been told the truth; in fact she had gone to Mechelen, where she knew she would find Charles and would be able to entrap him. Charles knew little of women, anyone could see that. I had no doubt that he was inept in the ways of love, most likely untutored even in lust. He remained an overgrown boy despite his high titles and undeniable authority. Maria Juana was seductive, and when I saw Charles approaching, with my half-sister walking sedately by his side, I could tell that she had disarmed him. My temper flared.

"See who I have brought you, Aunt Catalina," Charles said in a sheepish tone. "I found her weeping before a shrine, praying for a husband."

Maria Juana had deliberately deceived me, and had taken advantage of Charles's trust. Was it possible he knew nothing of her brazen conquests, her illicit liaisons? Or was he so taken with her that he cared nothing for her past? Or was it possible that she had convinced him that with the right husband, she could mend her ways?

It was all I could do to keep my composure. "So you decided not to visit the shrine of St. Walafrid after all," I began, glaring at Maria Juana.

"Pardon me, Your Majesty, but I did. Then I heard of the wonder-working powers of St. Juliana, whose shrine is at Mechelen, and I hurried there to invoke her aid."

As Maria Juana was speaking, Charles nodded benignly, looking more like a fond, approving father or grandfather than a captivated young man.

"I prayed to the saint most earnestly," Maria Juana went on. "I confided to her that many years ago, our father King Ferdinand instructed you to arrange an honorable marriage for me, but that so far you had not done so."

"What's this?" Charles interrupted. "I know nothing of this!" The hound, which had been sleeping at his master's feet, sat up and began to bark excitedly, making Maria Juana draw back in fear.

What she said was true. Years earlier, when I first came to England, my father had told me to find a husband for Maria Juana, and I never had. But my father was long dead.

"Old instructions from an old man," I said aloud. "I was a girl then, on my way to a new country and a husband I had never met. Poor Arthur," I added. "He was never very strong. He was so ill—"

The hound continued to bark. Charles looked pale.

"With your permission, dear Aunt Catalina, I must rest— The seas were rough—my stomach—" He put his hands to his belly and belched loudly.

"A proper English belch," I remarked, and smiled at him. I suddenly felt empathy for this boy, still so young, apt to be taken advantage of by everyone.

He did look pale and ill, yet I had no doubt that dealing with Maria Juana and her wiles had worn him down. I reminded myself that much rested on this young man's shoulders—and could not help but notice that while he seemed astute beyond his years in some ways, in others he was as innocent as a babe.

"My gentleman usher will provide what you need," I told him in a gentler tone, and summoning Griffith Richards, I put an end to our talk, leaving Maria Juana to find her own lodging—which I prayed would not be with my nephew.

It was not until the evening of the following day that Charles and I spoke again, this time without the disturbing presence of Maria Juana. The December night was cold and wet. We sat close to the blazing hearth, looking out toward the sea as the last pale rays of sunset light were fading.

He broke in on my contemplative mood, to tell me, somewhat abruptly, that he had made up his mind to marry Maria Juana.

"My counselors advise against this marriage," he told me. "They want me to choose between Isabella of Portugal and the French princess."

"Or Princess Mary," I was quick to interject. "Who would bring you all the lands and wealth of England."

"And who is a child of five," he said.

"Nearly six, and such a pretty, intelligent, sweet-natured girl."

"She comes from a line of women unable to bear strong sons. I require a fruitful empress."

"But not an unsullied, virginal one, it would seem."

He smiled, and drank deeply from his wine glass.

"Maria Juana pleases me," he said simply. "She makes no demands. She has been my companion for over a year." He set down his glass and looked at me. "I see no reason why I shouldn't marry her."

He paused, then went on. "Your daughter is my cousin, in a close degree of affinity. If I chose to make her my wife, the canon lawyers would require a dispensation from the Holy Father in Rome. No such dispensation would be necessary if I take Maria Juana to wife. We are not close in blood—"

"She is your grandfather's bastard!" I blurted out.

"So she never ceases to remind me. And she also reminds me that you caused her mother's death."

I shook my head. "I never did. No matter how often she repeats that lie, it is not true. I swear it on the Blood of Our Lord." It was as stern a denial as I had ever made.

The hearth fire crackled. Eventually I went on.

"You must not be distracted by spiteful gossip, Charles. Or led astray by lowborn temptresses. Maria Juana is not fit to become your consort. You must marry a princess of the blood royal. And then, if you feel the prickings of lust, you will do as my husband Henry does, and find your pleasures among the women and girls of your court.

"I am only telling you what your father and mother would say to you, if they were still able to advise you," I added after a moment. But Charles merely went on sitting quietly, now and then looking over at me, his expression thoughtful, and drinking his wine.

"Do you know," I began again after a time, "my husband Henry does not travel aboard the *Catherine Pleasaunce* as he once did. It was named for me. There was a time when he would not board any other vessel—except perhaps the *Catherine Fortileza,* which was also named for me. He ordered that ship made shortly after our marriage. He paid me honor then. Now—"

"It has been rumored he means to put you aside," was Charles's abrupt remark. "Best to face it, Aunt Catherine. I doubt whether it can be avoided. Not even by the Holy Father in Rome, Pope Adrian, whose election I took such pains and cost to ensure."

It was true. My nephew had used all his considerable influence, and—so it was said—a great deal of gold to persuade the College of Cardinals in Rome to elect his former tutor Adrian of Utrecht pope. It was a strategy Cardinal Wolsey would never forgive, as he coveted the office of Bishop of Rome for himself.

Charles stood then, and stretched out his hands to the hearth fire. "No, I doubt it very much. But should the worst happen, I will do my utmost to protect you—and to preserve the honor of our family. I cannot marry Princess Mary, she is too young and I must have an heir as soon as possible."

"But surely—" I began, only to be silenced by my nephew's shaking head.

"If King Henry means to put you aside and take a younger wife," he said, "then nothing on earth will persuade him otherwise. Once he makes up his mind, he will not change it. Not for all the gold in the Americas, or all the might of Spain."

12

No matter how hard I tried, I could not put my nephew's words out of my mind. Hours passed, and still his pronouncement lingered, making it impossible for me to think of anything else. That night I knelt on my prie-dieu, and asked for relief from the nagging worry that kept me from sleep.

"When he makes up his mind," Charles had said of my husband, "he will not change it. Not for all the gold in the Americas, or all the might of Spain."

His voice, hoarse and rough as always, held a note of warning. He seemed to be saying that there was no way I could escape a foredoomed future. My every instinct told me that I faced a major obstacle, one that might prove to defeat me.

The following afternoon I had a most unwelcome visitor.

"The Lady Maria Juana Ruiz de Iborre y Alemany!"

I looked up, to see my gentleman usher Griffith Richards standing on the threshold of my apartments, with Maria Juana behind him.

I hesitated. I wanted to send her away. Yet her presence in my apartments was a challenge, and I felt myself rising to the challenge. As a warrior would. As my mother, the great Queen Isabella, would have. (Oh, how I missed her at such times!)

I stood, my back straight, my head held high—all too aware, even as I did so, that I was a good deal shorter than Maria Juana, and that I did not look my best. I bore the marks of fatigue and worry, and of my lack of sleep the night before. Steeling myself, I told my gentleman usher to admit my half-sister.

She made no pretense of politeness. Gone was all trace of the simpering coyness she had shown when with the emperor. Instead she spoke plainly, and seemingly without evasion, of what concerned us most.

"Charles has been taking counsel with experts in the law of the church," she began. "Since I am always at his side, I hear what is said between them. Unlike you, Catalina, I was not tutored in Latin and Greek. I am not learned. But I have an attentive ear, and I understand much of what is said in these talks. I understand more, I'm sure, than Charles imagines."

I could well believe what she said. Maria Juana was shrewd and intelligent—and when it came to her own interests, quite ruthless. Or so I was discovering.

She shook out her skirts and took a few steps, heedless of the strict etiquette that she had learned to follow when she was a member of my household. Then, she would never have dared turn her back on me, or spoken to me without my permission; now, she moved where she liked, said what she liked, and flaunted her freedom. I saw Griffith Richards wince at the sight. Yet he remained silent, sensing that I did not want him to object or interfere.

"Before long you will be replaced as queen," Maria Juana was saying as she paced. "King Henry and his lawyers will use every argument they know to bring this about. One of their arguments will be that in marrying you, King Henry offended against the divine law. In the Book of Leviticus it is written that it is wrong for a man to marry his brother's widow. If he does, he faces divine punishment. The marriage is condemned. There will be no children.

"You were married to King Henry's brother Arthur, and then, after Arthur died, to Henry. Your marriage to Henry is cursed. Therefore King Henry must find another wife. One not tainted by a former marriage to his brother."

Maria Juana looked keenly at me, to gauge my reaction. I remained quiet. I had heard this same line of argument often before, from my husband and from my own confessor, each time one of my babies died, or I miscarried.

"Yet if Arthur was too weak or too young to take your virginity, then you were never truly married to him, and once he died, you were free to marry Henry just as if you were an untouched young girl." She paused, then added, "Only a few of the women of your household know the truth about your marriage to Arthur. I am one of them."

Her words left me shaking with anger. How dare Maria Juana presume to judge the soundness of my brief, sad marriage to Arthur? To be sure, he was a thin, weak young man and I a virgin when we were wed. Beyond that, only Arthur and I knew what had passed between us once we were husband and wife. And Arthur had long since left me a widow.

"I assure you, Maria Juana, that *I* know the truth—and unlike you, I speak the truth. You say whatever suits you, whatever benefits you. I say what I know to be true, whether it benefits me or not."

At this she laughed in derision.

"Surely, Catalina, you are not so naïve. Everyone serves their own advantage in what they say, whether they realize it or not."

But she had more to say. And in saying it she remained cool and detached. It was clear to me that my half-sister had made bargains before, and profitable bargains, to judge from her rise in wealth and possessions. In return for much gold and other riches, she had traded her body, her birthright as King Ferdinand's daughter, and her ability to keep and reveal secrets of the court. And now she was on the threshold of making the greatest bargain of her life: trading a precious secret she knew concerning my marriage to Arthur for the high honor and position of wife to Emperor Charles and mother to his children.

"Here is what I propose," Maria Juana was saying. "You, Catalina, are in hopes of preventing King Henry from setting you aside. I wish to marry Emperor Charles. We can accommodate one another, if you are willing. We can reach a bargain."

Skeptical, I asked what the terms of this bargain would be.

Before answering me Maria Juana looked over at my gentleman usher, who continued to stand all but motionless at the doorway of my apartments, as if to block Maria Juana from leaving. His expression was impassive but I noticed that his face was growing more and more red—a sure sign of vexation.

"If you should try to prevent the emperor from making me his consort," Maria Juana said in a low voice, barely above a whisper, "then I will reveal what I know of your wedding night with Prince Arthur. If you offer no objection, I will keep what I know to myself."

It was as though a blow had struck me, I felt such a shock. So she meant to lie, to distort the truth of what had happened on that long-ago wedding night, and indeed on all the nights of my brief marriage to poor unfortunate Arthur. She meant to betray me, and the memory of dear Arthur, who knew so well what his own weaknesses were, in order to become Charles's wife.

I looked at Maria Juana with newfound loathing. She was acting entirely out of spite. She had no need of wealth—she was already wealthy. She knew, better than anyone, that I had not caused her mother's death or harmed her in any way. She had lived in my household, watched me in my daily actions, observed my heartaches and triumphs. She had no reason to want to harm me—other than envy. I was the daughter of King Ferdinand and Queen Isabella, a royal princess and now a queen. She was my father's bastard, with no claim to his royal name or title. It was this vital difference between us that made her want to cause me harm. And she would surely do so—if she could.

"I welcome any *truthful* words you may say about my ill-omened marriage to beloved Prince Arthur. I pray daily for his soul. As to any lies you may tell, may God preserve you from eternal punishment!" I felt my cheeks grow warm, my voice rose and it was all I could do to prevent myself from slapping Maria Juana.

It was all too much for Griffith Richards. He could not remain silent any longer.

"Brazen strumpet!" he burst out. "Wanton worthless daughter of a pig!"

But Maria Juana had already slithered past him and escaped into the corridor beyond.

Nothing was as it had been.

It was as if Maria Juana was a bird of ill omen, whose appearing was a warning of dire things to come. Sailors see such birds from their ships, and quake with fear, knowing for certain that fierce storms and high waves will soon be upon them. In the same way I began to tremble with fear, and sleep badly or not at all, waiting for the first of the storms to arrive.

It did not take long.

"Traitor!" Henry bellowed on the day he learned that my nephew Charles had broken his word, and was not going to marry our daughter Mary. He howled in his rage and shook his fist. "Faithless cur! How dare he betray me!" He closeted himself with Cardinal Wolsey and I could hear more shouts of rage from the chamber where they were.

At the time I thought little of the fact that my husband did not include me in his talk with the cardinal that day, though later on my exclusion did seem significant to me. I see now that Henry was turning away, not only from me, but from his longtime reliance on Spain and her allies. Instead he had begun to fear them, as he had once feared King Francis.

Henry felt deeply aggrieved and betrayed—and in truth I did too. I had trusted my nephew to protect me and defend my interests as he had promised to do, come what may. And that meant making my beloved daughter Mary his wife, so that she too would be protected and defended. I never imagined that he would actually marry Maria Juana, no matter how potent her wiles. Her influence over him would be that of a persuasive mistress and nothing more.

Nothing more, that is, if the storms did not worsen.

But worse was yet to come.

For Charles was bent on making war, and for that he needed money—a great deal of money—and a formidable army. The army was already his to command. Our Spanish soldiers are well known to be the most feared pikemen and mounted warriors in all Christendom, only the Swiss can be compared with them when it comes to defeating the enemy—any enemy. When my nephew became King of Spain he had a force of thousands of armed men, superbly trained by the Great Captain himself, Gonzalo Fernandez de Cordoba, whose men at arms my mother had relied on in her long fight against the Moors.

As to the money Charles needed, it was his to command as well—if only he married his cousin, Isabella of Portugal. Her dowry of a million crowns was a temptation he found impossible to resist, and so he married her, and in less than a year, she gave him a son and heir.

He married her, and broke his word to Henry and to me. But the wars he waged made him ever stronger, ever more feared, and left those who had relied on him all but powerless to oppose him. In the end he became master of much of Italy, where he fought with the French and won.

Having crushed his rebellious imperial subjects in Flanders, he ordered his captains to march southward, into Milan and Lombardy, where he made King Francis his prisoner, and took the king's children hostage—which I thought was unspeakably cruel—and ordered them sent to Spain.

Nor was this the full extent of his audacity; he dared to threaten, and then to assault, the citadel of Christendom, the holy city of Rome.

———

Letters and messages began reaching my dresser Maria de Caceres from her two young cousins Rosa and Angela who were novices in the Convent of the Poor Clares in Borgo San Sepolcro. They wrote of trying to escape from the city when the first imperial soldiers began running through the streets, shouting threats and assaulting friars and nuns, seizing priests and bellowing "Pay or die!"

"I'll never forget that first terrible day," Angela wrote. "They were setting fires everywhere, shooting off their guns, making us all terrified. We had no way to escape them. We went down into the cellars where the sacramental wine was kept, but they had been there before us, and drunk all the wine. We tried to hide from them, we prayed that their commanders would stop them. But there were no commanders, no orders. Only confusion and hatred. We heard them cursing the Holy Father and all the priests and nuns—only they called us devils and whores.

"They smashed the doors of the church where Father Michael was saying mass. They rushed in and attacked him. He fell. Then when he lay helpless, pleading for his life, there before the altar, they cut off his head."

"We heard that the Holy Father, Pope Clement, had taken refuge in the fortress of the Castel Sant'Angelo," Rosa wrote, "but that did not prevent the terrible mayhem from continuing. The cruel soldiers dragged the sisters from their convents, not sparing the oldest of them, and raped them and beat them to death with sticks. They stole everything of value, even silver chalices and relics of the saints and martyrs."

Cardinal Wolsey had informants in the holy city and they sent messages to him filled with stories of damage and ruin. According to these informants, precious papal records were destroyed, documents burned, entire libraries thrown onto bonfires. Works of art were ripped with swords, graves of the holy martyrs desecrated, reliquaries made into chamber pots. Even altar cloths and vestments were stolen.

"The soldiers maimed or killed everyone and everything without mercy," Angela wrote to my dresser Maria. "Even the mothers in labor, and young children. I saw babies stuck on the sharp point of a lance, and children barely old enough to walk thrown against the stone walls and killed. There is blood everywhere, all of Rome is in mourning. If only you could have seen the faces of those men, the soldiers, filled with hate and eager to destroy all that lay in their path. They were pure hatred, pure evil."

"May God forgive them for what they have done," Rosa wrote. "I know I never shall."

I read and reread all the letters, shaking my head in wonderment and praying for the souls of those who were lost. All the time I kept thinking, surely it was not my nephew Charles who loosed those savages, those haters of the church, on Rome. I wanted to believe that the men had simply gone berserk and been maddened by all the blood, all the confusion and terror. I had heard of soldiers overcome with fury when their comrades were killed. Then, thinking only of avenging the deaths of their friends and brothers in arms, they struck out blindly.

"It is the way of war," my mother told me sadly. "Fighting, even for the highest and best of causes, creates tragedies. Losses. Men die needlessly."

Yet the thought that it was Charles, my sister's son, who was encouraging his men to kill and destroy, not only other men, but families and their shelters, their servants and even their animals ate away at me, day after day, until I could not bear to think of the holy city of Rome any longer.

"Babylon the great has fallen!" I heard one of my husband's councilors say to another. "And a good thing too. The Roman cesspit has been draining us of money for far too long. Perhaps now we can see where the real demons are, not in hell but in Rome!"

Another added, "I only wish they had killed all the apothecaries. The makers of poisons. They were the true masters of the College of Cardinals. If you can't overcome your rivals with swords and pikes, use poison! That was always the way of Italy, of the church of Rome. Poison!"

Hearing these words made me shudder. I had heard rumors of bishops and archbishops who died unnatural deaths, unexplained deaths. Was my nephew, my poor mad sister Juana's son, responsible for those as well?

In those sorrowful days I felt as if the world had been turned upside down. There was much talk at court about a battle far to the east, in a place I had never heard of called Mohacs, where an army of Turks had killed the King of Hungary. The cardinal shook his head in worry over this battle. "The Turk will overwhelm us all, in the end," he muttered to himself. "The Infidel will triumph."

So much had gone awry, the order of the world was in tatters. Maria Juana had indeed been a bird of ill omen. Then the worst storm of all arrived and my own small world was shattered. My husband had been struck by Cupid's arrow, the dart of love.

A poison dart, as it proved. For his beloved was the sullen, thin-lipped daughter of Elizabeth Boleyn, the prideful, willful girl who had been sent away from the Archduchess Margaret's court for the sin of lust. Anne Boleyn, whose father Thomas Boleyn had just been appointed Lord Rochford and whose lovely dark eyes and unchaste ways had captured my husband's obdurate heart.

At first I found it hard to believe. Elizabeth Boleyn's defiant, rebellious daughter who had shown me her scars, the marks of her beatings, and said, "Here is my marriage portion."

She had come back to our court several years earlier, and had been appointed one of my many maids of honor—far from the most alluring or beautiful of them, to be sure, but much improved from the unhappy, unappealing girl she had been when I advised her mother to send her to the court of Queen Claude.

Henry had named one of his ships the *Anne Boleyn,* as he had another vessel the *Mary Boleyn,* for Anne's bothersome sister, and another, as I have said, the *Catherine Pleasaunce,* for me. I should have realized that Anne was important to him, as he was sparing in his ship names and only christened a ship with the name of a woman he desired. I ought to have realized that his appetite was wide and deep, and his dissatisfaction just then very great.

Instead I paid Anne little attention, other than to notice that she danced well, and was tall, and could rarely keep still, she had so much energy. She complained about the peacocks that wandered through the palace grounds, she said they woke her with their cries in the early morning. She had a vicious greyhound named Grisaud that bit anyone it disliked and growled and bared its teeth at Griffith Richards. And there was another thing I noticed: at times Anne stared at me rudely, though when that happened and I looked back at her she quickly lowered her eyes.

I confess that I was paying a great deal more attention, in those disjointed days, to the betrayal of my nephew Charles and the ugly assaults of his soldiers in Rome. I lamented the destruction of the papal city when an equally devastating assault was being made on my marriage, my family.

Whisperings had begun, all of them having to do with Anne and my husband. It was being said that Anne had already borne Henry a child, or even two children, and that throughout the hunting season—when Anne's presence was not required at court—he kept her in a small hunting lodge in the forest near Esher, where he could visit her at his pleasure, and where she could bear his children in secrecy and hide them away, out of sight.

It was all absurd, to be sure. Had Anne been great with child she could not have hidden her swollen belly, beanstalk-thin and lean as she was. I and others in my household would have been aware of her condition, and its furtive cause.

Yet the whisperings persisted, and became mutterings, then shouted insults.

"Whore! Harlot! Jezebel!"

Anne could hardly leave the palace, or walk on the lawns, without hearing the abuse.

She had a small flat writing desk covered in gold that she kept in her storage chest at the foot of her bed. One day by chance I saw her lifting the desk out and placing it on a table by the window in the room she shared with two of the other maids of honor. The greyhound was lying at her feet. She was preparing to write a letter, and was sharpening a goose-quill pen with a knife. So intense was her concentration that at first she did not hear me come into the room, but went on with what she was doing.

When the quill was sharpened she took a letter from the pocket of her gown and began reading it.

I recognized my husband's handwriting—and the imprint of the royal seal. At the bottom of the letter were two hearts intertwined.

I gasped, the greyhound growled, and Anne, startled, turned and saw me.

In an instant she was out of her chair and standing, with her back to the desk, glaring angrily at me.

"I want a household of my own!" she cried, her voice quavering slightly. "I want eighty serving men and twenty women to attend me!"

Instead of reacting angrily I moved toward the table and, keeping my voice low and even, complimented her on her gold writing desk.

"How did you come by it?" I asked.

"It was a gift," Anne snapped. I noticed that she still gripped the quill, and that she was attempting, without success, to hide both the letter with the royal seal and the sheet on which she had been writing.

"A lovely gift indeed. I believe Bessie Blount has one just like it. And Madge Shelton, and others who have enjoyed my husband's favor. Is it, by chance, a gift from the king?"

Anne seemed confused. She said nothing, but bit her lip. I saw that I had shaken her confidence, but only for a moment.

She struggled for a response.

"If you must know, yes. Henry Norris brought it to me."

"My husband's groom of the stool."

She nodded, still unsure.

"And did Norris bring you the king's letter as well?"

"What letter?" she started to say, but I was too quick for her. I had already snatched the letter from her trembling hand.

"Oh please, Your Majesty, I beg of you—" Anne began, dropping to her knees and shaking with fear. "I swear I have done nothing. It was not my fault—"

But I had already begun to read the letter, which was in my husband's uneven, hard-to-read handwriting. I had always found the few brief notes he had written to me over the years difficult to decipher. He hated to write notes or letters, I had heard him say often that he found writing tedious and painful. Yet he had written to Anne. And the more I read the letter I had taken from her, the more I suspected that he had written others. And that, as the whisperings and mutterings and flung insults alleged, there was an intrigue going on between Henry and Anne, complete with secret letters and messages, furtive meetings and avowals of love, and worst of all, I feared, promises of marriage.

13

ALL AT ONCE, AS IT SEEMED, I WAS BEING TOLD WHERE I COULD and could not go and who I could and could not talk to. The new restrictions came from Henry, I was certain of that, but he lacked the courage to inform me of them himself. Instead he sent his messages to my gentleman usher Griffith Richards, who received them with an ill grace and passed them on to me.

"Your Majesty may no longer order the royal barge or walk abroad without an escort of ten men of the royal guard," I was told. "Dr. Vittoria may no longer serve as your physician and must leave our court at once." My serving men, cooks and laundresses were reduced in number and my gold and silver plate—brought from Spain when I came to the English court as a bride—was taken away and replaced with vessels and platters of inferior metal.

There seemed to be no end to the humiliations. It was as if I were a servant myself, some sort of higher servant, whose services had been found wanting and who was being demoted as a result.

My shrunken household was to operate on a far lower budget than in the past; rather than accept lower wages, many of my servants left in search of more lucrative positions. My seamstresses were informed that from then on they would be required to serve the Lady Anne, who was in need of a new wardrobe in the French style. I am glad to say that they all left court rather than serve "the king's harlot," as they called Anne—though I did hear them remark that the harlot had good taste in gowns.

When I entered the banqueting hall I was surprised to see painters on high scaffolds, repainting the ceiling, which had many images of the pomegranate—my symbol—entwined with the Tudor rose. All the pomegranates were being replaced with more roses. I was being erased, wiped away. I remembered when those pomegranates were first painted, along with my initials and Henry's intertwined. I looked up at the painters, indignant that they should carry out such an unsavory task. But they merely kept on with their work and ignored me.

That I was no longer allowed to speak with the imperial ambassador Inigo de Mendoza did not surprise me, though I protested loudly against this new restriction. But when the royal canopy of state was ordered removed from my apartments and I was told I must no longer sign any documents as "Catherine the Queen" but only as "Catherine, Princess of Spain," I felt a chill of fear and that night I was unable to sleep.

My world was crumbling. However I was determined not to show weakness, not even when I heard that the cardinal had convened a secret meeting of experts in church law to decide whether or not my marriage to Henry was a true and valid one. I wore out my knees in praying, night after night, kneeling on the stone floor beside my bed until my poor knees were bruised and bloody. I remembered that my mother had worn a coarse hair shirt under her clothes as a reminder to rebuke her flesh. A hair shirt! A torturous device that scratched and tormented her skin. I thought of doing the same, but realized that I did not have mother's force of will. I could not mortify my flesh as she had. But I could wake in the middle of the night to pray until my knees bled, as a sign of how sincerely I was entreating the Lord's aid in my time of need.

There was aid of a sort, though not exactly the sort I was hoping for. After a long day of hunting Henry came into my apartments one June evening and collapsed onto my bed. He called for a servant to relieve him of his boots and, sighing a deep sigh, closed his eyes and was soon asleep, snuffling loudly and tossing from side to side.

It had been a long time since he had come to my bed, and as I suspected, he did not intend for me to join him there. I slept that night in an adjoining small room, having left word with my dresser Maria de Caceres that she was to wake me in the morning as soon as the king arose.

To my surprise, I slept the night through. When Maria woke me the following morning it was to tell me that my husband was already up, and was hungry. He wished me to join him for a dew-bit, as he liked to call a huntsman's light morning meal. Maria had already laid out my clothes and helped me quickly into them. Then I joined Henry.

He sat awkwardly on the bed, chewing on a small manchet loaf and drinking from a goblet. I felt a twinge when I saw him there, a tug of familiarity and loss. He was still a handsome man, broad-chested and with muscular arms and legs. And his voice, when he spoke, was pleasing—the voice of a singer—unlike the thick, hoarse voice of my nephew Charles.

"Catherine," he began, indicating that I should sit beside him on the bed, "what I have come to tell you is this. My conscience has pained me for a long time. In an effort to ease it I have taken counsel with scholars and with my confessor. Wolsey has asked the opinions of men learned in interpreting the Scriptures. I have prayed and I have fasted."

He paused to eat more of his manchet loaf and to drink from his goblet. I noticed that no share of the dew-bit had been provided for me, though I was hungry.

"At last I have reached a conclusion," Henry went on. "I am convinced now that you and I have been living in sin these many years. A union such as ours is an abomination, not a blessing. Rather than continue it, or endure the indignity of a trial, I ask you in the name of all that's holy to make your profession as a nun and leave court."

"I will, my lord and husband, if you will do the same, and enter a monastic order."

I saw a fleeting smile cross his features, then disappear.

"Even if I agreed, I am king of this realm, and a reigning monarch cannot desert his subjects."

"Only his wife," I said, more tartly than I meant to sound.

"Catherine," he answered with unaccustomed patience, putting the remainder of his loaf and his goblet aside, "you are not my wife in the eyes of God. The deaths of our children bear out the truth of this. The Lord punishes false unions such as ours. I have borne this punishment long enough. I must end it."

He called for a serving man to bring him his boots, rubbing his chin and feeling the prickly ends of his unshaven whiskers. Just at that moment he gripped his belly and cried out, his face contorted with pain, his loud outcry carrying throughout my apartments.

"What is it? Shall I send for Dr. Huick?"

But Henry only gave another sharp cry, waving away the servant who came through the door carrying his boots, my gentleman usher and other servants drawn to the room by the sudden sounds of his distress.

"Out! Out! Get them all out!" He waved one hand in the air uselessly, pathetically as it seemed to me then.

"But milord husband—" I began, only to break off when he glowered at me. Hurriedly I told all the others to leave.

I stood where I was, watching anxiously as Henry's face grew contorted once again, then relaxed. He breathed quickly, shallowly, still holding his belly.

"I've begun a course—in physick," he managed to gasp out after a moment. "I see now—that it was unwise. The dog days are almost upon us, and the moon is waxing. Yet when this pain—grips me—I must find relief—"

His words came in snatches, he grimaced with each breath. I

could see that he was suffering, though the pain did not seem quite so intense as when he had first cried out.

"Dr. Vittoria," he was murmuring. "A pox on him! Where is he when he could be of use?"

"You ordered him sent away," I said quietly.

"Bring him back."

"As Your Majesty wishes."

Trained in Salamanca and learned in the Arab medical treatises as well as the Latin ones, Dr. Vittoria was both a physician and an apothecary, and often used his own herbal remedies to ease the pain of his patients. I had come to know him well during the years he had spent in my household, and I trusted him to carry messages to my nephew and bring messages back to me from the imperial court. That he had Moorish blood—he was dark-skinned and slight of build—had always made Henry uneasy, no matter how much he admired the doctor's skill. When my household was reduced in size, Dr. Vittoria was ordered not only to leave my service but to leave England. Henry called him a spy and an informant.

Once he had gone, I missed not only his learning and skill, but his intuition. His healing instincts were nearly always correct, and his methods flawless.

Before he left the doctor had told me privately that in his view the king was more ill than anyone at court realized. He had a putrid ulcer on his inner thigh that was slow to heal, and that the physician believed was growing worse.

"I have seen this sort of affliction before," he confided to me. "It robs a man of his ability to father a child. It affects his legs, then spreads throughout his lower body. The testicles swell and become tender. The pain grows worse. And then—" He did not go on. There was no need.

I had not shared the doctor's opinion with anyone, knowing how dangerous it would be to do so. If Dr. Vittoria was right, Henry would never have a legitimate son to succeed him. If he was wrong . . . then nothing much would change. Yet I had never seen my husband in such pain.

Then another thought struck me. What if Henry was so very ill that he had not long to live? What would happen to Mary then? She was not yet old enough to rule on her own. If Henry died and Mary became queen suddenly, unexpectedly, would I be appointed regent for her, as Henry had appointed me regent in his stead when he went to lead his army in France years earlier, before Mary was born?

Henry interrupted my thoughts. In a low voice he repeated his words. "Bring him back. And tell him to hurry."

I wrote a hasty message and dispatched a swift rider to begin the long journey to the imperial court in Mechelen where I was certain Dr. Vittoria would be found. It would be weeks before he could be expected to return to England—provided he would agree to return, knowing how Henry's moods were inclined to change. In the meantime I sent for Dr. Huick. But by the time he arrived my husband had fallen into a fitful and troubled sleep.

I remember hearing my mother say that there is a divine order behind everything that happens. As time passes, she would say, the Lord guides events so that the wicked are punished, and those who strive for righteousness are rewarded.

So it seemed in the Year of Our Lord 1528, the year of the shadow of death.

It began with a shiver. Then a twitch. Then a stink spread from the poor wretch. Then he felt damp, wet all over, so wet he had to tear his clothes off and pray for a cooling rain to fall.

By the time he (or she) had begun to stink, Dr. Vittoria said when he returned to court, there was no saving him. Not all the remedies devised by all the apothecaries, not vinegar and wormwood, rosewater and treacle, not even ground sapphires mixed with pure gold (the king's favorite remedy) could prevent the sufferer from dying—and quickly.

So many, many died in the first few days, even more in the first weeks of that summer of mortal illness. I sent Mary to the north where the disease had not yet spread so widely. Where the hand of God spared more than it slew. My husband's wealthy chamber gentleman Will Compton, struck down by the sweating plague, spent his last hours surrounded by his servants, who—so I was told—began plundering his possessions even before he was dead. In his will he left an ivory chest filled with jewels and treasure to Henry, but the chest could not be found. It had disappeared, along with his other valuables—all but his chessboard, which was thought to be of no value.

Anne shivered and twitched and grew damp, and I could see that she was terrified, her eyes wide and her hands shaking with dread. Her father Thomas Boleyn had sickened but recovered, yet Anne seemed more afflicted. I made certain that she was given extreme unction, and afterward, feigning concern lest her possessions be stolen as those of Will Compton had been, I ordered Griffith Richards to bring Anne's storage chest to my bedchamber.

Telling Maria de Caceres to guard my door and let no one enter, I opened the chest and took out the golden desk.

Tucked away in the desk was a bundle of letters, tied with an embroidered ribbon. All of the letters bore the stamp of the royal seal. I took a deep breath, untied the ribbon, and began to read.

"My mistress and friend," Henry wrote, "my heart and I put ourselves in your hands. To be apart from you hurts me more than I could ever have thought possible."

The words were like a dagger in my belly. I could not help but weep as I read on.

He wrote of "the great love I have for you," he swore to Anne that she was "the one woman in the world whom I most esteem." He could not bear to be apart from her for long, he wrote, for "the pang of absence" was too great. He was her loyal servitor and beloved, he sought no other.

At the bottom of his brief letters he drew a device of two hearts adjoined, and sent her a bracelet with his portrait.

I forced myself to read more, though with every page my sorrow and distress grew. There were so many letters, so many gifts had been exchanged, plans made and hopes raised. This was no passing infatuation. It seemed clear to me that Henry and Anne were of one mind and one purpose: to be together.

And now Anne was on the point of death.

The Lord was taking vengeance on them both.

I have asked myself time and again what it was about Anne Boleyn that led Henry to choose her as his great love. After much thought I have decided that he saw in Anne a remedy for his own heavyheartedness. He saw in her an elixir of hope.

In this Anne stood alone. Bessie Blount, who took pride in her title as Mother of the King's Son, had given him Henry Fitzroy. Anne's sister Mary Boleyn had given him pleasure—and a worthless, witless son whose existence no one ever mentioned, as he was mad and his madness was incurable. Madge Shelton offered him her charm and her dimples—but did not produce a child, no matter what gossip said. Yet Anne, with her giddy, exuberant restlessness, her willful nature, her very childishness, lifted his spirits. Had his eye fallen on Anne at another time in his life, I reasoned, he would not have been drawn to her.

Choosing her when he did, he was heartened. He saw a way forward, out of failure. From then on he clung to her as a drowning man clings to a floating bit of wood. And that was why, just at that time, he was so eager to free himself from me and marry Anne. He wished, with all the force of his ardor for Anne, that I would not be there to impede his hoped-for marriage. He wished that I would make everything simple for him, and enter a convent.

But Anne was ill, and expected to die.

Yes, there is a divine order at work in everything that happens. The wicked are punished, and those who strive for righteousness are rewarded.

Sometimes, however, this outcome is delayed.

As Anne lay between life and death, Henry sickened. I was prepared to ask that extreme unction be administered to him. And to send to the north to arrange for Mary's return, with an escort of a hundred mounted men and another hundred pikemen. For Queen Mary's return, I almost wrote, as queen she would have been from the moment her father died. And I would have been regent for her.

Instead, Dr. Vittoria arrived at last, bringing with him mandrake root and an unguent of his own mixing which he used to treat weeping wounds and black infections of the skin. I watched as, frowning in concentration, and making the sign of the cross over his pot of greasy cream which had the most appalling stench, Dr. Vittoria sat at Henry's bedside and worked his healing wonder.

For four days and nights he sat there, sleeping for a few brief hours when Henry slept, waking to swab him again and again with the foul-smelling grease. Through it all he prayed, quietly, to himself and nodded, smiling, as if certain that the wound was on its way to being healed. On the fourth day, when I looked in, Dr. Vittoria was sound asleep, but Henry, roused and looking more alert and happily expectant than I had seen him look in many months, was pulling on his own boots and preparing for the hunt.

"No time to waste," he called out to me as I stood in the doorway. "The stags are fighting over the roe deer, there are pheasants near the coveys and ducks flying over the marsh. I must be off!"

It was a miraculous healing. Not only had Dr. Vittoria brought Henry back from the brink of death, but Anne too had responded to the medicines he sent with Dr. Butts to give her. How much of Henry's newfound glee came from the relief he felt in his aching leg, and how much from the news reaching him of Anne's recovery I could not have said. But while Henry rewarded Dr. Vittoria with his most earnest thanks and the gift of a strong-legged young gelding, he generously rewarded Dr. Butts with the office of royal physician and a salary of a hundred and fifty pounds a year.

But by then the first leaves were turning to gold and red in Epping Forest, and in the capital, Londoners were expecting the arrival of Cardinal Campeggio, legate and judge, sent from Rome to decide, once and for all, the vexed question of whether or not King Henry and I were truly married in the eyes of the church.

The eminent Cardinal of Santa Anastasia had hardly been among us a week when I realized that his mission was a sham. He was not sent to England to pass judgment, along with Cardinal Wolsey, on my marriage to Henry, he was sent to avoid having to make such a judgment.

He did me the honor of coming to my apartments so that he could take counsel with me, something I would never have expected a man of his stature to do. I soon realized why. It was his intent to persuade me, as Henry had tried to do, to join an order of holy sisters, and thus to leave my marriage of my own free will. Once I had done that, Henry could marry whomever he chose. By discussing this matter in the relative privacy of my rooms the cardinal preserved my own dignity, indeed his intent was to make it appear to others that the plan originated with me, not with him.

"Your devotion to the Lord is well known," he told me after giving me his blessing and settling himself, with many a groan, into a nest of soft pillows Maria de Caceres had prepared for him. He was an old and weary man with sad eyes, his worn face wrinkled and his legs unsteady under him as he walked. He was said to be tortured by pain in his foot—which led me to wonder whether Dr. Vittoria's unguent might help him.

"Many pious wives choose a life of religious devotion," the cardinal was saying once he was situated among the pillows, "after their years of bearing children are behind them—" He broke off, coughing, and at my signal wine was brought, my servant offering it to the cardinal reverently, on bended knee.

"To devote oneself to a life of prayer and fasting, to enjoy the serenity of the cloister—" he coughed again "—is a blessing only those who have lived that life can understand." He smiled a wan smile. "The peace of the cloister," he began again, then his eyes slowly closed. He had drifted off to sleep.

I was determined not to allow the cardinal to try to lull me into submission. I was no trembling girl, I was Queen of England, and the daughter of the great Queen Isabella of Castile. How my mother would have bristled with anger to be counseled to enter a convent!

And yet, I reminded myself, my mother had worn a hair shirt under her gown. She had found a way to keep her worldly dignity while deepening her piety.

But then, my father had never sought to put her aside.

Cardinal Campeggio was not easily deterred from his goal. He made several more visits to me in my apartments, trying to persuade me to agree to become a nun. In the end, convinced by my stubbornness that I would not enter the religious life unless Henry did the same, the cardinal tried to convince Henry to allow our marriage to continue. To reconcile him to his fate. Henry objected, arguing, as he invariably did, that he had to provide the realm with a prince. And that I was now too old to give birth to one.

In response the cardinal produced a letter from Cardinal Wolsey describing a ceremony we had witnessed several years earlier. In that time-honored ritual, Bessie Blount's son Henry Fitzroy was created Duke of Richmond and Somerset and given other titles and offices reserved for the heir to the throne.

"There is now a prince of this realm," Cardinal Campeggio insisted, "and no need for any other. In due course, Henry Fitzroy will succeed to his father's throne. The Holy Father Pope Clement can acknowledge the boy as your son, bearing the royal blood of the Tudors. He can, and will, if need be, grant a dispensation to allow Henry Fitzroy to marry your daughter Mary. Though they share the same father, and are half-brother and half-sister to one another, nevertheless it can be permitted."

The thought of this alarmed me and filled me, as it always had, with repugnance.

"Any union, even one between brothers and sisters—or half-brothers and half-sisters—can be sanctioned through a dispensation from the Bishop of Rome. His power to dispense is without limit."

For a moment there was an uncomfortable silence. I felt only distaste, and even Henry was, for the moment, taken aback. He had not expected this proposal to be made. Especially not from the aged, sleepy cardinal sent from Rome. He had been outsmarted. He glanced at me, a worried glance.

"Indeed," the cardinal added, "the Holy Father can even grant a dispensation to allow King Henry to marry a second wife while the first still lives."

"Can he indeed?" was Henry's delighted response, his worries forgotten. But I could not keep silent. "What?" I blurted out. "How could that be?"

The cardinal was nodding. "Such a dispensation has been granted before, and no doubt will be again.

"Ponder these things," he said at length, "and may the Lord bless and guide your thoughts, that you may serve his good purposes in all you do."

14

"THE PAPAL COURT IN ROME IS A CESSPIT, MY DAUGHTER. I SPEAK AS one who knows."

I had gone in search of Cardinal Campeggio after spending several days in distressing thought. I could not resign myself to either of the courses of action he had proposed when last we met. To take the veil of a nun would be to retreat into silent obscurity. To leave the field of battle without mounting so much as a defense.

Yet to agree to become the lesser of my husband's two wives, the older, rejected one, the one without a son, was loathsome. Especially since I had no doubt that Henry would choose Anne to be his other spouse. That the daughter of Queen Isabella and King Ferdinand should share a husband with the granddaughter of a London merchant was abhorrent to me.

It had been hard enough for me to stand by, watching with envy, as Bessie Blount gave my husband a bastard son. That I should be expected to share the king with Anne and whatever children she might have, all the while smiling and making no complaint, for the rest of my life was impossible. No, abhorrent. I was bold enough to say so when the cardinal welcomed me to the richly appointed apartments he had been given in the palace, blessing me as he did each time we met. I thought he looked tired and dejected, and wondered whether his foot was giving him added pain.

Once we were closeted together, I spoke my mind, as openly and honestly as I could, confessing that I could not reconcile myself to being one of the king's two wives.

"I quite agree," the cardinal confided, nodding. "It is contrary to all vows of fidelity. It dishonors the marriage bed. But we live in extraordinary times. The end times, some say. The church has lost its way, and entered into the swamp of worldliness. All is greed and lies, and the lust for power. We must make our way through the swamp as best we can, any way we can."

I watched the aged prelate's sad eyes as he told me, gravely, that the papal court was a cesspit, and that having lived there and experienced its evils, he knew it well.

He told me of the malice and hatred that divided the members of the College of Cardinals, the brawling and conspiring that went on behind the altars of the venerable churches in the papal city, the church offices that were sold and the biblical teachings of love and forgiveness dishonored.

"The Cardinal of San Onofre had a priest who was his secretary," he began, "a strong, hefty man, young and full of energy, a priest who would rather tussle than say mass. The cardinal wagered his jeweled ring that this priest could wrestle any man to the ground in the time it takes to count to one hundred. Within minutes many had bet against him. Suddenly the church was a public fighting arena, with men shouting and jewelry and coins clinking and fighters with bloody faces clutching their ribs in pain. It was a spectacle I hoped never to see again—but I did see it, time after time. The church of San Onofre became a gambling hall and remained one, with women upstairs to relieve the gamblers of their winnings."

I was about to ask whether the strong young priest did in fact wrestle many a man to the ground in the time it took to count to a hundred, but the cardinal had gone on to recount other stories of corruption and vice, all having to do with money.

I had to remind myself that it is said to be the love of money that is the root of all evil, not the money itself.

He had gone on to say that the pillaging and destruction of Rome was nothing more or less than the just judgment of God against his faithless children who for years had bought and sold church offices, pardoned unpardonable crimes, indulged in every sort of vice.

"My own palazzo was ransacked, my treasures stolen, my servants attacked and four of them killed before my eyes. I could not protect them."

After a silence he said, simply, "May they rest in peace."

Then he looked at me, as if assessing me, weighing my worth, though by what measure I could not have said.

"We have spoken of two paths you may choose to take, Catherine. One leads to the convent, the other to, as it were, the king's bed, only it must be shared with another wife.

"A woman in your situation, Catherine, if she were a Medici, or perhaps a Wolsey, would follow a different path."

At the mention of Cardinal Wolsey's name I became curious, then more alert than ever.

The cardinal limped to a corner of the room where a large old chest stood against the wall. Taking a key from the pocket of his robe he unlocked the chest, lifted the lid, and drew out a small green ceramic jar. He brought it over to a table near where we had been sitting.

"The healing medicine in this jar," he told me, "was given to me by Dr. Vittoria. It eases pain and causes wounds to close and aids digestion. When dried for a year and then ground into a powder, twenty-five spoonfuls of this a day can do wonders to soothe morning sickness in women with child and men, such as the king, with infected sores.

"When preserved green, however—" The cardinal said nothing, but merely made the sign of the cross.

"This jar is full of preserved green ginger. Should any of it be consumed by an unwary person, its effects would be almost immediate. Yet the source of those effects would be impossible to discover."

It was the perfect poison.

My every instinct told me to leave the small room at once. Yet I could not seem to move. I was in the presence of evil. I was certain of it. Frightened and horrified as I was, I was mesmerized. I began to tremble.

The most I could do was to move away from the green jar. I cursed my cowardice! Yet I did not, I could not, leave the room.

"You would not need to fear discovery, should any of this medicine do harm. Should harm befall—anyone—it would appear that he or she had simply collapsed suddenly from an unexplained cause."

I could not bring myself to object when the cardinal told me that the jar was mine to keep, should I ever need it. "Take the jar, Catherine. Put it somewhere safe. And let us both pray that it is never needed."

I did not use the dread preserved green ginger, but I did pay the Count de Cabra's son to marry Maria Juana and take her back to Spain. The old count had died, and his eldest son and heir was full of pride and ambition but short of money—the fate of many of the Spanish nobles in my household. The young count could not have been more pleased with the match, and Maria Juana, tiring of waiting for her opportunity to injure me, gave her grudging assent.

My nephew Charles, as I hoped, made no objection—for reasons of his own.

Maria Juana had become an intolerable nuisance, with her gossip about how I had failed to save her mother but had let her drown during the fierce storm at sea, how I lied about my marriage to the king's brother Arthur and how in fact Arthur and I had slept together, not once but many times, before he fell ill and died. Two hundred escudos and the income from one of my estates in Estremadura was a small price to pay to rid myself, at least for the time being, of my half-sister.

I did not delude myself that Maria Juana would never trouble me again. I hoped, however, that with time she might settle into her new life as the Countess de Cabra and lose some of her spite. And when at last Cardinal Campeggio and Cardinal Wolsey convened their court the following spring, Maria Juana did not attend it.

The court that assembled in the great hall of Blackfriars was imposing indeed—though we were distracted from its solemn proceedings by loud shouting and the tramping of marching feet and clanging steel from the militias drilling nearby. Fear was spreading through London on the day that the court opened in that spring of the Year of Our Lord 1529. There were rumors that Emperor Charles's soldiers would soon land on our shores in their thousands and conquer the capital. And then go on to conquer the entire realm. It was being said that the emperor's men would take me away to Flanders or Florence (not to Rome, I hoped), rescuing me from the strict judgment of the cardinals who were intent on depriving me of my crown. Intent, as it then seemed, on declaring my marriage to Henry invalid.

I remember well the joy I felt when I entered the great hall on the arm of Griffith Richards.

"Our good Queen Catherine!"

Cheers and shouts of encouragement followed me with every step I took. Much heartened, I held my head high and smiled, though my face was partly veiled from the onlookers by the black lace mantilla I wore over my jeweled headpiece. The long mantilla that swept almost to my knees had been my grandmother's, then my mother's, before it came to me. I cherished it, it was among my most prized possessions. Each time I wore it I saw Henry wince. To him it was a galling reminder of who I was and what my ancestry was. I was the proud heir of the Trastamaras; Henry was a mere Tudor, and as everyone knew, the Tudors were latecomers among the ruling families of Europe. Scavengers of the crown, as it were, rather than true inheritors of it.

I was aware, even as I heard the many outcries of support, that my deep purple gown and the floating black lace of my mantilla must have looked dark and dull when compared to the scarlet robes of the cardinals and the shining cloth of gold that covered the royal throne. The splendor of the bishops and court officials, the tall gleaming gold crosses held aloft by Cardinal Campeggio's attendants, the high narrow windows with their rich blues and reds all outshone my dark, dignified attire.

Somewhat to my surprise, Anne was present in the great hall, sitting with her father who had just been awarded new honors and titles. She looked away as I passed, but I could see that she was fidgeting uneasily, nervously.

I had a sudden impulse to break free of my gentleman usher's firm, reassuring arm and announce, as loudly as I could, that Cardinal Campeggio had supplied me with a strong poison to use against Anne or Henry or anyone I chose. The thought both horrified and exhilarated me. I, Catherine, could bring to light the iniquities of the papal court. What the cardinal had called the swamp of worldliness.

I could say, the cardinal himself handed me poison, and instructed me in how to use it! And he as much as told me that Cardinal Wolsey had used poison to try to gain the throne of Saint Peter for himself!

Saints seek the Beatific Vision—I had been granted, or cursed, with a vision of hell—the hell made by the corrupt cardinals of Rome.

But of course I would not disrupt the solemn court. I would not make a scene. I could hear my mother's voice—the voice of reason—advising me against it.

Who would believe you, Catherine? the voice was saying. You are eager for revenge, not justice. You would say anything to injure the men who are sitting in judgment against you. No one would believe you, no matter what you said. It would be whispered that you had gone mad, like your sister Juana.

I let the impulse pass, took Griffith Richards's arm once again, and let him lead me to my seat.

The tribunal did not proceed quickly, despite the threat of an imperial invasion and, as May turned to June, the return of the sweating plague with its fearsome toll of suffering and death. My advocates pleaded my case eloquently and at length—but in vain. Days passed, then weeks, and the cardinals did not reach a conclusion. Instead delay after delay made the long proceedings even longer. Meanwhile there was a distraction, one that had nothing whatever to do with the law: a rumor spread that Anne was pregnant with the king's child.

Could it be true? The French ambassador thought so, according to tales reaching me from more than one trusted source. My nephew Charles feared so as well. My women thought they could detect in Anne the rounded cheeks, the bilious stomach, the long naps and tearful scenes of a woman with child. In vain I pointed out that Anne had always been moody, querulous and demanding, full of vexation, by turns giddy and tearful. No, they assured me. This was different. And besides, her breasts were growing round and ripe with milk and her stomach was swelling.

If it was true, if Anne was indeed carrying my husband's child, then all the legal arguments were worthless. The court itself was of little weight. Henry would marry Anne, knowing that Cardinal Campeggio would obtain a dispensation from Pope Clement to sanction his taking a second wife. I would be cast into the shade. Anne would have her child, Mary's rights would be disregarded, and the King's Great Matter would cease to matter at all.

I remembered reading, in Henry's letters to Anne, about a gift she had sent him, "a present so beautiful that nothing could be more so." He thanked her for "the ship in which the lovely damsel is tossed about." Seated where I was in the great hall, I was close enough to Henry on his raised golden throne to see what he wore each day the court met. Among his jewels and finery was a simple gold chain with a pendant in the shape of a ship. Was it Anne's gift? If so, it was a sign of his devotion for certain. But was it also a symbol of approaching fatherhood?

I had to forestall disaster, if indeed disaster loomed. Anne might or might not be pregnant, but if she wasn't, she might become so before long. I had to act, and soon.

I summoned my courage and said my prayers. Then, without notifying my advocates or preparing anyone around me for what I intended to do, I rose from my seat on the next day the court convened and made my way to where Henry sat on his gleaming throne.

I heard gasps and cries from the onlookers, and saw both cardinals frown. I could tell that Cardinal Wolsey was about to rise from his chair and protest but his colleague put out a restraining hand. I went up the few steps to the throne and knelt.

"Milord husband," I began, my head bowed, "I beg you not to let this dishonor continue. For twenty years and more I have been your wife, your one and only true wife. I have borne your children and wept with you when the Lord took them—all but one. I have suffered the shame and humiliation of your faithlessness—"

"Now then, Catherine, you are overwrought," Henry began, doing his best to raise me to my feet.

I stayed where I was, on my knees. I could hear a disturbed murmuring in the crowd of those watching.

"I have suffered," I repeated, "the shame and humiliation of your faithlessness, though I did not deserve it. I have kept silence when I could have cried aloud. The pain you have caused me is greater than any woman should be asked to bear."

Once again he attempted to grip my arm, to lift me off my knees and raise me up. But my long mantilla was in the way. He fumbled with it, grunting audibly, and in the end gave up. He heaved a sigh.

"Nothing would give me more pleasure than to learn from this esteemed court that our marriage is indeed a valid one. Yet I cannot rid myself of my fears. Only my love for you, Catherine, has kept me from giving in to my conscience. Like you, I have kept silence. But I owe it to my people to end that silence and allow this court to render its judgment."

I waited no more than the space of a breath, then got to my feet and stood facing the onlookers. I took another deep breath.

"I Catherine protest the authority of this court. I assert my privilege to appeal to the supremacy of the Holy Father in Rome." My words rang out through the great hall.

A hush fell. No one spoke. No one called me back as I went down the few steps and began the long walk toward the entrance to the hall, the only sound the clicking of my heels on the tile floor.

I had not gone far when I heard Cardinal Campeggio's voice ring out behind me.

"Catherine! Come back into this court, or I will hold you in contempt!

"Catherine!" he shouted a second time. "Come back into the court or I will hold you in contempt!"

But I had gone too far to turn back, and besides, I felt liberated. I had entered the hall on the arm of my faithful gentleman usher. I left it on my own, feeling stronger and full of daring. In that moment I felt as if I could take on the world.

I was in contempt—and in disgrace. Yet the proceedings collapsed without ever reaching a conclusion, and less than a month after I made my protest the Cardinal of Santa Anastasia adjourned the court and it never met again.

15

THE COURT PRESIDED OVER BY CARDINALS CAMPEGGIO AND WOLSEY never met again, as I have said. But as it had reached no decision, the old strains and questions it was meant to decide remained unresolved.

As far as I was concerned, I was and would remain Henry's one and only true wife, and Princess Mary was his heir.

But his desire for Anne, and for a son, ate away at him, and as the months passed the atmosphere at our royal court dissolved into a chaos of wrangling and rancor. Through it all, one thing remained clear: Anne did not love Henry. Of that I was certain. She did not show him any of the kindness or constancy or even simple fondness that women in love cannot help but show.

Instead she was harsh and impatient and filled with bitterness.

Hardly had the proceedings at Blackfriars ended when Anne's loud accusations began to ring out through my household. She was still my maid of honor, living in my apartments, but she acted as though she ruled all. (And indeed I was no longer allowed the title of queen, instead I was addressed as "Mistress Catherine.") I was Anne's superior in rank, and certainly her superior by birth, but she expected to be made queen soon, and when Henry failed to marry her she berated him at the top of her lungs, for all to hear. She seemed not to care that in shouting like a fishwife she revealed both her inferior birth and her ignoble motives.

Henry came to seek her out, there among the women of my chamber, and they quarreled. Anne accused him of failing to keep his word and end his marriage to me, of cowardice, of forcing her to squander her precious youth and sacrifice her good repute. And all for nothing.

The more Anne shouted, the more he protested, until, weeping with rage, Anne threatened never to speak to him again, and demanded that he return the token she gave him—the golden ship with its cargo of the maiden tossed about in stormy seas.

What happened then astounded me. I never thought I would witness such a sight: the king, tall and strong as he still was, fearsome as he could still be, at the mercy of a woman such as Anne. Her threats and tears reduced him, I greatly regret to say, to fearful, whimpering dread. To helpless tears of his own. And all this within the hearing of my servants and household officers. Of even the kitchen boys, the laundresses, the poor women who brought me cherries and strawberries and songbirds in cages and newborn pet lambs in hopes of earning a coin or two.

This dishonorable spectacle went on far longer than it should have, and happened again and again. I and the others heard Anne warn Henry that she would leave him, heard him beg her not to, and then, heard him attempt to placate her by bringing her gifts. And not just any gifts, but lavish, costly ones. Lengths of Bruges satin and silk from Florence and Brescia to be sewn into splendid gowns and kirtles. Jeweled collars for her surly greyhound Grisaud. Strings of Orient pearls and rings set with rubies and sapphires. I knew that Henry had sent his groom of the stool Henry Norris to visit every goldsmith's shop in the Strand to seek out gold hearts set with diamonds for Anne to wear in her long glossy black hair.

I saw the way my chamber women looked at Anne when she caused these shameful scenes. How they scorned her company afterward, partly out of fear—for who knew where the rude shafts of her anger might land next?—and partly, it must be said, from envy. At their most spiteful they muttered to one another, just loudly enough so that Anne could hear them, that she was not so young as she once was, and might never marry anyone, and besides, her only beauties were her thick curling hair that fell to her waist and her fine dark eyes.

They reminded one another, in Anne's hearing, that others of the king's favorites had surpassed Anne in loveliness. Bessie Blount had a far more pleasing face and a more bountiful figure, Madge Shelton more grace and charm, not to mention a much more pleasing disposition. In fact, they whispered, every one of my maids of honor was far more pleasant in manner than the shrew Anne. Didn't she realize that the more she argued and accused the king, the less desirable she appeared?

Every time I heard these remarks I took more satisfaction from them. I only wished I had the courage to repeat them to Anne. Yet to descend to such rude behavior—the behavior of a lowborn woman, not a queen who was the daughter of Queen Isabella and King Ferdinand—was beneath me. Or so I told myself, day after day. In truth there was another reason. Anne, it appeared, was in the process of forming a queenly household of her own.

She was about to take my place.

She was not only berating Henry, shaming him into making her his queen, she was actively preparing to take on my role in every detail.

One by one she was choosing those she wanted to serve her: her women, her butler and pantler, her almoner, her cupbearer and the master of her plate and jewels. One by one, each of them began to receive liveries in Anne's colors and offers of wages—rather high wages—too tempting to resist. Some were lured away from my household, others brought in from outside. In the wake of the sweating plague, which had carried off so many gentlemen of substantial fortunes, many a large household had dispersed, and there was no shortage of servants in search of positions.

However, when Anne was bold enough to offer Griffith Richards twice what he earned as my gentleman usher if he would agree to abandon my service and become head of her new household, he took offense.

"Do you really imagine that I would leave Mistress Catherine to serve an adulteress?" was his ringing response.

Anne, nonplussed, offered him three times what he earned.

"And having served the queen from the day of her coronation, would I desert her now to earn a trollop's coin?"

It warmed my heart that he called me queen, even though Anne's reply galled me.

"Your wage would assuredly be the king's coin," she said, "and when he hears your response, you will regret having made it."

Others in my service were less loyal, and willingly accepted the higher wages offered them to serve Anne. I could not match those wages; for some time, in fact, I had been unable to pay my servants much of anything. I was reminded of this whenever Anne displayed the jewels and other finery the king gave her. One of her lovely rings would pay all two hundred of my staff for a year. No, I must amend that. I no longer had two hundred servants to pay, as many of them had left me to serve Anne.

I tried not to feel dispirited, to maintain my outward composure amid the shifts and changes of loyalty surrounding me. But it was becoming more difficult, as the tide of royal support seemed to be turning toward Anne. I was sent away for a time to live in the country, but did not stay long. It suited Henry to have me and those who still served me remain nearby, for reasons he alone knew. He even brought Henry Fitzroy to live at court, though Anne complained stridently about this and it led to more conflict. Nearly everyone, including the servants, bickered and fought, with some supporting me and others Anne. There were broken heads and bloodied noses, wounded limbs, torn stockings and doublets slashed to ribbons. And chaos when now and then even the beggars and other low folk at the palace gates took sides.

That we all lived in such close quarters made every slight, every resentment more wounding. My nerves grew more and more frayed. Each new shaft of malice went deeper than the one before. Meanwhile the sudden, unpredictable reversals of royal favor led Anne's father Thomas Boleyn to rise in wealth and status, even as Cardinal Wolsey plummeted. Boleyn was already rumored to be the richest man in Kent, with properties, offices and honors and even a profitable lumber mill to sustain his fortune. In the Advent season of the Year of Our Lord 1529, higher honors came to him. He was made Earl of Wiltshire—a new creation—and, soon afterward, Lord Privy Seal. Cardinal Wolsey, on the other hand, was attainted for treason, and died in disgrace.

The cardinal was gone, but his horde of gold and other valuables remained. All was now forfeit to the royal treasury. Henry was eager to survey his new possessions, and took me with him when he went downriver to Greenwich to take stock of them.

Not since I left my mother's palace had I seen such treasures. Paintings and embroidered hangings covered every wall of the rooms where the valuables were stored. Heavy gold vessels and bowls gleamed from the cabinets, jeweled trays and flagons were arrayed on long tables of carved wood. As we passed through each of the rooms I marveled at the sheer abundance of precious things. What need did the cardinal have for a dozen canopied beds, each more splendid than the last, or for gilded chests seemingly without number?

That he possessed precious clerical vestments and gold chalices for serving mass did not surprise me, though the overall value of everything that he had left behind seemed shockingly high for one sworn to follow the austere, unselfish teachings of Jesus.

"I swear, the fellow had more than I ever did," Henry remarked, half to himself, as we surveyed the spoils of the cardinal's ruin. Three clerks walked along behind us, writing down each tapestry and goblet and silken bedcurtain. "I can't imagine where he got it all."

"Perhaps he had a gold mine no one knew about," I remarked. Henry had been searching for gold within his kingdom for years. Though the search had not yet led to a discovery he continued to hope that it would, and even brought a wealthy miner turned banker from Augsburg, Augustus Hochstetter, to court to continue it. Herr Hochstetter claimed that he had found rich gold mines in Peru, and was confident that England held equally productive mines. He claimed he could make England very rich indeed, and Henry was as eager as a child to believe him.

This was the side of Henry that I took most pleasure in. He could be filled with excitement over some remote possibility and then dwell on it endlessly, his face alight with expectation.

"There, you see?" he said to me when we had gone through each of the rooms and the secretaries had completed their long lists of treasures. "Thomas was wealthier than I am, and now by dying he has enlarged my treasury. Just wait till the moneylenders see all this—and Anne too, of course," he added, glancing at me. I knew better than to comment on his mention of Anne, as it seemed, just then, as though Henry's hopes to find a way to marry Anne had stalled.

It was not merely that he was still, under church law, my husband, after all he had been offered the possibility of having more than one wife at a time. No, it was something else, a wearying sense of futility that sometimes showed itself in his expression. At times exultant, at times deeply unhappy, it was hard for him not to lose heart. And in truth it was hard for me as well, though I was heartened from time to time by unexpected support.

Anne's aunt, Elizabeth Howard, Duchess of Norfolk, swore to me that she would always be on my side in any dispute with the king, come what may. She had been among my ladies-in-waiting for twenty years and more, and often confided in me as I did in her, though always careful not to carry our friendship beyond appropriate bounds. Her loyalty to me, and sympathy for me, was more important than her loyalty to her husband's family. She assured me that she would declare herself for me and against her niece Anne, whom she despised.

"Anne is no better than my husband's mistress Bess Holland," Elizabeth told me indignantly. "The churl's daughter who used to wash my children's clothes." Had she spat on the floor she could not have been more eloquent.

Elizabeth told me how she was made to suffer when she complained about her husband's keeping company with Bess. How the duke humiliated her by shouting at her and confining her to a distant manor house, then keeping her there, a prisoner, while his guards mistreated her. I remembered her saying that her possessions had been taken from her and that she had had very little to live on, never knowing when or if she would be released.

"If you complain about Anne," she said in low tones, "you could find yourself the king's prisoner, without hope of ever being free again." Her warning continued to haunt me on long prayerful nights when I could not sleep. She was right, I could be attainted of treason, just as Cardinal Wolsey had been. Or I could simply become another victim of the sweating plague, alive one morning and dead by afternoon. Many women did not live to reach the age of forty, especially if, like me, they had had many pregnancies. I was already well into my fifth decade.

I did my best to push such morbid imaginings from my mind as the Advent season approached, with its message of hope and reconciliation. However, reconciliation seemed less likely than ever. The widening breach between Henry and the Holy Father in Rome was much talked of; indeed the king was warned that he would suffer excommunication unless he sent Anne away from court. Far from sending her away, he showed by his generosity to her just how great his appetite for her had become.

Among the many gifts he gave her that New Year's were twelve dressmakers from Brussels, brought to court to sew for her and carrying with them chests filled with lengths of wool and silk and costly hangings in cloth of gold and silver and crimson satin. A number of the late cardinal's tapestries were also presented to Anne, along with much of his plate. Anne in turn gave the king a set of throwing spears for the hunt, and a trio of musicians—a fine lutenist, a viol player and a boy soprano with a high angelic voice and a face as sweet as a girl's.

"They will play at our wedding," she announced to Henry, boasting to whoever would listen that the wedding would take place very soon. For as the king himself was proud to say, there was nothing to hinder their union. All opposition had been swept away. No matter what the Holy Father in Rome might say or think, I, Catherine, was not his true wife.

Legal scholars by the score had declared it so. Many cardinals had agreed; after all, he paid them well to agree. And the English clergy, in solemn convocation, had given the king the new title "Supreme Head of the Church and Clergy of England." As head of the church he answered to no one—except, of course, Anne.

And Anne was more determined than ever to take my place.

The mirthless Advent and New Year's celebrations had passed when Anne dealt me her most daring blow. She brought the Countess de Cabra back to England, to bear witness to what she knew—or claimed to know—of my marriage to Arthur.

My first thought, when I saw my half-sister Maria Juana, Countess de Cabra, was that she looked much older than when she had left our court to marry the count and live in Spain. Thin and irritable, her face lined and her mouth turned down, she was impatient with the younger women in my household and snapped at them in a hoarse voice. No doubt she envied them their youth and high spirits, I thought at first. She was a widow, the Count de Cabra having died valiantly in battle leading his knights against the army of Suleiman the Magnificent, but I did not think her aging or bad temper came from sorrow or grief. Rather, I suspected, she felt wronged, and wanted satisfaction.

Each time I saw her I was reminded of our father Ferdinand—a much older Ferdinand. Her fleshy cheeks were sunken, her close-set eyes underhung with sagging pouches. Her curling hair was still abundant, but much of it was gray, and—this was most striking of all—she seemed not to care any longer whether she was thought handsome or seductive. The occasional flashes of fire in her dull brown eyes were not sparked by lust, or the desire for conquest. They were sparked by revenge.

"Your sister the countess has been telling me about your marriage to Prince Arthur," Anne said to me when, at the king's command, the three of us sat together in Anne's spacious bedchamber, adding, "Her memory is keen."

On Henry's order Anne had recently begun to live apart from the other women of my household, in a suite of rooms all her own. In the bedchamber of her new suite was a large bed he had given her, resplendent in coverings of gold and silver. A bed more suited for a queen than a maid of honor. Also in this room, on one wall, was a carefully drawn, branching tree of descent displaying Anne's ancestry—a largely imagined ancestry, as I was told indignantly by the Countess of Norfolk—stretching back to the generation of William the Norman nearly five hundred years earlier.

"She remembers well your wedding night," Anne continued. "How ardently you and Arthur embraced, how she and others witnessed and displayed the bloodstained bedsheets afterward—"

Here Maria Juana nodded vigorously.

Anne went on. "She recalls how Arthur boasted of his conquest, not once but many times—"

"Yes, many times," Maria Juana put in, continuing to nod in agreement.

"And that you, Catherine, having lost your maidenhead, blushed and smiled and stammered that you were now a true wife."

"I did no such thing!" I interrupted. "I said no such thing! And well Maria Juana knows it! If she had any truthfulness in her, she would ask my forgiveness for her lies!" I paused for breath.

"I am sorry to hear you speak so disparagingly of your sister," Anne said smoothly, "when she has come all the way from Aragon to bear witness to your union with the prince. Her words carry much weight."

"Maria Juana is not my sister," I snapped, "though she is said to be the daughter of my father's whore. For all I know, her ancestry is as uncertain as your own." I glanced with contempt at the genealogical tree as I said this.

In truth I was shocked by the bitterness and ugliness of my

words. I had always thought of Maria Juana as my half-sister, and had never denied our shared paternity. I had not realized, until that moment, how angry I was at both Anne and Maria Juana, who were doing their best to put me in a trap from which only supporters long gone or long dead could rescue me. Until that terrible afternoon I had been the outwardly calm, composed one, Anne the quarrelsome, accusing harridan. I had had the upper hand. Now that Anne had the all too willing support of Maria Juana, however, she felt that she had triumphed, and that left me furious and spiteful.

Nonetheless my retort was swift.

"No matter what lies this faithless woman tells, my almoner Master Reveles and many others in my service at the time will refute them!"

"What others?" Anne demanded.

"My confessor, Fray Diego—"

"The drunkard? The debauched friar, who, I believe, was sent away in disgrace?"

"My duenna, then."

"I believe she is deceased."

Anne knew a good deal about my household as Arthur's wife and widow. I concentrated, I searched my memory.

"My duenna, Doña Elvira," I repeated.

"Doña Elvira has gone to be with the angels," Maria Juana put in.

Who was there, I asked myself. Who remained, out of all those who had served me so many years earlier, who could recall the intimate details of my marriage to dear Arthur? Dear, weak, frail Arthur?

I could not think of a single one who could truthfully refute Maria Juana's lies.

Anne, seeing that I had run out of servants I could appeal to, smiled, a knowing smile. She had triumphed.

To underscore her triumph the dour, morose churchman Thomas Cranmer came himself to inform me, in mournful tones, that any hope I had of remaining King Henry's wife was without merit.

"It is plain that you were indeed married to Prince Arthur,

Mistress Catherine. Therefore any later marriage you may have entered into cannot be looked on as valid. Nor can it be made so by any dispensation granted by the Bishop of Rome, nor by any person in heaven or on earth!"

He allowed his chill words to hang in the air, final and unanswered, until I turned and left the room in disgust—or, more truly, in dismay. Cranmer, a renowned scholar, had been my last hope. If he could not defend my cause, my right to remain Queen of England, then I could expect no other aid. And the learned Cranmer had called me Mistress Catherine and not Queen Catherine. He had been convinced by the king, or by the king's money and power, to abandon me—and Princess Mary—and to lend the weight of his learning to Anne.

I threw up my hands in despair and paced up and down the length of my apartments, which had never seemed so empty. Then I prayed, swore, asked forgiveness for my swearing and prayed again.

In my aching head I could not stop hearing the scholar's dire words. My marriage to Henry, he had said, was no marriage, and no power in heaven or on earth could change that.

16

WE SAW STRANGE LIGHTS IN THE SKY ALL THROUGHOUT THAT summer, and they went on appearing long into the fall. Streaks of green and blue, yellow and deep glowing violet lit the nights, and in the days, there were odd luminous clouds, no larger than a man's fist, that grew brighter and brighter until they gave forth lightning in quicksilver bursts.

No one doubted that these prodigies of nature were omens of disaster.

"Evil days have come upon us," my dresser Maria de Caceres was fond of saying, shaking her head. "Evil days indeed."

As if in sympathy with the signs in the sky there were rumblings under the earth, and shakings, so strong and violent that buildings fell and great trees crashed to the ground, their limbs and branches slapping the turf until it quaked afresh.

"It is that whore Anne Boleyn," people said. "That evil-tongued, proud, scheming witless Mistress Anne, who bears the devil's marks. She has brought these evils among us. England is undone!"

Fishermen told of giant sea creatures, longer than ten boats, that swam up the Thames and beached themselves on the shore to die. Of tides flowing backward, and balls of fire the size of human heads falling out of the skies. Everyone in my household was afraid, even Griffith Richards, who I thought of as the bravest of men. It was he who brought me word that my chamberlain's twin sons, Donald and Daniel, had hanged themselves in the meat locker, and that their father, in despair over their loss, threw himself in the river, leaving me all his possessions.

There was a written message with them:

"Done because I am undone," the enigmatic message read. "O my sons, my sons—"

Each day brought some new tragedy or omen. I began to be fearful myself, though I tried not to show my fear, lest I lead others to commit desperate acts. When my old horse Griselda, the filly I had had since she was foaled, began to stagger and lose her sight, I quietly told my groom to feed her on poppyseed cake until she fell into an unending sleep. I did my utmost to face each dire event courageously, and not to bleat and cower like the others, or give in to the terror of madness. But when I grew damp and hot with fever and could hardly stand upright from dizziness I felt my courage failing, and prayed to be delivered from hopelessness.

Feverish dreams assailed me—of smothering under the weight of great fish, of being tortured and hanged, as men of unnatural desires for other men were hanged. Of familiar faces twisted and distorted in anguish until they were almost unrecognizable. I pray most fervently, as I write of this, that I shall never have to endure such fevers again.

Throughout my feverish ordeal an old saying echoed and re-echoed in my head, one that I had heard recited and sung when I was married to Arthur. It was a chanted prophecy:

> *A queen shall be crowned*
> *In the hall of the kings*
> *And the queen shall die.*

When my fever was at its worst I imagined that I was the queen who had been crowned in the hall of the kings, and who was doomed to die.

My apothecaries bled me and dosed me with strong purgatives that made me vomit. I grew weaker by the hour, I felt myself giving in to the force of the old prophetic words. In my delirium I imagined Henry, greatly weakened by the pain in his leg, unable to reign any longer. I saw him handing his crown to Henry Fitzroy and disinheriting our daughter Mary. Then I saw myself led out to the kitchens, where grim-eyed cooks forced me to eat poppyseed cake until I could not stay awake any longer and sank down into the earth, to be covered, as I had ordered Griselda to be covered, with sweet grass.

I was awakened from these dark fantasies by Maria de Caceres, who was noisily opening my traveling chests and removing my things from them.

"He is taking that accursed woman to France," she told me. "He requires your traveling chests. She has too few of her own."

So Henry was acting at last, I thought. He was determined to marry Anne. He feared to carry out the ceremony in England, knowing what an outcry the people would make. To avoid this he would take Anne to France, and marry her there. But I would not lend her my chests.

"If she lacks traveling chests, let her buy more," I said firmly. I had thirty fine chests covered in Cordovan leather, and several dozen inferior ones as well, all bearing my name and emblem. They had been brought from Spain when I came to England as a bride. They had held everything that was precious to me. I had no intention of letting Anne have them—or even borrow them.

"And there is one thing more," my dresser was telling me. Her voice was soft, apologetic. I was instantly on the alert. She sounded tenuous. She knew I would be loath to hear what she was about to say.

"The king requires your jewels."

"Tell the king my answer is no."

Maria turned pale. "I cannot tell him that, Your Highness."

"Then summon him, and I will tell him myself."

So this is how it is to be, I thought. He intends to marry his whore mistress, and to take from me all that I value: my title of queen, my household, my most precious possessions. All these he means to squander, at my expense, on the least deserving of the women at our court: Anne Boleyn.

And for what? For a fleeting passion, and the hope of a son.

"Madam."

While I was lost in my musings, Henry had come into the room.

Instinctively I knelt, as I always had. He was my sovereign. And something more: my husband, my partner and lover. My old friend and ally. And now, because of Anne, my enemy.

He reached out his hand, the hand with jeweled rings on each fleshy finger, and raised me up. Standing before him, he towered over me. I had shrunk, over the years. He had expanded, in height as well as girth.

"Catherine, I require your jewels."

"To adorn your mistress."

"To adorn my wife."

"I am your wife."

"As you please. In any event, I will soon have another."

"She shall not have anything of mine."

There was a pause, then Henry said, more softly yet urgently, "She has my heart."

A retort sprang to my lips, but I remained silent. I knew in that moment that my cause was lost. I knew it, as surely as I have ever known anything in my life. And still I argued, and fought over my rights. I clung to the symbols of my rank. I am ashamed to write this, but I quarreled with Henry, as loudly and bitterly as Anne ever had, until he threw up his beringed hands and cried for Wolsey— the late Cardinal Wolsey—lamenting that Wolsey had always known how to make necessary things happen without bickering and strife.

Back and forth we went, Henry arguing that I had no further

need of my jewels, that I was ill (he was right about that) and could not leave my apartments and in any case, I was no longer queen, as all the experts in the law of the church agreed. Therefore it was only right that I should hand over my jewels to him—in actuality, I was sure, to Anne.

I in turn argued, fiercely, that Henry was far more ill than I was, that the pain and stinking infection in his sore leg were likely to get worse and that even if he made Anne his wife he was too old and sick to become a father once again.

I told him, bluntly, what my physician had told me: that with the worsening infection in his leg he might very well die—and soon.

"You made me regent while you were away fighting in France," I reminded him. "We were much younger then, to be sure. And I was carrying a child. Do you remember that?"

He nodded.

"I fought off the Scots. I lost the child in my womb. I wept—but I did what needed to be done, as ruler and guardian of the realm, in your stead. Do you truly believe that Anne could do the same, should you become ill and unable to rule any longer? Has she the valor, the strength? Would the soldiers fight for her, if the imperial armies of my nephew Charles invaded England?"

My arguments struck home. Henry knew he was on weak ground, to imagine that Anne could do what I, Queen Isabella's daughter, had ordered done on Flodden Field.

He had his answer ready nonetheless.

"I assure you, madam, that I will not die. Yet if I should, my councilors will serve as my regents until such time as my heir can rule. Now, I will have your jewels—and your traveling chests."

"Not while I breathe," was my own harsh reply.

"As you wish—but I *will* have them," were Henry's parting words.

And as sure as night follows day, five of his chamber gentlemen came with royal warrants to retrieve both the jewels and the traveling chests within the hour.

Henry was indeed taking from me all that I valued: my place at his side, my role as his queen, my dignity. What were a few jewels and traveling chests compared to these?

Signs and wonders continued to appear in the skies in the autumn of the Year of Our Lord 1532, and Mistress Anne, my husband's beloved, ordered her wedding clothes sewn and embarked for France.

The Scandal of Christendom, that's what they were calling her in Calais. The king's harlot. The Whore of Babylon. So my friend Elizabeth Howard told me in her letters carried by swift messenger during the month of October.

None of the respectable women of our English court would cross to France, and only a few would serve as Anne's attendants. As for the women of the French court, only King Francis's mistress, Mme de Vendôme, would meet or welcome Anne, and that in itself was a scandal and a disgrace.

Yet according to what the duchess wrote to me, Anne continued to announce that she and Henry would soon wed. They were lodged together in the old Exchequer in Calais, with the handful of women who had attached themselves to Anne's household in attendance nearby. Elizabeth and Thomas Howard, Anne's uncle and aunt, were lodged in another part of the old Exchequer, from which vantage point the duchess could observe much of the goings-on.

"Your half-sister Maria Juana is there as well," Elizabeth informed me. "Anne has promised to find her a rich French husband. But it will be difficult, as none of the ladies of Calais visit Anne or even acknowledge her presence. How then can Anne find an available wealthy man to marry Maria Juana?

"Not only do the French ladies ignore Anne, they ignore all of the English women around her," the duchess wrote. "Apart from the king, who delights in her, Anne is completely on her own. Her serving women obey her commands and gratify her whims; to all others, she is as remote as the moon—and as cold."

The duchess described, in her long letters, the atmosphere surrounding Anne during the visit to Calais: the quarreling among the women, the rising resentments and jealousies. According to the duchess, Anne disliked Maria Juana (who was, I must admit, the more graceful and seductive of the two), and was envious of her. The wedding finery created by the Belgian seamstresses displeased Anne, I was told, and the insulting remarks the Belgians made about her appearance displeased her even more.

"Of course the kirtle doesn't fit! Her belly is growing bigger and bigger!"

"By the mass, she's going to have twins!"

"And if she does have twins, which one inherits the throne?"

"The firstborn, you fool!"

"What if the firstborn is an idiot?"

"Then the other one!"

"What if one is a prince, the other a princess?"

On it went, Elizabeth wrote, with much muffled laughter at Anne's expense. It sounded to me, from the letters and other messages I was receiving, as though Henry was wavering in his decision to make Anne his wife. She was proving to be more fearsome and demanding than he had expected. And less pure.

The duchess was certain that my husband was sleeping with Anne, just as if they were already married. But according to Henry's old friend and jousting partner Charles Brandon, Anne was keeping company with another man as well.

My prayers were being answered. Anne's true nature was showing itself, and Henry would see through the veil of lustful illusion at last. He would return to me, his true and only wife. He would return to me.

As it turned out, of course, the illusion was mine, not Henry's. For a few days I expected to have good news in the duchess's letters, the good news that my husband had seen through Anne's façade and rejected her. Instead, Anne soon found a way—the most obvious way—to bind him to her with lasting bonds. Her seamstresses were right after all. She was carrying the king's child.

This changed everything.

I was urged, for my own safety and wellbeing, to return to Spain at once. If I stayed on in England I would only be in the way. A troublesome presence at best, at worst, an obstacle to the security of the realm.

Besides, I was told, I would be sure to suffer, watching Anne preside over court festivities, wearing my jewels, sitting at Henry's side in the place of honor as I had done for so many years. I would not want to see her married, or crowned, or to hear of the birth of her child. If I left England and returned to Spain I would still know of these events, to be sure, but they would seem less painful.

Something in me rebelled against leaving. It would be as if I left the field of battle, conceding defeat to the enemy. I was not bred to yield, to give up. I was determined to fight on, quietly, stealthily if I must. But I would not lay down my arms. I would stay and fight on.

It was the Spanish ambassador who first brought me word that my husband had pledged himself to Anne, and she to him, in a hasty ceremony with only a few witnesses present. It had taken place toward the end of January.

"One of my informants knew of it," he told me, "but only an hour or so before the vows were exchanged. It was only by chance that he was able to find out what was going on.

"Anne was ill," he learned, "but not too ill to repeat her wedding vows. The king was trembling and shaking. When he repeated his vows his voice was low—almost a whisper."

"How ill was she?" I demanded.

"It was the sickness of the mother-to-be."

Fateful words. So the Scandal of Christendom had conceived a child, and knew herself to be pregnant by the end of January. That meant that she would deliver her child in the fall, unless—

I banished all such dire thoughts from my mind. I will not even record them here. Unless—

Many things could go wrong, as I knew only too well. The

midwives were never completely certain there was a healthy child in the womb until it quickened. Anne's quickening would not be expected until the spring. And by then the outrage of my husband's pretended marriage to his impure mistress would be avenged.

The time had arrived for my nephew Charles to come to my defense. I sent him a message, urging him to act, to threaten invasion if Henry persisted in flaunting his feigned union with Anne. To invade England if his threats brought no result.

When I received no immediate response I sent a second message, and then a third, all of them signed defiantly "Catherine the Queen." I waited for an indication that the imperial armies were on their way, or that Charles himself would land on the English coast in his flagship. Day after day I expected an envoy from the imperial court. An informant, even. A messenger at least.

But there was nothing. Gradually the truth became clear. It was no longer in Charles's interest to defend me or protect me. I was not important: Henry was.

There could be no other reason for my nephew's inaction.

My chamberlain Lord Mountjoy brought me the instructions Henry was too ashamed or too preoccupied to deliver himself. In delivering them the chamberlain called me, not "Mistress Catherine," but "Princess Dowager."

"It is the king's pleasure that you send no letter or message to the imperial court," he announced. "Nor will you be allowed to receive any."

He was unctuous, as always. He meant to be ingratiating, despite his harshly negative message.

Before I could demur he went on.

"You will remain in your apartments until more suitable quarters are provided. In the meantime you will not be receiving any allotment of funds from the royal treasury, or from any other source—"

"What? Am I to provide for my household from the few coins I brought from Spain as my dowry, when I married Prince Arthur? I could not feed a lapdog on that pittance!"

As my own ire rose, Lord Mountjoy seemed to become increasingly pleased and self-satisfied. He was a handsome man, tall and slender, and he danced gracefully and well—an ability much prized at our court. He was preening, as he stood there before me. My words had no effect—or rather, they had the effect of making my chamberlain ever more aware of the security of his own position and the fragility of mine.

As I was to learn later, Henry had promoted him to first gentleman of the chamber—at Anne's insistence. My household officials and servants were being won over, through bribes and promises of promotion, to betray me. Had my nephew come to my aid with his arms and his fortune, Lord Mountjoy would have been put in a cold, cramped dungeon and I in my rightful place, on my queenly throne beside Henry. Not complaining angrily to an indifferent household official who was hiding a slight smirk—or was it a yawn?—behind one gloved hand.

The question about Anne remained: Was she or was she not carrying a prince, a future king?

Whatever the truth, Henry decided to take the bold step of presenting her to the courtiers as his wife and queen, the future mother of his son.

Throughout our marriage it had always been his custom on Holy Saturday, on the eve of Easter Sunday, to attend mass with me. We made a ceremonial entry to the chapel together, and I sat to his side in a throne appropriate to my state. On this Easter Eve in the year 1533, however, it was Anne who accompanied him, not me, amid a loud and prolonged fanfare of trumpets, and with sixty waiting women in attendance.

Yes, sixty! Among them were many of those who had pointedly declined to attend Anne when she accompanied Henry to Calais. They still resented Anne's usurping my role and my status— Elizabeth Howard assured me of that—but they dared not refuse the king's command. Some had been won over by gifts or promises of future benefits, others by threats or the fear of blows. All the women were stiff and tense, the duchess told me, ill at ease in being forced to take part in a ceremony that felt false. There was many a frown, many a murmur of resentment as they made their way along.

What was especially galling to the women around her was the splendor of Anne's adornments. She had not been crowned queen, yet at Henry's order she was dressed in regal finery for this significant occasion. From head to toe she shone with gold, her trailing mantle made from cloth of gold, the jewels at her throat and on her fingers gleaming with a gilded luster. Nor were these mere garnets or amethysts or Orient pearls: these were crown jewels, priceless gems from the treasure house in the Tower.

"All the gold and jewels the king heaped on her only made her look worse," were Elizabeth Howard's first words to me after the mass ended and she came to tell me how it had gone. "I overheard many criticisms from among her attendants. The shadows and the darkened chapel could not hide her flaws. Instead they revealed all her shortcomings. She is not beautiful. She is not young. Her nose is far too large and she has spots on her cheeks. She lacks the grace to walk like a baroness, much less a queen. And as for her swollen belly—" Elizabeth shook her head, her mouth turned down in disdain. "It is more a shame than an honor to the realm. If the king married her in January, as they say, then she was already with child when they said their vows."

Her words were scalding reminders of all that gave me pain, yet they were at the same time gratifying, I have to confess, especially when she described the deepgoing resentment Anne gave rise to among the women of the court. Even the men, the duchess told me, had to be nudged by Henry into acknowledging Anne with bows and murmurs of "Your Grace."

"No man, whether highborn or low, likes to be forced to show honor to a pregnant whore," she concluded.

The following morning, "Queen Anne" was prayed for at the Easter mass, and hearing the unwelcome form of words, some of the worshippers actually rose and left the church. If only I had been there! I would have led them out myself. But I was imprisoned in my rooms, far from the outrage being committed against me, doing my best to observe the resurrection feast in reverent solitude.

"Queen Anne" indeed! She had no right whatever to that title, only my husband's command that it be used. No formal judgment had ever been issued dispossessing me of my claim to the title of queen. Despite this, elaborate and costly preparations were already being made for Anne's coronation.

"It had better be done soon, before she gives birth to the prince!"

"Or will the crowning and the christening be combined?"

Londoners laughed and jeered in an effort to mask their dread, but it did seem, as the hastily arranged coronation festivities took form, as though the natural order had been turned upside down. Anne's triumph was the triumph of disorder and wrong. It was seen as fearsome, as a sign of evil having come into the world. Not everyone gave in to their fears, but a great many did. For Anne, who bore the devil's marks on her body, was just one more of the many strange signs and omens of disaster to be feared.

And as Anne's coronation came closer and closer, the strange events multiplied, and the number of bodies pulled from the river and discovered under the stairs and in lonely fields on the outskirts of the capital grew higher.

"From dread and despondency, and the fear of unknown evil, good Lord, deliver us," prayed my confessor on the eve of Anne's coronation. That night, toward sunset, a ball of fiery light appeared above the horizon and hung there, glowing, then spitting fire, until dusk. Londoners turned out into the streets in droves, certain that the end of the world had come, and it was nearly dawn before the forces of the Lord Mayor and the guilds, the soldiers and the booming of the Tower guns could force them back into their homes.

17

THERE WAS REBELLION IN THE AIR THAT SPRING, WHAT WITH THE signs and wonders in the sky and the quaking of the earth and the high tax levied on every Londoner to pay for Queen Anne's coronation, which could not be long delayed.

The Londoners were incensed.

"You should hear them shout, 'Not a groat for the whore Nan Bullen and her crowning! We'll have none but Queen Catherine!'" Ambassador Chapuys told me gleefully when he came to visit me at Buckden. "London is yours, Your Grace, and always has been."

Henry had ordered me moved to the Huntingdonshire countryside so as to be away from the capital when Anne's coronation solemnities and festivities went on. I had no wish to hear the uproar, much less to join in all the clamoring myself, though I would have liked to hear the shouts of support and loyalty from the people. Shouts of support for me, not for Anne.

Buckden was a spacious estate with an empty, lonely feel to the great old high-ceilinged hall and large apartments. It had been a bishop's palace but the bishop and his priestly staff had been moved elsewhere. My footfalls echoed in the bare, chilly rooms. The ambassador's boots were even louder as he walked through the apartments, looking around at the stark bare walls and sparse furnishings.

I shivered, and moved closer to the hearth where my groom Francisco Phelipe had ordered a fire laid. In the past my chamberlain Griffith Richards would have seen to this task, but he had not been allowed to come with me to Buckden; like many others who had been members of my dwindling household, he had gone to serve Anne, by order of the king. I still had my serving women, my confessor George de Atequa, my cooks, kitchen turnspit boys and grounds keepers—Buckden had large grounds and gardens, and stands of fine old trees—and most important, my physician Miguel de Lasco and my apothecaries Juan de Soto and Philip Grenacre.

In charge of all were my captors—as I thought of them—Sir Edward Chamberlain and Sir Edmund Bedingfield, assigned by my husband to keep me confined, oversee the estate and defend it should the need arise. They were scornful of this task, seeing it as far beneath their status. The look Edmund Bedingfield gave the ambassador when he was admitted was perfunctory, he and Sir Edward hardly paused in their afternoon dice games, played in the guards' chamber, far from my own principal chamber with its welcoming hearth.

"When is the coronation to be?" I asked when Ambassador Chapuys and I had seated ourselves before the fire.

He was uncomfortable. "Not until one more matter has been settled—legally."

"And what is that?"

He fumbled for words. "It is a mere formality," he said at length. "A proceeding in the archbishop's court, a point of detail."

I saw through his evasiveness, and demanded to know more.

He sighed. "A correction must be made, an adjustment in status, for the sake of the succession." He spoke hurriedly, dismissively. "I recommend that you pay no attention. Simply ignore whatever is said to you, or required of you." He cleared his throat, then said, "Archbishop Cranmer is about to order you to appear before him at Dunstable, where he means to arrive at a judgment concerning your marriage to King Henry."

So it was to be done at last. The unfinished work of Cardinals Wolsey and Campeggio was to be completed by the dull, dour Archbishop Cranmer—who, I reminded myself, had once been Thomas Boleyn's humble chaplain. Thomas Cranmer was about to decide whether or not I was Henry's true wife and queen. He could only decide one way—against me and in favor of Henry's freedom to marry Anne.

No wonder the ambassador was looking down at his feet rather than at me.

"It is only a form, a show. It means nothing," he was saying. "The only true authority is in Rome—" He broke off, cleared his throat. He looked at me apologetically. I had been given ample evidence that Rome had fallen into such a state of corruption and sin that the authority of the Holy Father was all but nil. His earthly authority, that is.

Whatever the unfortunate state of affairs in Rome, and however great my contempt for the archbishop, I was determined not to cooperate in any judgment he might arrive at that would weaken my claim to be queen.

I wrote out a protest, refusing to heed the summons to attend the archbishop's court, and saying that he had no authority to make a ruling. I might have added that the archbishop himself had been married twice—so it was said—and that in my opinion neither of his marriages was a valid one as he had taken holy orders. To add this would have been to act out of spite, however, and besides, not everything one heard was true.

I trusted that my letter would be delivered.

I waited—and in due course the ruling came down. I was declared to be in contempt of the archbishop's court, which found that Henry and I had never been married at all. Words might have been spoken, vows taken between us, but in the archbishop's judgment, we had never been man and wife.

Which meant, however it hurt me to imagine it, even fleetingly, that Princess Mary was not the heir to her father's throne, and that our son who had had so short a life so many years earlier had never been a true heir either. I was no more than a contumacious Castilian heiress who had overstayed her welcome in England by many years.

I knew, to be sure, that this was nonsense. That any judgment pronounced by a cleric in the pay of the Boleyns was one-sided and without merit. Yet the words stung. They roused me to renewed anger against this imposter whose alluring ways had robbed me of my place at court, my rightful place at the king's side. Even as I railed inwardly against her I knew, of course I knew, that it was as much Henry's doing as Anne's. His was the highest power, the power of the throne. All decisions were his. All betrayals were his as well. Henry had shaped and defined the judgment of the archbishop's court. Now it was up to me to do what I could to rob it of its force.

There was little enough I could do while at Buckden. But I could at least send my dresser Maria de Caceres to London in my place, to buy cloth and thread to make new garments to enhance my meager wardrobe (all my queenly finery having been taken away) but in truth to be my eyes and ears.

I asked Ambassador Chapuys to send an urgent message to the king saying that my few remaining gowns were in rags and my torn kirtles a disgrace, and making me sound more pitiful than demanding. Because I was no longer looked on as an impediment to Henry's plans my dresser was permitted to go to the capital and spend a small sum at the cloth market.

Maria de Caceres lost no time in setting out, escorted by three of the ambassador's men. It was a modest enough group of travelers, unlikely to draw attention. On arrival, however, she was glad to have the protection of the mounted men, for she found London a bedlam, loud with shouts and slanders against the queen who was about to be crowned and filled with resentment. And the cloth market was at the center of it all.

"You want to buy *what*?" my dresser was asked rudely when she tried to order five ells of woolen cloth dyed in my favorite shade of light blue. "Are you mad? We have no woolens at all, and barely half an ell of sour green sarcenet, and that a ruined scrap, dragged out from under the wheels of a cart!"

"Don't you know that there are no more ships from Flanders, there is no more cloth at all!" another indignant merchant told her.

Others simply shook their heads, or threw up their hands in exasperation. Even the moneylenders were at their wits' end, Maria told me in a message she sent to Buckden. There was no trade, no borrowing or lending. Everyone expected war—and soon. No trade could go on in the shadow of war.

"You wait and see," one burly drover told Maria as he passed her with his five thin cows. "A year from now we'll all be ruined. All! Unless the king takes Good Queen Catherine back, and casts aside his whore!"

Maria took a chance and told the man she was hoping to find some cloth for the queen—"the true queen, that is," she added.

Squinting, he looked her over, then her companions.

"You'll find all the cloth you want at the Steelyard," he told her. "They are Germans there. Subjects of the Emperor Charles, though they do business here in England. They have no use for Nan Bullen, I'll tell you that for certain! Their warehouses are full of woven goods, made in Flanders—but they won't trade it. They know—we all know—there will be war."

He told her where to go to find the German merchants whose walled community was on the north bank of the river. "Go carefully," he cautioned. "Their knives are sharp—and their tongues are even sharper."

Maria found her way to the Steelyard and, once she explained who she was and that she had come to London on an errand for me, she was welcomed into its embattled confines.

She told them how I was all but imprisoned by King Henry and kept from coming before my faithful people, prevented from receiving their aid and encouragement. And she confided to them that I was ill, and in great need of cheer, to strengthen me and bring me back to health. If only they could make some sort of demonstration to show their support for me! Could they not show their loyalty to me on the day the unworthy queen Anne was to come to London?

The merchants assured her that they would, then let her choose from among their stock of woolen cloth and would not let her pay them anything.

And on the day Anne passed through the capital in procession, the merchants of the Steelyard made their contempt for her evident, by placing the arms of Aragon and Castile—my arms—and the imperial eagle of the Hapsburgs, my nephew's arms, higher than Anne's own emblem of the white falcon.

The meaning of this challenge to Anne's rank and title was not lost on the crowds of silent Londoners who watched as she was carried through the narrow streets from Fenchurch and Gracechurch to Leadenhall and then along Fleet Street and the Strand to Westminster. Musicians played to her, the Tower cannonry saluted her and loud trumpet fanfares demanded respect for the very pregnant, very bilious Anne as she was borne past in her regal litter, covered in a white satin canopy and drawn by two patient long-eared mules with gilded saddles.

There were hundreds in the procession, the noblewomen in gowns of cloth of gold that glinted in the sunlight, the lord chancellor and royal councilors, even the members of the leading guilds (whose livelihoods were being choked off by the stark decline in trade with Flanders) in velvet and gold chains. A seemingly endless procession winding past the silent crowds.

"We were kept behind staunch barriers," Maria wrote to me. "We could not have disrupted the procession, even if we had wanted to—and there were many who wanted to very much. I heard them murmuring to one another, cursing Anne under their breath.

"When I finally saw the harlot Anne, sitting in her litter, with her hair hanging down like a virginal young girl, and her gown sewn with emeralds and rubies, I wanted to reach out and snatch away all her finery. I saw that some of her ladies in their crimson gowns and ermines looked as aggrieved and outraged as I felt—or so I imagined. None of them wanted to be there, appearing to support the imposter who had stolen the king's affections and brought harm to the good queen, Queen Catherine.

"All the fanfares and grandeur in London could not make any of us greet Anne," my dresser Maria let me know in her message, sent to me at Buckden. "She is hated. And she looked as if she was about to be sick."

I had warned Maria that the coronation ceremony, held the following day, would be lengthy and tiring. I remembered my own coronation well, how I became very hungry and thirsty after three or four hours of prayers and anointing and knowing that the end was not yet in sight.

But I had not been carrying a child on that long day, and Anne was.

"The longer it all went on, the more pale she became," Maria wrote in her last message to me, sent at the end of the coronation day. "I overheard people commenting on how she looked as if she were going to faint. No one wanted to be there, or to take part in creating her queen. She didn't deserve it. Imagine! A commoner raised to be anointed queen! And all of us forced to watch each anointing and robing and praying over her.

"I could tell how much she liked it all, even though she was feeling so poorly. Every now and then I saw her smile. When the Duke of Suffolk brought the crown, and it was placed on her head amid singing and praying, she could not have looked more pleased. I think what pleased her was the humiliation of the others, all of them of higher birth, forced to pay homage to her and show that she had attained the highest rank possible for a woman, next to being born a queen, of course.

"She stumbled and nearly fell when her father led her out of the abbey after she had been crowned. Oh, she was tired! But he held on to her arm very so tightly that I saw her grimace, and made sure she managed to walk the length of that long aisle while he held her in his grip. The choristers burst into loud song and the trumpeters blew more loudly than ever and we all felt more and more tired ourselves."

Thanks to Maria I was able to imagine the ceremony, and almost felt my own stomach churn as I read over her account. She wrote how afterward, there was much talk of midwives having been in the abbey just in case Anne went into labor during her crowning.

No one seemed to know when the child would be born. It was being said that the king had brought to court astrologers and seers to predict the date and time when Anne would give birth. That the baby would be a prince no one doubted, though according to Maria, not every conversation she overheard or every comment made to her was very astute.

"You would think the king would have had the courtesy to wait until she was delivered before making her go through all this!" was one remark she heard again and again.

"Of course he couldn't wait!" was the usual answer. "Had he waited, her child would not have been born to a king and his anointed queen. His claim to the throne would have been questioned. Princess Mary's claim would have been better—or even Henry Fitzroy's!"

Other remarks, made in low tones by Anne's enemies, were more astringent. "Why make a queen of such a woman! And she of such low birth! Why not crown the girl who feeds the pigs!"

But what Maria overheard most often were loud grumbles from the overtaxed Londoners complaining that they had to pay for all the lavish pageantry and finery, the tourneying and banqueting, the costly gowns and even for the wine that flowed freely from the public fountains. How could they be expected to bear, in silence and without complaint, the burden of such a high price for the elevation of a brazen, insolent woman to the rank of queen? How, when the docks were all but empty of merchant ships and the merchants' coffers empty of coins, could Londoners accept Anne Boleyn as the true wife of King Henry? Especially when the Holy Father in Rome had made his extreme disapproval known?

For he had most certainly done so. Even before the archbishop had placed the crown on Anne's unworthy head, Pope Clement threatened to declare the marriage annulled and to excommunicate Henry.

When the last of my dresser Maria's messages had reached me, and she herself had returned to Buckden to give me an even more lengthy report on all that she had seen and heard, I was dejected. I could not help but mourn the loss of what had been mine—for how could it not be a loss, now that Anne had her crown and—what was much more important—now that she had the next Prince of Wales in her belly?

I began to make plans to leave England, to return to Castile and devote myself to a quiet retirement from the world. It seemed the right, the dignified thing to do. I even thought, for the length of one wet afternoon, of wearing a hair shirt under my gown as my mother had done. I would found a convent, and visit the nuns on each holy day to ensure that they were not falling into lives of sin as so many monks and nuns were said to do.

But if I went to live in Spain, I would have to leave my beloved daughter Mary behind. Mary, I felt certain, would soon be wed to a prince or nobleman. When her own new household was formed, would she permit me to join it? Or would my own notoriety as Henry's rejected wife and Anne's humiliated rival haunt any court I joined, and overshadow Mary's own legitimacy?

Whatever move I made, it would have to be one that preserved my dignity and my independence. I would need quiet time to pray and ponder. To survey the land, so to speak, as any wise commander does before returning to the fray.

Even as I thought over these things, I resisted inwardly. I was never one to leave the field. To retreat was not in my nature. Not until I had used every weapon at my command, every fighter loyal to me, to regain what I had lost. Still, I wanted to make a wise decision, not a hasty one.

To this end I asked Ambassador Chapuys to visit me again, and he was soon back at Buckden.

"I have been thinking of leaving England, of going to live in Castile, perhaps even in the Alhambra or nearby," I told him when we sat once again before the hearth fire in my rooms.

"I could rest in quiet there, it seems a fitting way to remove myself with dignity from all that has happened."

The ambassador looked at me searchingly.

"Why would you enter a convent now, when you refused to earlier?"

I had no answer for that. The ambassador went on.

"If you imagine that you could retire from life, or hide yourself away like a recluse, you couldn't be more wrong, if I may say so. You have become a cause, a symbol."

This took me by surprise. "What sort of symbol?" I asked him.

"Why, of resistance to the king's vanity, his dishonoring of his marriage, his refusal to submit to the authority of the church. Consider the harm he is doing to the kingdom by attempting to put you aside, knowing full well he would bring on himself and his subjects the ire of the Emperor Charles. You, Catherine, represent stability and safety. The king has put his people in peril.

"And no monarch dares do such grave injury to his people without suffering many a penalty," he added, his tone becoming ominous. "Why, you ought to have heard the slanders and insults flung at Anne behind her back—and at the king as well. I heard many a tavern oath to 'No queen but our Good Queen Catherine!' on the eve of the coronation—and after it was over."

I remembered what Maria de Caceres had written to me about the silence of the crowds that watched Anne process through the capital. I questioned Ambassador Chapuys about this.

"True enough, they were silent when her procession went by. But it was not out of respect. They were withholding their shouts of loyalty. They were denying her their fealty. They were refusing to offer her their heartfelt support and love."

Listening to the ambassador, I took heart. So my support among the people was growing stronger, not weaker. I stood, and began pacing back and forth. I felt more tenacious, more determined to stand my ground. Still, I thought, this ever widening support for me means that I am a growing threat to the future peace of the realm and the restoration of good order, and to the authority of the king and his new wife. I said as much to Ambassador Chapuys.

"Ah, but that is where you are wrong. You are no threat at all if he believes, or at least he constantly tells others, that he does not expect you to live much longer."

Caught unawares by the ambassador's blunt words, I had to catch my breath. "Is that what he truly believes?" I asked at length.

Instead of answering me directly, he asked me whether I had not noticed that little attention was being paid to who came to visit me, or to how often my physician and apothecaries came and went, giving me medicines and offering advice on my illness?

I agreed that I had noticed this, and with some surprise. I sat down again.

"He has convinced himself that your illness will soon put an end to your life. Which, I assure you, none of us who support you believe, or want to believe. You will recover. You will enjoy a long life. But I urge you, Your Majesty, do not think of leaving England. Not just yet."

"But there is no place in England for a dethroned queen."

"The more supporters you have, the more defenders will protect you."

A collation was brought in, and we supped and drank in subdued silence as the summer dusk fell and the logs crackled in the hearth. He had given me a great deal to consider, and I found myself somewhat at a loss over what to make of all that he had revealed to me. I knew that ambassadors were prone to exaggeration, and to viewing events and circumstances in a way that benefited their own interests. Yet what if he was right? What if Anne's position as queen was more tenuous than I imagined? Kings and queens had been dethroned by their angry subjects in the past. Royal fortunes were altered by war, or mischance, or—as the Holy Scriptures show clearly—by the hand of God.

Suddenly I felt more hungry than I had in a very long time. I ate what was before me and called for more. I drank my wine. I felt my spirits rise within me.

"Do not think of leaving, not just yet," Ambassador Chapuys told me before he left. "Things are far too unsettled. The people are fractious and unruly. They are as displeased with Anne as the king is pleased with her. It is best that you remain here in England—at least for a few months."

"Until Anne delivers her child, you mean."

"At least until then, yes." He hesitated, then added, "Or until the king realizes just how strong a daughter of Castile and Aragon can be."

Pondering all that I had seen and heard that night, and smiling, I went to bed, but it was a long time before I could get to sleep.

The blow fell in that warm, sunny summer of the Year of Our Lord 1533. The Holy Father in Rome declared that Henry's marriage to Anne was not a valid union—and that his marriage to me was the only true one. The child Anne was carrying would be born a bastard.

Everything that had been done since the start of the year—Henry's marriage to Anne, my removal from court, Anne's crowning and assumption of the rights and role of queen—all had to be undone immediately, and the former royal hierarchy of the court restored.

I rejoiced. Henry was irate, and truculent. He refused to do as Pope Clement ordered.

This was something the soothsayers and astrologers had not foreseen, just as they had failed to predict the death of my sister-in-law Mary, Henry's younger sister and my longtime friend. Mary, Henry's favorite sister and wife of his companion and jousting partner Charles Brandon, had died only a scant few days before the papal ruling was issued.

It was another omen, those in my household said. Another dark foretaste of things to come, like the wonders in the sky and the rumblings and quaking of the earth. A sign—as if more signs were needed—that the time was out of joint, with divine disfavor at work among us.

Caught between anger and mourning, Henry received his sentence of excommunication with ill grace, his foul temper fueling his bitterness.

I had no doubt that he knew the nature of the eternal torment he faced: to be cut off forever from the church of Rome, the church of St. Peter and St. Paul, the source of all Christian order, law and belief. To be driven from the community of Christian believers. To be denied the blessings conferred by the sacraments, and burial in consecrated ground. And—most terrible of all—to be condemned, after death, to endure the agony of neverending terror and anguish, without hope of relief.

It must have seemed to Henry, in his most fearful hours, as if God himself had turned his face away, and denied him his mercy.

Certainly his fellow rulers were turning away. One by one they registered their shock and anger that the English king, that very King Henry who had written a treatise against the heretic Martin Luther, had incurred the harshest sentence the Holy Father could impose. One by one they registered their blame and censure. If Christian rulers defied the head of the church in Rome, then there would be no armies of Christian knights to defend Christendom against the advancing Turks.

I heard Sir Edmund and Sir Edward, my jailers, muttering that "the Turk will get us all in the end!" as they went to and from the guards' quarters each afternoon. Revolts rose up everywhere: in Ireland, in Scotland and in the borderlands, and increasingly, in London, where, I was assured, my supporters were strong and contempt for Anne greatest.

It was Anne, people said, who had brought down the punishment of the Holy Father. She had no fear of the eternal torment caused by excommunication. She welcomed the breach with Rome. She was a heretic!

The king's new wife was a heretic, the king was an excommunicate, the realm was churning with rebellion and under threat of
invasion. It was no wonder my captors shook their heads and condemned the state of things. The time was indeed out of joint, and we all
stood in peril—if not from the Turks, then from the avenging sword
of the divine.

18

I WROTE TO HENRY TO ASK WHETHER I COULD BE ALLOWED TO attend the funeral of his sister Mary, who had been my dear friend. One of the royal secretaries brought me a curt and impersonal response. I would be allowed to attend the burial service. He told me when and where it would be held, at Bury St. Edmunds in Suffolk in two days' time.

Keeping in mind that Henry believed I was close to death, I set out for the burial site, taking my physician and apothecary with me and accompanied by six mounted guardsmen. Although I wore a sober black gown and concealing veil, and no jewels or other indications of my rank as Princess Dowager, still in each settlement I passed, dozens of villagers called out greetings to me and shouts of encouragement.

Once arrived at the chapel where Mary's body was to be laid in its tomb, I had to be helped out of my litter and could barely manage to kneel without help as the prayers were said and the final interment made. I coughed, again and again. I wept freely—heartfelt tears, for Mary's death saddened me and she had been a strong supporter of mine and opponent of Anne. I'm sure that I was pale in my grief.

I gave the impression, or hoped I did, that Henry was correct in what he was telling others: that I was very ill and would not live much longer. I wanted to seem an aging, sympathetic figure, one that elicited sympathy.

While the last of the prayers were being read I looked over at Henry, who as chief mourner was standing close to the bier, leaning on a thick wooden cane. He too looked pale, and tearful. I felt an unaccustomed wave of pity for him as he stood there, wearing sober black just as I was, and shorn of all adornment. I was taken aback by his appearance. His customary jeweled doublet and flashing rings, the gem-laden gold collar he wore around his neck, his fur-trimmed cap with its rubies and pearls, even his gleaming gold dagger: all were missing on this day. He was naked in his grieving, it seemed to me, no longer king but the bereaved brother of a loving sister, one who had brought him much joy in life and who had died far too young.

There was no sign of Anne. She had not chosen to support him with her presence in his time of sorrow. Or had he commanded her not to attend the burial, preferring to be on his own, without her interference?

On an impulse I asked my apothecary Philip Grenacre for a scrap of paper and a bit of charcoal, and wrote the words, "We will hold fast." It was the message Henry and I had exchanged many years earlier, when we were both young and besieged by difficulties, Henry by his father's cruel constraints, I by the fear and uncertainty of my years of widowhood. We had been drawn together then, we had become allies in our season of distress.

I asked Philip to give the paper to the king, once the solemnities ended.

When next I looked up, I found that Henry was standing beside me, looking as vulnerable as I had ever seen him. He was never good at dissembling his grief—only his fear. He had no bravado, no anger to hide behind when in the grip of sorrow.

He stood there, gazing down at me, and I struggled to stand, coughing as I did so. He hesitated—but only for a moment—then offered me his arm. His chivalry was stronger than his pride—or his inner torment. Without saying a word, he led me out of the chapel, amid the whisperings and murmurings of the mourners. He waved his attendants away, and led me into the sunlit chapel garden, full of the scent of flowers and new-mown grass.

We had not spoken for many months. The silence between us was awkward. I dared to break it.

"We made a pact once," I said softly, "you and I. We agreed that whatever others said or did, we would not let it sunder us."

I could see that my words pierced his heart, torn as he was by strong emotions just then—grief, loss, perhaps even regret. He shook his head. He did not look at me, not even when I coughed and faltered as we slowly walked past the flowering stalks and bushes.

"I remember well," he muttered under his breath, then added, "I should never have let you come here today."

"Had Anne been here, I would not have come."

He shrugged. "She is ill."

He paused as we were walking, and drew out of his plain black doublet a miniature portrait. I recognized it at once. It was of Mary, as a young woman, her dark curling hair framing her lovely face, smiling and happy.

"She was twenty when this was painted," he said. "And today she is buried at thirty-seven. And still so beautiful."

"The Lord in his wisdom—" I started to say.

"No! I'll have none of that drivel about how we each have a given span of years!" He shook his head, a lion shaking his mane. "She was weak, she sickened. I was not kept informed. I would have sent every physician in the realm to save her!"

Startled by the sudden sharpness in his tone, I swayed on my feet, and he helped me to a stone bench where we both sat down. I noticed that some of the royal guards were watching us from a respectful distance, and wondered whether they might interrupt our conversation. But Henry had more to say.

"Such a waste! All that beauty, that sweetness. Brandon did not let me know how ill she was. I thought, when she kept to her bed these last few months, that it was a ruse. I thought she was avoiding coming to court. I knew she objected to my marrying Anne."

She objected to your treatment of me, I wanted to say, but held my tongue. Instead I asked the question that was uppermost in my mind.

"If I may, I would like to ask a boon. Buckden is cold and full of drafts. I am quite miserable there. If you would allow it, I would like to return to London. To Durham House."

He looked at me, scrutinizing my pale face. Thinking, I had no doubt, that if I did move back to the capital, I would not be there long, as I was in my last weeks or months. He looked away then, and for the first time I saw a fleeting smile cross his lips.

"Crum won't like it, but yes, you may."

I sighed with relief. "Thank you, Your Grace."

Within a week I was installed once again at Durham House in the Strand.

It was not long before Henry came, alone, to see me in my new residence. I wondered at first whether he had come in hopes of finding me in extremis, with a priest at hand to administer the last rites. But it soon became apparent that my state of health was far from being his main concern. He had come to talk, confident that he would find me to be—despite all—a sympathetic listener.

I sent my servants away and prepared to hear what he had to say, keeping in mind that he believed me to be weak and suffering.

"Sometimes, Catherine, I imagine that there is indeed a curse on my house. I thought that it would lift when I married Anne. Instead—"

"Instead?"

He shrugged.

"Mary has died. Your nephew Charles and his armies are at my doorstep. The accursed Bishop of Rome has condemned me—not that his condemnation has the effect he thought it would. I am being forced to find another way to worship."

I could not help wondering what that other way might be. I looked at Henry expectantly.

Gripping his cane, he got to his feet. "There is to be a new church," he said. "A revitalized church. One free of the bonds of Rome. One with the sovereign himself at its head. An English church, not an Italian one."

I thought, what breathtaking arrogance! To take to himself the leadership of the faith. Is he to tell us all what and how to believe? Is he to be the chief theologian?

"It is time the old ways of Rome were discarded," he was saying. "The ruler of the realm will be the ruler of the church as well."

How like Henry, to try to conquer what he cannot control. To conquer it—or to destroy it.

"Whatever changes you make, Your Grace," I began to say, "you will still have the Lord's displeasure to contend with." As soon as I said the words, I feared that I had said too much. But I could tell right away that he had come to the same conclusion, and was fearful. Presently he asked me, "Do you know the story of the Mouldwarp?"

"I have heard the servants relating it, yes."

"The old prophecy from the days of King Arthur, and his wizard Merlin. The prophecy of the cursed king who brings on himself the punishment of God." He was trembling as he spoke, there was a catch in his voice. Still he forced himself to go on. His words came in gasps.

"The Mouldwarp—was a great hero to his people—a champion—a defender against all the enemies of the realm." He began to shout. "He was strong, valiant—"

"But doomed to fail," I went on, as Henry began shaking his head and crying, "No, no, it must not be! It cannot be!"

In his anguish he shook his head more and more violently, like a beast shaking off a heavy harness, or a bear being baited by dogs, trying in vain to free itself from their tormenting jaws.

"Yes, doomed to fail," I repeated. "Because he surrendered all to his pride. His lust. He was vain and willful. He took to himself a woman unworthy of him at his best. A woman who will lead him to destruction! Or so the servants say, when they speak of the Mouldwarp. But that is only legend, only servants' talk when they go to their pallets at night, and cannot sleep."

He swallowed, blinking rapidly and attempting to recover himself. He did not look at me. "I—" he began, but could not go on. I waited for his sense of panic to ease.

"I tell you, Catherine," he said after a long minute of silence, "I cannot remember when I last slept the night through." At last he slapped his knees and got to his feet, evidently about to leave.

"I—" he began again, then thought better of it, and bade me a swift farewell.

Living as I now was at Durham House, it was not difficult at all for me to remain in close contact with my former gentleman usher Griffith Richards, who served in Anne's household and who was often sent on errands to all corners of the capital. He made certain that his route came near my residence, so that he had an excuse to bring me news and encouragement. He had never ceased to be loyal to me, despite his unwanted position in service to Anne. And because my own guardians had become much more lax in their oversight of me and my visitors than they had been in the past, Richards was a frequent and welcome visitor.

He could not wait to tell me all that was going on in Anne's chambers.

"If only you could see how she flaunts herself, Your Majesty," he said one warm afternoon as we sat overlooking the river. And oh how it warmed me to be called by my former title, instead of the demeaning one of Princess Dowager!

"She shames herself," he went on, "with her fat belly, dressing in her long red silk court gowns and wearing masses of jewels. Some of them yours, Your Majesty, I'm very sorry to say.

"And the way she talks and laughs, it is so unmannerly, so

brazen. She boasts about how your nephew Charles doesn't dare bring his armies ashore, for fear her own relatives would raise an even larger army and defeat him.

" 'Let them come,' she says. 'Let them try to take our land. The Howards will put ten thousand fighting men into the field and fight them and kill them all.' Her taunts are rude and braggardly. Not at all fit for a royal chamber.

"She has ordered hundreds of workmen to renovate her apartments, and hundreds more to build her a new hall and gallery where she entertains. And such pastime it is! With dancing and music, merrymaking and flirtation going on hour after hour, and on into the night. I tell you, Your Majesty, such scenes would never have gone on in your apartments, in your gracious presence."

"What sort of scenes?"

He lowered his voice. "There is not only laughter and merry-making, but secret meetings, hidden pledges of love. Furtive mutterings in corners. Betrayals of love and honor. I have seen men of a goodly age visit Anne's rooms without their wives, and meet there the young girls who are their lovers. I tell you, it is worse than anything that ever went on in the Maidens' Bower, there beside the river, where the king met his favorites, far from the eyes of his chamber gentlemen—"

"Or his wife," I put in, reminding Richards that Henry had had more than his share of liaisons with other women while married to me. And that I knew all about them.

"But this is different," my former gentleman usher insisted. "This is bold and outrageous, as if Anne is daring the whole world to rebuke her and all those who serve her. Offering the most shocking example to everyone. She is without a shred of modesty or dignity." He shook his head. "It cannot last," he said. "It must not."

What Griffith Richards was telling me went a long way to explaining Henry's disturbed, confused state of mind. Anne was acting in a way that upstaged him. He had always been the most flamboyant, the most dramatic figure in any room he entered, anywhere; now, it would seem, his starring role had been taken over by his consort. (I cannot bear to write, "by his wife.") And the effect of her supplanting him was damaging, far more damaging than he had imagined. He knew, to be sure, that Anne was domineering and importunate, that she insisted on having her own way. But her newfound arrogance was leading to a harshly adverse result; it was undoing all that he had done to elevate the tone and power of his rule.

Anne, Richards was telling me, was cheapening the good name of the court by besmirching the wholesome reputation of the queen's household—a reputation I had shaped and guarded over many years. She was inviting the taint of scandal to dirty the court, overshadowing it with her own ill-behaved style, her loose, sensual attitudes and tastes. Everything from her bearing, the careless way she carried herself, to her likes and dislikes in music and dancing and dress. Her entire sensibility was wayward and ill suited to the dignity necessary in a queen. She was as headstrong as a child, with a child's fickle, contrary demands and passions. Henry had seen this, I was sure, but he had shut his eyes to it—until now. And he found it to be both confusing and galling to his pride.

"She is giving the gossip-mongers a great deal to talk about," Richards was saying.

And giving all the courts of Europe a reason to look down on England, I was thinking. Lowering the repute of the king, the awe in which he had formerly been held. His prowess in the tournament and the chase, his good looks and high spirits, his courtly accomplishments. Everything that had set him apart, indeed above, his royal peers. Now he would be ridiculed as his new queen's fool. Unless, of course, she presented him with a son.

"She is blamed for setting an immoral example. It is even whispered that she brought her own wizards to court to cast spells on the king, to make him do her bidding. How else could she have captured his heart and broken his will, and made him turn his back on you, Your Highness?"

Richards described Anne's own new favorite, the sweet-faced little singer Mark, who was always by her side. "She treats him like the fool he is. He dotes on her."

"Does the king never intervene in these—these entertainments?" I asked.

"He is ill at ease there."

"But surely he is pleased about Anne's child."

"Indeed yes. He has brought in soothsayers and conjurors to read the boy's future. They all agree—all but one, an old hag from Norfolk named Mabel Brigge, who tried to kill the king with her witchcraft—that he will be handsome and strong like his father, and will live to vanquish all his enemies."

I could not help but ask what happened to the witch from Norfolk.

"The king had her seized and thrown into his dungeons, where she rots. Meanwhile Anne has ordered all those who serve her to wear her new livery." He removed his heavy outer garment. Beneath it he wore a doublet of blue and purple silk, embroidered with Anne's motto: the words "La Plus Heureuse." "The Most Happy."

"And is she, do you think?" I asked. "Is she truly the most happy woman at the court?"

"I cannot say. She is certainly the most giddy. The most prideful. The most insolent—"

I interrupted his list of vices to ask whether Anne had yet taken her chamber. It was August, and the birth could not be far off. I had always followed the long-established custom that a queen should retire into her birth chamber a month before her baby was expected—and Anne's child was said to be due in September.

"She has not," my former chamberlain told me, "but I will be certain to bring you word when she does."

As it happened, word of Anne's withdrawal into seclusion was not long in reaching me—but it came in a surprising form. I was ordered to provide, for the new baby, the christening mantle and robes that Princess Mary had worn at her own christening seventeen years earlier.

I still had the treasured garments; I had preserved them in a carved wooden chest lined with purple satin. I had been hoping—indeed I had not yet quite given up hope—that they would be worn by Mary's firstborn when she married and bore her first child.

I lifted the gold hasp of the chest and brought out the small robes. They smelt faintly of oil, their crimson cloth of gold shone in the candlelight. The long ermine-trimmed mantle looked as fresh and new as it had the day Mary's christening ceremony had taken place.

No, I said aloud. Anne's ill-begotten child shall not wear these precious garments. I will not allow it.

I called for my supper and put the small clothes back into their chest. Later, however, as I ate, lingering over my meal as I had very little appetite, a thought occurred to me. Why not agree to provide the christening gown and mantle after all—but on condition that Henry allow me to join the throng that awaited the birth once Anne's labor began? My grief would be lessened, I could say, by passing on the christening garments that Mary had worn to the new heir to the throne. I would be enhancing my dignity, not lessening it.

I sent my groom Francisco Phelipe to the keeper of the queen's chamber with this message, and the following day I was given permission to bring the garments to the palace myself.

I found all in turmoil at Greenwich, where in the rooms anterior to Anne's dark, stuffy birth chamber many a drama was playing itself out.

The astrologers Henry had summoned to court were in one anteroom, the visionaries who had received divine messages about the coming birth in another. The two groups disagreed about the disposition and character of the prince who would soon be born, the astrologers certain that he would be a stern, serious judge, commanding in his power and authority, while those who heard heavenly voices were equally certain that he would be an avenging angel, God's warrior, quick to strike the enemies of the church and the realm.

While royal guards kept watch at the birth chamber door, relieved at intervals by tall halberdiers, Anne's maids of honor and chamber women busied themselves with preparations for the masques and banquets soon to be held to celebrate the prince's birth. New garments had to be sewn, new headgear designed and fitted, dances practiced and music learned. And all of it carried out with an ear kept cocked for the sounds of Anne's impending delivery from the other side of the thick oak door.

The royal herald paced nervously back and forth before the door, waiting to make his announcement of the new heir to the throne who, it was said, would be given the name Edward or Henry. Scribes sat waiting to fill in the birth proclamations, messengers to carry them on the first stage of their journey to far-off courts. My nephew Charles would receive such a proclamation, I thought to myself. He had sworn to descend on England to seize the throne should Anne's child be named heir instead of Princess Mary.

Henry Fitzroy too was close by, in case Anne's child died at birth or proved to be a malformed, freakish thing, more monster than child. I had seen such births, they were not at all rare. Griffith Richards had told me how much Anne hated to have Henry Fitzroy at court, let alone in her apartments. She called him an albatross, a bird of ill omen, and swore that he would bring her bad luck. But Henry insisted that young Fitzroy be on hand, along with his fiancée Mary Howard, Anne's cousin, and according to Richards, Anne's objections only strengthened Henry's resolve.

Having never before been part of this activity outside the birth chamber—I was always the royal mother-to-be, awaiting my labor pains and then undergoing my good hour, as the agony of labor was known—I had not realized how crowded and full of movement and exertion the outer rooms were, with seamstresses coming and going, tailors and shoemakers fitting garments and taking measurements. So many voices called out across the rooms, conveying urgent messages. Servants were berated, scribes and secretaries put to urgent tasks. The king's armorer was summoned, and told to await the order to repair and polish His Highness's jousting armor in time for the tourneying. Grooms from the stables were sent for and informed that the warhorses ordered from Flanders had been lost when the ship that was carrying them went down in a storm; more large, strong horses had to be found to replace them, and quickly.

And as if this was not enough, preparations were under way for the wedding of Charles Brandon with his ward Catherine Willoughby, a wedding to be held the following morning. I heard much criticism of this marriage. After all, Brandon's wife Mary had only been laid in her tomb a short time before, and he was marrying young Catherine (who was barely fourteen) because she was a wealthy heiress.

"Greed, sheer greed," it was whispered. "He was not content to wed the girl to his son. He had to have her money himself. And he a man in his later years, and she a mere stripling!"

Despite the gossip and the censure, many of Anne's maids of honor were attending to their finery for the wedding, making ready to garb themselves quickly on the following morning. They hoped for wealthy matches of their own, and a wedding such as this, between the Duke of Suffolk and his ward, was certain to bring together dozens of eligible young women and men with good fortunes and titles, looking for fruitful, compliant young wives.

I had thought that my presence would cause more of a stir in the busy rooms. I was far from ignored, to be sure; I received many soft words of welcome and even a few guarded, whispered predictions of doom for Anne and her child. But I was far from being the center of attention, much less a disruptive presence. Indeed I found myself in the midst of increasing strain as gossip flew: about the child soon to be born, about the likelihood of war, and above all, about the king's new favorite, a young charmer said to be not much older than Catherine Willoughby. A young girl-child who was the opposite of Anne in every way: gentle, softspoken, obedient. Blond and simpering, artless and undemanding.

Before long the gossip gave way to greater excitement. Anne, awaiting her feared birth pains, and maddened by jealousy of this unknown favorite (Henry kept her in the Maidens' Bower, away from the palace but nearby), shouted her complaints to the empty air, imagining that Henry would be on the other side of the chamber door. Her shouts grew louder, her language more rude. A temporary hush fell. Activity in the room slowed.

Then all at once there was a terrible shriek from the birth chamber: Anne's labor had begun.

19

Anne's screams grew louder and more anguished. I confess that I took pleasure in hearing her cries, knowing well how much she must be suffering. The pain of childbed is the worst pain of all—just ask any mother. I endured it many times, only to endure, when it ended, the cruel distress of loss.

Knife-sharp pain, a sword-thrust in the belly, each assault worse than the one before: that was the good hour, the hour of childbirth. Pain past all bearing, so cruel and unsparing that even death seemed a comfort. I knew it well. I remembered it well. And each time I heard Anne scream I smiled inwardly.

Time passed and the mild fall afternoon turned to evening. Plates of comfits, ripe apples and sugared cakes were brought in and the hearth fires lit, and still Anne's moans continued. Tension rose in the small rooms while we waited there. Every cry, every gasp from the birth chamber was met with nods or frowns. The first baby always takes longest to be born, the women were saying, nodding in agreement with one another. "And boys take longer than girls."

Evening lengthened into night, and still we heard no newborn cry. Fresh logs were laid on the fire and I closed my eyes, overcome by drowsiness despite all.

It was near to dawn when I was awakened by loud shouts. Anne was groaning and weeping, now crying out for her mother, now damning the midwives and cursing the day she had first met the king.

The king! He was nowhere to be seen, though his councilor Thomas Cromwell entered and left the room at intervals, looking to see who had arrived and who had left over the lengthening hours.

"What of the wedding?" I heard people murmuring as the first light of dawn filtered in through the high windows. "How can they be wed, while the queen endures her pains and the prince is likely to be born at any time?" Still I noticed that, even as the question was asked, those who asked it were dressing in their wedding finery, preparing to witness the marriage of the Duke of Suffolk and his young bride.

My legs and back were stiff, I was hungry and needed to eat and then to walk until my legs were free of cramping pains. No sound came from beyond the guarded door of Anne's chamber. All had gone quiet. I wondered why. Was it possible that Anne had fainted, or that—just possibly—she had given birth to a stillborn baby? All at once the door of the birth chamber was flung open and the head midwife emerged, her apron bloody and her arms and face dripping with sweat. She called loudly and insistently for the surgeon.

I heard Anne gasp and then begin to moan and grunt like an animal shying from the slayer's knife. Shrieks of torment. High-pitched screams. Then silence once again. The wedding guests were filing out, on their way to the chapel.

During the uneasy silence that followed, I ate, sparingly, from a plate of food brought to me and drank from a cup. I hardly tasted the food, I was too tense, wondering why those of us in the outer rooms were not hearing any further sounds of labor, yet no announcement of the royal birth had been made.

All the noisy bustle and even the murmured talk around me had subsided. Everyone was listening, keenly, for the newborn's cry.

What had happened? All those around me were whispering the same questions, giving voice to the same fears. Was Anne still alive? Had the baby choked and strangled in her womb? Or was it a freak, a pitiful misshapen thing, without sense or feeling? What had happened? Was Anne growing weaker? Was there, after all, a curse on the king and on the Tudor line of kings?

I had the christening robes with me, I was glad no one had asked me for them. If Anne's child died, or was unfit to reign and likely to die, then I would not have to give up the robes. To give them up would be a symbol of defeat.

My mind went back to another September day, to that terrible, bloody day almost exactly twenty years earlier when I had urged on my men, my warriors, out into battle against the fearsome savage Scots on Branxton Moor near Flodden Field. They had come pouring out of their camp in their thousands, their sharp iron pikes gleaming in the dull morning light, to face our English bills, our guns and arrows.

We stood strong against them that day! We were invincible. How I wish I could have led the men myself, in the vanguard, as my mother did when she rode into battle against the Moors. But I could not. I was carrying a child in my womb, and hoped to give Henry a son. I did not dare risk the baby's life. Still, I did the best I could to stand among the valiant English, mounted on Griselda, waving the men on and encouraging them as rain fell and the ground under Griselda's hooves turned to mud and gore.

Though two decades had passed I could still recall how bravely the men fought, what great deeds we did that day. How I saved my husband's throne, or so the soldiers said. I saved England. And in truth we were stalwart, merciless. We met and overcame and pursued the enemy Scots, and turned them back.

I knew glory then, and great pride. Yet I also knew great sorrow and loss. For what was left, at the end of that battle, but broken swords and shattered bills, bleeding men and dying horses. Banners torn. Mounds of bodies. The overwhelming stink of death. On the bloodstained field men lay writhing and gasping and dying horses pawed the air and whinnied piteously. The memory made me recall what my mother had once told me.

"To fight on," she said, "no matter what the odds, is a valorous thing. But in any retreat, the wounded are left behind. It cannot be otherwise. Their suffering is the price of victory."

Remembering her words I shivered, and felt a chill. I drew closer to the hearth and grasped the christening robes and held them against me. I wished I had never come to the palace.

On Flodden Field, at the end of the long day of battle, it had been the Earl of Surrey who brought me the torn surcoat of the Scots king James, bloody and sweat-stained, and I sent it to Henry in Tournai. The christening robes my daughter Mary had worn were destined to become my symbol of defeat, when they were handed over to be worn by Anne's child. Unless—

An hour passed, then another. At last, as the wedding guests began to return to Anne's apartments, we heard agonizing cries, the worst so far. The chief midwife opened the door of the birth chamber and at that moment we heard a cough, then a high-pitched cry that grew steadily louder. A cry such as I had heard when my son, the New Year's Boy, was born. My weak, shortlived son.

The midwife, looking more frightened than exhausted, beckoned to the herald who was waiting beside the door.

He cleared his throat, then announced loudly and evenly that the queen had given birth to a princess.

I clutched the box with Mary's christening robes tightly to my chest. I could hardly breathe. Anne had failed. My prayers had been answered.

The courtiers, shocked and silent, seemed hardly able to move. Ashen-faced, the astrologers and soothsayers filed out, murmuring apologies and excuses, humiliated that their predictions had not come to pass. The baby princess continued to wail and cry as the herald proclaimed her name and title.

"A princess! A princess! It is a princess!"

The word was carried from the birth chamber out into the corridor beyond, I heard running feet and cries of surprise and vexation.

"Does it live?"

"It lives, it breathes!"

"What of the queen?"

"She lives."

Mortified, Henry strode into the birth chamber just as I was making my way out into the outer hallway. The midwives fled at his approach. As I left, the christening robes secure under my arm, I heard his voice boom out.

"Cancel the tournaments! Cancel them all, I tell you! Bring Fitzroy forward! No, let it be called Elizabeth, after my mother. It will have to do until there is a prince!"

As proud as on the day of our victory on Branxton Moor, I made my way to the river stairs, where my bargemen waited to take me back to Durham House.

20

"YOU REALIZE WHAT THIS MEANS, DO YOU NOT?" AMBASSADOR Chapuys was gloating, rubbing his hands together and looking very pleased with himself. "The king has an excuse to take you back. God is punishing him for putting you aside, and marrying a heretic. She is unable to give him a prince. It is a clear sign of divine displeasure. Worse punishment will no doubt follow."

I had never seen the grim, determined ambassador look so impassioned, so convinced of his purpose. He spoke crisply, decisively. There was no doubt in his mind that everything had changed, especially my future. He had come to see me at Durham House on the day following the birth of Anne's daughter. In his overjoyed state he forgot his usual deference to me, and was speaking with me on very familiar terms—which, just then, I did not mind. I was as hopeful as he was.

The Londoners had exploded into noisy protest on hearing the news of Anne's giving birth. Almost from the moment the Tower cannons began to roar their acknowledgment of Anne's baby, the clamor in the streets began.

"The Great Whore has foaled a Little Whore!" came the shouts of the unruly crowds in the streets near the river. "Get rid of the whore Nan Bullen! Take your wife back! Take back Good Queen Catherine!" They laughed and stomped and cried out long into the night, and repeated "Ha ha ha!" in derision. Banners and crests with the initials H and A—for Henry and Anne—had been mounted in many parts of the capital ever since Anne's coronation. Now they gave rise to laughter and taunting. A reminder that Henry and Anne, together, had produced, not a prince, but a weak princess.

No one had asked me for the christening robes for Anne's daughter. The christening itself was accorded little attention, held early one morning and without many members of the court in attendance. The event came and went quickly, all but overlooked except by those forced to attend because of their rank and nearness to the throne. It did not seem to matter that the gown and mantle the baby princess wore at the ceremony were not the ones my daughter Mary had worn seventeen years earlier.

Henry's attention shifted to his bastard son Henry Fitzroy, Bessie Blount's son, and to the boy's forthcoming marriage to Mary Howard, Anne's cousin. Young Fitzroy would succeed to the throne if Anne had no son. Anne's daughter, the tiny, red-faced princess who had been given the name Elizabeth, was thought to be too weak to survive, like my own baby son Henry, who had died after only a few brief weeks of life.

"She isn't likely to live long, little slip of a thing that she is," the ambassador told me. "The nursemaids complain that she won't suckle. Odds are she'll be dead in a week.

"The rude folk say it is the curse of the Mouldwarp," he went on. "The accursed king of old story who cannot pass on his kingdom to a son. He is condemned to reign as year by year his realm withers, his subjects suffer. Then invaders come, and drive him out. The Mouldwarp must lay down his crown and flee. King Henry, they say, is this accursed being come to life. You, Catherine, must prove them wrong—by becoming his true wife once again. You must counteract the curse and remove it."

I knew well what the ambassador was envisioning, and I confess that it gladdened my heart. I could save the throne and the kingdom from ruin. I could resume my place at Henry's side, Mary would once again be recognized as his heir. Mary's husband, when she married, would be at her side to reign; their son would continue the Tudor line of kings.

All this would be sure to come about—if only Anne continued to fail at her task of providing the realm with a prince.

I was not the only one thinking these thoughts, to be sure. I learned from Griffith Richards that Anne was dreading the very outcome that I hoped for, and blaming me for her failure.

She had found out that I was among those in the rooms just beyond the birth chamber during her long hours of labor. She had become convinced that I was there to savor my triumph and her great disappointment—otherwise why would I have come at all? I must have been certain that her child would not be the prince Henry so greatly desired. Therefore, I must have brought the sad outcome about, by some means or other.

"She finds it very satisfying to blame you," the ambassador had told me. "You can well imagine why."

I could indeed. Anne resented my very existence, of that I was certain. She resented the loyalty and support the people continued to show for me, a loyalty she herself did not command. No doubt she resented Henry's visits to me, the influence I continued to have, such as it was.

But there was more than mere jealousy at work, of that I felt sure. Anne had always been inclined to imagine things, to fear and dread the worst. That fear was lurking beneath any confidence she managed to acquire. I had seen her tremble when she ought to have been at her most secure. I had heard the quaver in her voice when she tried to speak most firmly. It was not hard to guess that when her daughter was born, all her fears leapt up within her more forcefully than ever, and she had to find someone to blame. She chose to blame me.

Richards told me that Henry found a more convenient victim: Mabel Brigge, the hag from Norfolk. She had said all along that the child would not be a prince. She had cast spells and brought about the catastrophe. He had the woman stretched on the rack, her torment all but unendurable, but she did not confess to bewitching Anne or her child to ensure that the baby would be a girl. Then he called back as many of the astrologers and soothsayers as he could find (though he was too late in this, as they had been among the first to flee the court when the birth of a princess was announced) and had them punished.

I was told that when one of the unfortunate prognosticators tried to insist that although the princess had the form of a girl, she had a man's heart and strength, Henry became so infuriated that he had the man castrated.

"There!" he shouted. "Now you see what it is like to have the form of a woman! Now tell me of your heart and strength!"

Strange and ominous happenings continued to surprise and alarm us all in those uncertain days. It seemed as if the very earth itself, and all that was in it and around it, was calling us to wakefulness. Warning us to be aware of the unsettled times we were living through and the dangers that threatened.

One night not long after the princess's birth I watched the most vivid sunset I had ever seen. Layers of rosy light turned to fiery red, then to scarlet, crimson, and at last to a purplish hue, the color of dried blood. For an hour and more the intense color lingered, and when at last it faded, I could not help falling to my knees in wonder, convinced that I had seen a marvel. What it meant I could not have said, but I believed that the hand of God was at work, and that I must heed His message.

And there was something else, something equally disturbing: the people were once again rising in aggrieved groups, outraged by the tyranny of the court. The king was oppressing and betraying his loyal subjects, they said. He was ill-using his rightful wife (by which they meant me, of course), even inviting heresy into the realm. The grievances, as relayed to me by Ambassador Chapuys and Griffith Richards and the few others daring enough to visit me, were diffuse and fitful, but they went well with the odd events and unsettling sights of that fall and winter.

I continued to pray for understanding of all that was happening, and for further signs that would lead me aright in all that I said and did.

Then, with the new year, came another jolt. Anne, it was said, was once again carrying the king's child. She hoped for a boy this time. By April the midwives were nodding in approval of her goodly belly, and saying that the Princess Elizabeth would have a brother by harvest time.

Once again preparations were made at court for the lying-in of the royal consort (even now I cannot bear to write "for the lying-in of the queen"). New midwives were engaged, lest the ones who had delivered the princess be found inadequate. Most important, a surgeon was brought from Pisa who, Henry was assured, had never yet attended a birth where either the mother or the baby died. Much hope was placed in this surgeon, I was told, especially by Henry. The midwives were said to resent the Pisan but their complaints were ignored.

The birth chamber was made ready, the golden cradle put in place as it had been the previous fall. But this time I was not asked to provide Mary's christening robe or mantle for the new baby, and when Griffith Richards came to Durham House he told me that Anne was insistent that I be kept as far away from the birth chamber as possible. There must be no excuse for me to bewitch the child or impair it in any way.

Every precaution was taken, every procedure in the long list of procedures drawn up by Thomas Cromwell observed. And yet there was an air of uneasiness, of nervousness about this pregnancy. The baby had to be a boy, a prince. And not only a boy, but a healthy, strong boy with powerful lungs and a robust, thriving body. He had to arrive hungry and noisy, Richards told me with a laugh. Not like the little princess, who though she lived, was a runt and did not clamor to be fed.

Meanwhile the people, Chapuys told me, were reviving another old prophecy along with the one about the Mouldwarp. I remembered this prediction well—in fact I had once thought it must apply to me.

> *A queen shall be crowned*
> *In the hall of the kings*
> *And the queen shall die.*

Anne had been crowned in the hall of the kings, just as I had. She might well be the one to die.

But for the moment, she was surviving and felt the baby kicking within her. The midwives and the Pisan surgeon swore to this, and their assurance made Anne bolder than ever, Richards told me. She told all who would listen that God had led Henry to leave me and marry her. And that his clear purpose must have been for her to give the realm the prince I had not been able to bear. It made sense—but not to the crowds that gathered wherever Anne went and shouted insults and threats, and called her the queen who could not bear sons.

"Do you know, Catherine, the guards that used to chase away all those who taunted Anne are nowhere to be found! The king has dismissed them." So I was told by Francisco Phelipe my groom whose cousin Hernan was in the royal guard. "And Hernan says the king is going to spend the summer hunting, not going on progress with the queen."

As the spring advanced the thing I had been dreading most— next to some vengeful act Henry or Anne might carry out against me—came to the fore. Amid the doubt and turmoil about the future one thing had to be settled by law: the order of succession. And so it was. By statute Mary was disinherited; Anne's children, born and as yet unborn, were declared heirs to the throne. And all of Henry's subjects had to swear on oath to uphold this law.

I refused. How could I not? I would not disinherit my own

daughter, the rightful heir to her father's throne. I would not abandon my own inheritance, the many long years I had spent in England as the bearer of the blood of Trastamara. This inheritance, my inheritance from my splendid heroic mother Isabella and my royal father Ferdinand, had been passed on to Mary, and would live on in her children in their turn.

Henry sent a dozen royal commissioners to instruct me that I had no choice but to take the oath to uphold the heinous Act of Succession. When I refused, he sent an even larger and more solemn array of officials. These men informed me that there was no evading the oath, not for the highest born nobleman or woman or most exalted churchman or councilor. No one, absolutely no one, was exempt.

Suddenly I was under siege. I was not allowed to see anyone or converse with anyone, not Mary, not my most trusted servants, not Ambassador Chapuys. Henry's own occasional visits stopped abruptly. The comfort of the confessional was denied me, as was my old prie-dieu, brought from Spain long ago, where I knelt to say my prayers. I hardly need to add here that my prayers were redoubled in those fear-filled days. I had no idea what would happen, only that I knew I must do as my mother would have done in my place. She would never have taken the oath. She would have been steadfast.

I was told that unless I took the oath my entire household would be dissolved, my servants denied me. Those of them who refused along with me would be severely punished. I would never see them again.

Those closest to me, most faithful to me over the years, continued to refuse, out of loyalty to me. One by one I saw them respond to the officials' cruel threats with stony silence. I can hardly write how proud I was of them, or how they strengthened and inspired me to remain stalwart in my own decision. I could not give in to the royal command if they did not.

Then I heard that a great many others in the kingdom were refusing to obey, among them the revered John Fisher, Bishop of Rochester and the upright, uncompromising Thomas More. The moment had come, it seemed, for the best in the kingdom to rise up against Henry's wrongs. To resist his wayward will, and follow their own consciences.

Or rather, I should write, to follow our own consciences. For I felt that in that moment, each of us had to search our minds and hearts and do what those best guides in life told us to do.

Inevitably, the day came when I was put to the ultimate test.

I knew that those who refused the oath were being imprisoned. Some had died. Others were being tortured, or threatened with torture. Henry and his ministers were showing no mercy. Durham House was surrounded by soldiers and members of the royal guard. Again and again I was ordered to take the oath; again and again I refused.

Then I was shut in a dim chamber, the only light a small window high up in one wall. I was given very little to eat or drink, but every hour I was instructed—indeed commanded—to take the oath. I had nothing to read, no comfort of any kind. I slept on the cold tile floor and ate at a wooden bench. Every day I commended my soul to God, thinking that it might be the day of my death.

I cannot say for certain how many days I was confined in this way, and threatened with being shut away forever unless I obeyed the royal command.

I prayed for a sign, for guidance. In my uncomfortable solitude, broken only by the coming and going of a single young serving girl, not one of those I knew well and trusted, I began to wonder whether I was being foolishly stubborn. Was I serving my own pride rather than following my conscience? Would I indeed be put to death, and would I die in vain, never to see Mary again or to live long enough to know my grandchildren? Had my life been a waste? I was glad that my mother did not live long enough to see me in my present state. I hoped I had not disgraced her name.

Tormented in mind, my thoughts ever darker and my prayers less infused with hope in God's mercy, I was visited by yet another cluster of royal officials. It was late in the day, their solemn faces were in shadow. I remember glancing upward toward the one small high window, praying for more light. Anything to make the walls seem less as if they were closing in around me.

"Princess Dowager," the leader of the delegation said when all the men had filed in and the heavy doors had been shut loudly behind them, "we have come to disperse your household. All your women have been locked in the cellar. Your physician, who is ill, has been sent to the friary and your confessor and apothecary will be put in the Tower dungeon, where they will be persuaded to tell us all they know of your wizardry against the queen."

I got to my feet, though unsteadily. I was dressed only in a loose woolen gown and shawl, my graying hair untidy—for I had no one to arrange it—and my hands without rings or bracelets. Around my neck I wore a gold cross bearing a relic of St. Lawrence. St. Lawrence the Martyr, who had been roasted alive.

"I am no wizard, but the true queen of this land," I said, my voice trembling despite my efforts to keep it strong. "I have done nothing to harm Mistress Anne."

One of the men slapped the leather bag he carried against a low table. "You will call the queen by her rightful name and title!"

I was silent. I could feel my legs wobbling. I reached for the bedpost and held on.

I realized that none of the men standing before me were royal councilors. Not a single face was recognizable to me. Henry had not sent his highest-ranking ministers to command me, only those most vehement and coarse.

Another man spoke. "You will swear to uphold the statute!"

"I will not."

More voices shouted their single demand. One added, "If you do not swear, you will be hanged. Hanged, do you understand?"

"I will pray for the Lord's mercy on my soul. But I will not swear."

I clung to the thick wooden bedpost. I was aware of its every crack and splinter.

One of the men pulled out his short sword. "I assure you, madam, that you will not escape the king's justice, should you continue in your obstinate refusal!" The voice was educated, cultivated. A student of the law, perhaps. Or an executioner in training. He had more to say.

"You may have heard that prominent men of law and the church have refused to take the oath. They are being put to death as we speak."

I faltered. I nearly fell. No one put forth a hand to help me.

"If you do not wish to have your servants suffer the same fate, you will obey in this and all other royal commands."

To this day I cannot say how it was that I found the strength to respond. But I did respond, and afterward, I felt, not weaker, but more empowered.

"I will not."

The men began to murmur.

"Then you will follow the chancellor and the Bishop of Rochester to the gibbet!" one of them shouted.

I stood as straight as I could, and let go of the bedpost. "And which of you will be the hangman?"

"That is not for you to know."

"Do you dare to hang me where all can see, and where the people will lament and mourn and curse the king? Or will you bring out your rope at midnight, in some foul alley, and do this thing in secret?"

The men conferred among themselves. Then the boldest of them stepped forward, coming so close to me that his angry face was glaring down into mine, so close that I could see the throbbing veins at his temples.

"Once more, Princess Dowager, on the king's order, you will swear to uphold the statute!"

I was silent. Guardsmen were called, and I was led down into the cellar, where I found my women in tears. They cried aloud at the sight of me, and we comforted one another as best we could for the rest of that long dark night.

21

I FELT AS THOUGH I HAD BEEN SPARED A TERRIBLE FATE AND GIVEN another chance to live. There was only one reason Henry did not order me to be put to death, as he has so many others: my nephew Charles was at last gathering his forces to rescue me.

Ambassador Chapuys brought me word that hundreds of skilled fighting men were being assembled in Spain, hundreds more mercenaries from Andalus and from as far away as Florence and Brescia hired to follow the imperial banner and invade England. England: that renegade land ruled by the tyrant King Henry (as he was increasingly seen) where the Holy Father and his holy church were cast aside and the king's own will and desire made supreme.

Ships were being assembled in the harbors of San Sebastian and Bilbao and Santander to carry the soldiers across the rough waters to the Dover coast, loaded with provisions to feed them and weaponry to arm them. I was assured by the ambassador that my nephew was bringing together the largest force of men and arms ever seen, and that he possessed more than enough gold and silver in his treasury to keep them equipped and paid for years. I was also assured that Henry had very few ships of his own to resist the vast invading fleet and turn it back, nor could he quickly mount any sort of defense on land. He relied on his coastal fortresses (I had often gone with him to visit them, and knew how proud he was of their strong walls) and the men who guarded them. Yet it had been so long since hostile ships in any number had arrived in English harbors that the invaders were sure to succeed in their conquest.

"He sleeps badly at night, for fear of the Spanish soldiers," the ambassador told me. "His spirit is not at rest. He fears the wrath of the divine—as well he should."

Chapuys had a small army of his own—an army of spies. He paid servants in the royal household to inform him of the king's eating and sleeping habits, how often he sent for his physician and apothecary, when and how often he howled in pain at the ulcer on his leg and what abuse he hurled at his grooms and ushers. In short, all he said and did and how he spent his days. Nothing was overlooked, the ambassador insisted, by these vigilant informers who were well paid for their observations.

And they were of one mind in this: that Henry was profoundly afraid. He could find no relief from his fears, no ease or peace.

Certainly there was none to be had from his consort. Anne taunted him, shamed him, goaded him past endurance—and from what the ambassador was hearing, her ceaseless prods and goads were even worse than the prickings of Henry's own conscience. He endured it all, and at times exploded in rage. But his very rage caused his blood to pound and the pain in his leg to worsen, and his head to ache, so that in the end he suffered more than ever.

Anne's taunts and criticisms were only one source of strain. The clamoring of his critics was growing louder. My own plight and that of our daughter Mary aroused much aggrieved talk.

"Your very own former gentleman usher, Griffith Richards, confided to me that if he were only twenty years younger he would gladly join the emperor's army," Chapuys told me. "He says the king's gone mad with all his ill fortune, and his fear of worse to come. He's quite out of his mind."

Hearing this, I remembered how Henry's father had acted very much like a madman, terrifying others in his wild raging and punishing his son, young Henry, far more cruelly than he deserved. My long-dead first husband Arthur had been his favorite, Henry was the son he despised. I saw it clearly, and resented him for it, even if he was my father-in-law and king of the realm. Now, it seemed, the prince that had been punished had grown into the image of his cruel father.

"They say he is an angry bull, pawing the ground and snorting, lowering his head to charge," according to the ambassador. "Whoever resists him is sure to be gored and trampled."

I knew well that Henry could be bullheaded, and that he left in his wake a path of ruin and even of blood, as he had shown only too clearly by the recent executions. But I could hardly imagine that he had no feeling whatever for our daughter. And Anne had not yet given him a son.

In fact, Anne herself was said to be suffering. According to Chapuys's informers among Anne's waiting maids, she was being tormented just then by stories she was hearing about Henry's pursuit of other women. She worried that he had tired of her, that he had deserted her and would never return to her bed. One tale after another gave her nightmares: it was whispered that Henry was weary of dark-haired, dark-eyed women such as Anne and sought a blond mistress; that he kidnapped and ravished young girls for his pleasure; that he boasted about being able to possess any girl or woman who caught his eye and aroused his lust.

"She is too old and too dark," he had said of Anne, and the words stung. On hearing them Anne dismissed the youngest of her maids of honor and those with the fairest hair and whitest skin. I had to remind myself that I too was more fair than dark—or at least I had been when I was a young girl and first came to Henry's bed. Did she suppose, even for a moment, that Henry missed my company, my body beside him in bed?

We women are prone to strange fancies, as men often say to our detriment. When we are frightened, or threatened, we imagine all sorts of things. I was sure Anne was no exception to this truth. Events were to prove that I was not so far wrong.

Henry went on progress that summer, despite the messages from Spain and the imperial lands that an invasion force was being readied. He traveled with his officers and servants from one country house to another as he usually did, as if in defiance of the danger from abroad.

But as Francisco Phelipe's brother Hernan had predicted, his intent was to hunt, not to spend days and nights in feasting and revelry, and Anne did not accompany him He moved on every few days, following reports of where the swiftest and strongest harts and bucks were to be found and taking Henry Fitzroy with him. Anne, her belly growing larger (according to reports), was left to go her own worrisome way, upset by stories of Henry's conquests and feeling—so I was told—more and more isolated and alone, her fears increasing.

It was clear to us all that Henry had decided to try to turn the ailing, weak boy Bessie Blount had presented to him fifteen or so years earlier into a fit heir to the throne—in case Anne was unable to provide one. By all accounts, young Fitzroy was well-meaning and as sweet as a girl, though his arms and legs were as thin as dry sticks and his voice—oh, his voice!—was shrill and high. As everyone knows, boys' voices turn to men's when the boys reach the age of fifteen or earlier, and Fitzroy's still had not grown lower. I had heard the grooms of Henry's chamber snicker that it never would, that he belonged among the castrati, the Italian boys who sang so beautifully, their voices soaring higher and purer than the voices of women.

Be that as it may, Henry seemed determined to toughen his bastard son and make a man of him. This alarmed Anne, who saw the child in her womb being deprived of his rights (always assuming her child was a prince, and not another princess) by the son of Bessie Blount.

Then word reached us all at Durham House that Henry Fitzroy had suffered an accident. He had never been a skilled rider like his father, who seemed able to make any mount do his bidding and even appeared to be genuinely fond of each of his horses and to be able to communicate with them. Many a time I have heard Henry speaking softly to his horses while stroking their muzzles, saying again and again, "So ho, so ho, my minion," and hearing them whicker and snuffle in response. Henry Fitzroy lacked this talent and was even said to be afraid of his more spirited mounts, unable to curb a horse when it shied. Horses sense fear, all riders know this; my own Griselda, the gentlest filly ever born, knew when a frightened rider was on her back and became uneasy.

The news of Fitzroy's accident set everyone talking—and speculating. It was said that a new horse he was riding threw him, and when he fell he broke one of his stick-thin legs and injured his back. He could have died, had one of his grooms not been there to break his fall and another to catch the maddened horse and calm him.

What caused all the talk was that the new horse had been given him by Anne. Or rather, by someone Anne paid to buy, in secret, a costly, unruly Barbary stallion and make a gift of him to the king's son. Anne wanted Fitzroy to die.

Enraged, Henry was quick to find out the truth. According to Ambassador Chapuys, the horse dealer was caught, beaten and forced to confess what he knew. Bleeding and weeping, terrified of Henry's vengeance, he admitted that Anne had sent him money and jewels in return for his gift of the stallion to Fitzroy. Wringing his hands and begging for the king's mercy, he was not executed but instead was sent, in chains, to be an oarsman on a ship Henry was outfitting to sail westward, to search for gold in the New World. All this I learned from Griffith Richards and the grooms in the stables at Durham House.

In my view it was Anne who should have been punished, but she still carried the king's child in her belly. That child was her protection, and she knew it. She would do anything, it seemed, to promote her unborn son's right to the throne—if the child was indeed a son.

Meanwhile I was afraid for Mary's safety. Anne feared Mary, that was certain. She had been heard to say, more than once, "She is my death and I am hers," and now that we all knew she had made an attempt to kill Fitzroy we had no doubt that she wanted to remove Mary as well.

But for the moment, in midsummer, Anne was distracted by Henry's dalliances with other women and the remarks he made about her being too old and too dark to attract him. At first I paid little attention to any of this, knowing Henry as I did and aware that he was accustomed to saying disparaging things (as he often had to me during our long marriage) and to seeking out new women to charm and seduce. But given Anne's condition, and her heightened fears, I wondered whether the present circumstances might give me just the opportunity I had been praying for, my chance to regain my place at Henry's side.

I sent a message to my trusted friend Lady Wingfield to say that I had come across a remarkable aid to making my face look youthful again. I told her how I treated my complexion with lemon juice three times a day and then applied the costly cream called dead fire, a precious substance that erased all the lines around my mouth and eyes and the pouches and scars and age spots that made me look like an old woman. If only I had known about this remarkable ointment when I was younger, I told her, I could have preserved my youth intact all these years. As it was, I seemed to be growing more youthful and more lovely each time I smoothed on the dead fire; the years were falling away and I felt beautiful, even though I would soon be an old woman of fifty summers.

I felt certain that Lady Wingfield would tell Anne of my discovery, and that Anne, feeling the sharp sting of Henry's rejection, would want to try it for herself. And indeed everything I said about the potent cream was true; it did indeed wipe away every blemish and wrinkle from a woman's skin—but it did much more, as I learned from the surgeon Henry brought to court to aid, if needed, in the delivery of Anne's child.

Luis de la Borda had indeed studied at Pisa, and was renowned for his ability to assist at difficult births. But he was Aragonese, not Pisan, as I discovered when Ambassador Chapuys brought him to Durham House to pay his respects to me. And he instructed me in the use of dead fire.

He meant well, to be sure. He was sympathetic to me, not only as a fellow Aragonese and the daughter of the great Queen Isabella, but because of my plight as the discarded wife of the king. He believed that he was offering me a chance to restore my lost beauty—which had never been outstanding—and fend off the deepest wrinkles that arrive with age. He cautioned me not to use too much of the remarkable cream he gave me to try or it might burn my skin. I was cautious; I spread some on the tail of a marmoset I kept in a cage, a sad-faced, fearful creature that spent its mournful days watching the comings and goings of my servants and now and then pelting them with bits of orange peel.

At first the cream seemed to have no effect. But then the marmoset began baring its teeth and screeching, running in frantic circles around the cage. I called for Francisco Phelipe and told him to wipe the animal clean, which he did.

"The tail is beautiful," he told me. "Smooth and without blemish. But the smell is terrible. And the poor creature's heart pounds more loudly than the royal drummers at an execution."

I have no excuse whatever for what I did in passing on news of the wonder-working dead fire to Lady Wingfield, knowing she would tell Anne about it. I have asked for forgiveness, I have prayed to be free of a spirit of revenge. But I must admit (how could I not?) that I wished Anne harm. I truly felt that she deserved punishment for what she did to Henry Fitzroy and what she no doubt wished to do to Mary.

I am at fault. But even now I confess that I burned with a desire for vengeance. I burned just as fiercely as my marmoset did when the dead fire ate away at his tail.

Besides, Anne had only herself to blame for what happened. I knew that she would be strongly tempted to try the dead fire, especially after learning from Lady Wingfield that I was looking more youthful because of it and that I was more than content with its effects. Anne was never moderate or cautious in anything she did. When she insisted that Lady Wingfield demand my entire supply of the precious cream, and when having gotten it she spread it immoderately over her swollen cheeks and chin and lined forehead, she ignored any thought of caution and soon, like my marmoset, she became frantic and began screaming in pain.

Lady Wingfield did her best to rub away the cream, but Anne, maddened as my poor monkey had been, was beside herself with burning irritation.

"It did lighten her skin a little," Lady Wingfield told me the following day, when the whole ordeal was over and Anne's entire household had been restored to a semblance of peace. "But her teeth are black and her breath smells as though she had swallowed the outscourings of an entire butcher shop. I never did smell anything so rancid! If the king were with us, instead of stag hunting in heaven knows where, he would make sure to stay as far from Anne as he possibly could."

I prayed for forgiveness, as I have said. I prayed for deliverance from Henry's anger. I prayed for a sign.

And then the sign came.

We expected Anne to take her chamber to await the birth of her child soon after St. Swithin's Day but the holy day came and went and still she did not withdraw.

Days passed, then weeks. There were questions, murmurs. Had the Great Whore given birth in secret to another Little Whore instead of a prince and was she hiding the truth in order to avoid Henry's anger? Ambassador Chapuys, Griffith Richards, Lady Wingfield and all those concerned about me and about Mary waited eagerly for news. What could have happened?

Then the midwives and the surgeon left the country house where Anne was staying, saying only that there was no announcement to make about Anne's condition.

"If you ask me," Lady Wingfield said when she came to Durham House, "there never was a child. Or if there was, she lost it very early on, and was too frightened to admit it."

I never knew for certain what was true and what was gossip, or whether (as I feared during my sleepless nights) her health declined because of the dead fire. One thing alone was clear: she had not given Henry a prince. With summer's end the court returned to the capital, Henry brought home his trophies from the hunt, Fitzroy limped on his injured leg that never seemed to heal and tended to hold his hand to his painful back with every step he took. The summer's follies and mischances were over. And my nephew Charles, once he heard the welcome news that there was no prince to succeed to Henry's throne, decided not to invade England until the following year, when the weather warmed and the French might be persuaded to join him.

Anne was said to be getting fat. She was stuffing herself with comfits, fruit and nut candies and licorice-root sweets. She slept badly at night and had nothing to do during the day, not even look after her small daughter who had nursemaids and laundresses, footmen and grooms and even her own almoner to fill her every need.

It was said Anne rarely held her child, and when she did, she wept as if she could not stop. Anne hated the sight of Mary and avoided Henry Fitzroy even though he was married to her cousin, and thus was part of the powerful Howard family—in addition to being the king's son.

Rumors continued to swirl through the court and to reach me at Durham House; rumors about Henry who was said to be enamored of a young blond girl who he kept in a hunting lodge, hoping that she would agree to wed him and bear him a son. When Anne learned that he had told this girl that he had been "struck with the dart of love" (the same words he had used years earlier to woo Anne herself) and that he would not eat or sleep until the girl agreed to become his mistress, Anne raved and shrieked (so Lady Wingfield told me) and swore that she would have the girl sent away. Meanwhile she continued to devour her favorite comfits, and to plot her revenge.

So all stood as the new year opened. Henry was ignoring Anne, and little Elizabeth, and attempting to arrange a marriage for Mary with the son of King Francis. My nephew Charles was pitting his powerful armies against the Turks in far-off Africa—though Ambassador Chapuys assured me that if at any time Henry threatened me or made me suffer and fear for my life, the emperor would send his troops immediately to defend me.

As it turned out, I had little to fear from Henry; it was Anne who had become my deadliest enemy—and Mary's.

There was a visionary in Kent, known as Friar Gawen but in truth no friar at all but a common thief who in his youth had languished long in the pillory for stealing his master's oxen. The people of Kent revered him, though as I was to discover, Anne gave him money to invent his visions. She paid him to say that he had had a revelation that Anne could not bear the king a son while I lived, nor could Anne's daughter Elizabeth thrive while Mary lived.

We were at great risk of being killed.

Friar Gawen drew crowds with his ranting and his tales of being awakened by an angel who told him to get down on his knees and prepare to hear divine messages. For a time the Kentish folk were in awe of his visions and his heavenly voices, and even Henry was so afraid of him that he shut him away in Penshurst Castle, where he predicted that soon many monks and even a cardinal of the church would die at Henry's order. (How he knew this I cannot imagine, but as it happened he was right.)

The friar was more mad than holy—and more greedy than mad—but his visions and voices spread fear, especially after Henry began ordering harsh punishments of monks and priests who opposed the immense changes he was making in the English church, depriving the Holy Father in Rome of all authority and putting himself, King Henry, at the head of all.

It was a spectacle of horror that spring, the spring of my fiftieth year, as one by one those who refused to swear loyalty to the king instead of to the Holy Father in Rome as head of the church were brought to their deaths. I was ordered brought to Tyburn and compelled to watch, though from a distance, as the first group of monks, all of them wearing their robes, all of them thin and weak from fasting, were led out to be hanged.

The crowd that gathered to watch the executions was large and greatly dismayed. How dare King Henry add this sacrilege to his long list of sins, that he should order holy men to their deaths? Few in the crowd were bold enough to voice their criticisms aloud; they knew well enough what punishment would follow if they did. But they were in anguish all the same.

Though ordered by the hangmen to stop their praying, the condemned monks continued to repeat the familiar words of the Lord when he prayed for his persecutors and asked for them to be forgiven. The starkness of those holy words, the thin chests and gaunt faces of the monks when their robes were stripped away, their unflinching offering up of their bodies made many in the crowd weep and add their own prayers.

That the cruel hangmen plunged their knives into the men's thin bellies and drew out their bowels while they still lived, causing a great stench and forcing many of the onlookers to retch and choke added to the horror. People sopped up the red gore in their handkerchiefs, and kissed the bloody ground, and afterward, when the men's severed hands and feet were borne away to be nailed to the city gates, they kissed these relics as well, showing their reverence for those the king had treated with such barbarity.

Not long afterward an even larger crowd gathered on Tower Hill to do reverence to the frail, elderly Bishop Fisher, who during his imprisonment had been named a cardinal of the church by the Holy Father Paul III. As soon as he emerged from the chapel it was clear to all those who were there to watch him die—really to honor him—that he was far too ill and feeble to walk unaided. He had to be helped to climb the steps to the scaffold, his unkempt white hair all but covering his wrinkled cheeks. Yet throughout the agony of his punishment he looked resolute, stern, and as strong as a much younger man, or so I was assured by those who recounted his suffering to me afterward. And when his severed head was mounted on Tower Bridge, it was said that his face resembled the face of a much younger man—as if he had found his youth renewed amid his suffering.

No cardinal of the Roman Church had ever been executed in England. Pope Paul declared the realm to be accursed of God, and called for a holy war against it.

Then, as if in response, rain began to pour down, heavy rain, day after day, flooding the Tower courtyards and the gallows at Tyburn, ruining the crops in the fields, filling the Thames until it overflowed its banks and washed away boats and docks, shiploads of Flemish cloth and English wool, wrecking the king's sport and rotting the heads of the condemned traitors that grinned down, black and stinking, from their heights on Tower Bridge.

22

ICOUGHED ALL SUMMER LONG AND HAD A RHEUM IN MY CHEST FROM the constant rain and cold. It rained, as I have said, not only for forty days and forty nights but until the first frosts and even after that. Many people feared the rain would never stop, but would sweep all before it, until the Lord's vengeance had been accomplished and all life came to an end. So I told Ambassador Chapuys when he was finally allowed to see me in my new residence, Kimbolton Castle, where I was taken when I fell ill.

We laughed about this—Chapuys brought a jester with him who made fun of those who feared the world's end, and I could not help but be amused—yet I continued to cough and sneeze and the medicines given to me were not much help in making me well again.

I drank wine to ease the rheum in my chest, and my surgeon bled me and gave me a purgative. Yet the pains I felt in my stomach by summer's end were much worse than my cough. I was not able to eat much and slept hardly at all; when I did fall asleep I was awakened almost at once by a feeling as if a clawed hand had gripped my belly and would not let it go.

My spirits sank whenever I looked in the pier glass and saw my pale, gaunt cheeks and called for Maria de Caceres to bring me powdered ochre to redden them. I hardly recognized my wrinkled, blue-veined hands with their long thin fingers; my shoulders were bony and my stomach so flat it almost disappeared beneath my ribs. I knew it was the constant cold that caused this, the cold and the rain. When the frosts began my bedchamber was icy cold, and my blankets thin.

I had not been allowed to bring my apothecary Juan de Soto to Kimbolton. His assistant, young Philip Grenacre, was well meaning but far from fully trained in the lore of medicines and philtres and still had much to learn, as I had often been told. I would rather Ambassador Chapuys had brought a seasoned apothecary with him than a jester! But then, as the ambassador told me in subdued tones, Henry had refused to give him permission to see me at all for many months, and he felt he could not make further demands.

Still, I told him I wanted to move to a warmer and healthier place. The decayed old bedchamber I slept in at Kimbolton was dark and small, the floors sagged and creaked and the old stone walls were chinked by gaps that let in the cold, rainy air. The furnishings looked and smelled as though they had not been cleaned or changed in a very long time. How I would have liked to change them all—no, to move to another house entirely, as I told the ambassador. To a healthier place with a sunlit garden. In such a place, I felt sure, I would get well again.

During the long cold afternoons I daydreamed of returning to Spain, to the Alhambra, with its green arbors and splashing fountains. In my memory it was always hot and sunny there, the sunlight so bright we had to seek shade and fanned ourselves while we drank cooling fruit drinks mixed with brandy. I imagined feeling the refreshing air on my cheeks, and hearing one of the young servant girls singing a tender, plangent melody for our pleasure.

For some reason I remembered the spiders, how as winter was approaching (the warm winter of Andalusia) the spiders scuttled in under the ceiling tiles and mother told me they were searching for their mates. She made it sound like such a welcome thing, so good and natural that the spiders should seek one another out to love and mate. But I learned soon enough that the bright green spiders stung, and the long-legged black ones could jump up and bite a child and kill him (as they did one of our baker's sons) and that there were poison caterpillars climbing the trees in the fall and if I touched one of them or tried to rub its fur my hand and arm itched for days.

All this I told Chapuys as my foolish thoughts wandered back to my childhood and he suggested that I must be thinking of spiders because of the pouch of live spiders that Henry always wore around his neck to keep him from getting the sweating plague. He spoke to me often of trifles, light things of no consequence that made me laugh. He described how Henry was gambling heavily at cards, playing Pope July and Primero and growling and frowning when he lost, which he often did. I insisted that he call me "Your Majesty" and told him that I shivered whenever I heard the words "Princess Dowager." He merely nodded.

I asked about Anne, knowing that she was in disgrace, having failed to give birth to a prince, but he dismissed my questions without really answering them. There was a rumor that Anne was pregnant yet again, and suffering from the stomach pains all mothers endure. Her pains could not have been as sharp or as piercing as mine, I thought—and chided myself for wishing even worse suffering on her for all that she had said and done against Fitzroy and Mary.

Besides, I was sure that Anne must be suffering anguish and worry knowing that Henry had found someone whose company he preferred to hers. His favored companion is plain, sensible Jane Seymour, who I know to be kind and docile, the opposite of Anne in every way. The Seymours are fruitful and have sons . . . and I hope . . .

Kimbolton Castle, February 1, 1536
To His Imperial Majesty Charles V from his envoy Eustace
Chapuys:

With the greatest respect and in profound regret at the news
I must send to Your Imperial Highness, I must inform you of the
circumstances which have kept me here in Kimbolton Castle
since Advent and continue to detain me here.

As Your Imperial Majesty is well aware, I was summoned to
Kimbolton by the Princess Dowager's physician who informed
me that she was gravely ill and that I should come at once. She was
asking for me. I made my way to the castle as soon as I was able,
though the roads were full of snowdrifts and my breath turned to
frost in the cold air.

I found the Princess Dowager very ill indeed, surrounded by
her household officials and by her lesser servants as well: her
laundrywomen and grooms, her gardeners and ewerers and
musicians, even her pastrycooks. All were praying most fervently
for her recovery and bringing her gifts to lighten her spirits.
There were nightingales in a cage, and half-grown lambs curled
up on her blankets, a singer and a lutenist and a boy with a high,
clear voice who sang Spanish songs.

When I entered the bedchamber the Princess Dowager held
out her arms to me and told me that she did not wish to die alone,
like a brute beast in a field, but in the embrace of one who cared
about her and shared her belief in the Roman church. Mary was
not allowed to be with her, and she feared that at any moment I
might be sent out of the bedchamber and not allowed to return.

Her strength was failing, she could barely speak above a
whisper. Maria de Caceres brought her soup and wine, but she
could eat only a mouthful or two of the soup and though the taste
of the wine made her smile, she drank only a little, then slept.

When she woke again it was evening, and all the lamps were
lit and the dingy old room looked less neglected. I stayed by her
side, as I could plainly see that my presence gave her comfort. She

pointed to a leather trunk that had been brought in and put in one corner of the room. In that trunk, she told me, was a record of her life, written by her own hand. She regretted that she had not been able to complete it, but that she hoped I would take it to Your Imperial Majesty. She also gave me her prayer book, brought from Spain when she first came to England to marry Prince Arthur. And her black lace mantilla that had belonged to her grandmother. These she wished me to present to her daughter in the hope that Mary would keep them near her always.

I stayed with the Princess Dowager for four days, at her bedside for most of that time. She ate only bread and a few sips of tea. She laughed at the foolishness of my jester and was glad when I told her that she would soon be moved to a fine new palace the king was building in the south, where the sun was warm and she would never feel cold again. It was not true, but it gave her comfort.

She received the last rites and forgave the king whatever wrongs he may have done her. Then one by one her servants came to her bedside and knelt before her, and she thanked and blessed each of them and gave each one a gift. She had no jewels left, but gave what tokens she had, books and combs and lengths of lace, vials of scent, her clove-scented pomander, embroidered patches with the arms of Aragon and Castile that she and her women had sewn. To Griffith Richards she gave a pair of her favorite hunting gloves, to Maria de Caceres her choice of what garments still remained to her. No one left empty-handed, not even the weeping head pastrycook, a large, sad-eyed woman to whom the Queen Dowager handed a small green ceramic jar saying "for your comfits."

As Your Imperial Majesty is aware, the Princess Dowager surrendered her spirit on the afternoon of the seventh day of January, and her frail body was opened at once to determine the cause of her death. I heard it said by the chandler who opened her that her heart was black, as is the heart of any person who dies of poison. I found this hard to credit. Nonetheless I am duty-bound to report it to you. The chandler and his assistants were alone when they did their work; the Princess Dowager's physician Miguel de Lasco was not permitted to be present, nor was the Bishop of Llandaff, who heard her confession. It was said that the Princess Dowager succumbed to illness after drinking Welsh beer, but as Your Imperial Majesty knows, royal courts are filled with such rumors, and in all my time with the Princess Dowager I never saw her drink anything but wine, unless there was no wine to be had, as happened at Kimbolton and on occasion at Durham House.

She was buried two days ago. May the Lord have mercy on her soul.

As Your Imperial Majesty knows, the concubine Anne has miscarried another child. It was said to be a prince, though as it was barely three months in the womb, no one can say for certain. The king swore and broke his golden walking stick over his knee when he heard this news, especially as it is rumored that the concubine miscarried after eating a surfeit of comfits made with green ginger.

Note to the Reader

Once again, dear reader, a caution and a reminder: *The Spanish Queen* is a historical entertainment, in which the authentic past and imaginative invention intertwine. Fictional events and circumstances, fictional characters and whimsical alterations of events and personalities are blended. Fresh interpretations of historical figures and their circumstances are offered, and traditional ones laid aside. I hope you have enjoyed this reimagining of the past.

Turn the page for a sneak peek at
Carolly Erickson's next novel

Confessions
of
Bloody Mary

Available October 2015

Copyright © 2015 by Carolly Erickson

Prologue

WHEN JOHN HOOPER STAGGERED OUT, BLINKING, INTO THE COLD light of that February morning in the year 1555 he hardly knew where he was.

He had not slept at all the night before, so damp was the stone floor of his cramped cell and so dank the wind that blew incessantly through it.

He had prayed all night, his arms around himself for warmth and his tears flowing freely down his thin cheeks.

He had not been outside the dark, narrow cell for eighteen long months, and he cursed the weakness in his legs that made him stumble as he left it now, in chains, and was led out into the courtyard to die.

Snow lay thick on the ground in the courtyard where the place of execution had been prepared, and the courtyard itself was full of shivering, weeping women and men, crossing themselves and murmuring prayers.

"Spare him! Show him mercy!" the bravest of them cried out to the guards as Hooper approached.

"He is our bishop, blessed and consecrated by God to lead and serve us!" a man's voice shouted, only to be silenced at once by a frown from a guardsman, his thick wooden club upraised.

"He is no bishop!"

"He is a heretic!"

"He teaches only evil!" came other voices from among those watching, shivering in the cold.

"He deserves to die! The queen has ordered it!"

"He has suffered long enough!" came the dissent. "Can you not see how thin he is, how ill he looks!"

"Then death will be a deliverance for him, and no punishment!"

On the voices went, heedless of the menace of Hooper's captors with their thick batons, as the sun rose higher and a tall three-legged stool was brought forward. The trembling Hooper, his chains loosed, was lifted up to stand on the stool. He looked out over the growing crowd. His face was haggard, his eyes red from lack of sleep.

"Good people!" he managed to call out. "Good people, I pray you, do not condemn what the Lord Himself has brought about! I may yet be spared, if He wills it!"

His voice broke as he tried to speak further, and he shivered.

"Do not endanger yourselves—" He went on as best he could, the trembling that overtook him growing until his knees knocked so violently that he could barely keep from falling off the stool.

"Pray for me," he called out. "Save your consciences—"

Praying and keeping vigil through so many long cold nights in his cell, a cell that reeked of piss and foulness, had weakened him, and he struggled now to endure the taunts and curses of his wardens.

Much as these foul taunts roused his anger, he struggled to contain the curses that rose to his own lips. He felt his fists clench, and forced himself to loosen them.

A stout, burly man came toward him from among the onlookers. A man Hooper recognized. A friend.

"Cuthbert," Hooper gasped. "Have you come to help me then?"

He smiled. For a moment Hooper allowed himself to imagine that this familiar face, these strong arms were indeed a sign of divine mercy.

But he was mistaken. He knew it as soon as he saw that his friend was struggling to hold back tears.

"May the Lord forgive me," Cuthbert mumbled, "but I am appointed to make the fire."

The look of pain and disappointment that for a moment crossed Hooper's wan cheeks was dreadful to behold.

"Yes, of course you are," he managed to say. "You are a woodsman, are you not?"

The man nodded, head bowed, his own wretchedness evident to those nearest them both.

"Then you must do as you are ordered."

It was all Cuthbert could do to force himself to obey the guards who were threatening him, telling him that if he did not bring the kindling and build the fire at once that he would suffer the same fate as Hooper.

For John Hooper, as now seemed inevitable, was to be burnt alive for heresy.

His mouth was so dry he could barely speak above a croaking whisper, yet he managed to urge his friend on, assuring him that he, Hooper, freely forgave him. All the while sticks and bundles of reeds were being put in place around the stool and set alight, but as there was a high wind, the kindling did not fully catch fire, making Hooper cough and choke and gag from the smoke.

Then his hair caught on fire. He screamed until he was hoarse from screaming.

"For God's love," he called out then, as loudly as he could, "spare me this agony! Let me have the gunpowder!"

As was well known, bags of gunpowder were tied to the legs of sufferers to shorten their final, most excruciating moments. One of the guards gave Cuthbert a push.

"Do it!"

Trembling and gagging, half blinded by the smoke, Cuthbert

lifted one of the bladders filled with the black powder and fumbled with the rope that bound it. Just then a gust of wind tore it out of his hands and tossed it up into the air, above the heads of the crowd of onlookers.

Now the black powder rained down, causing those nearest the suffering Hooper on his high stool to run stumbling away in fear, clawing at their faces and tearing at their garments.

Few were left to pray for the dying Hooper. He made no sound, though Cuthbert thought he saw his friend's blackened lips move and imagined that he tried to beat his scorched chest with one bloody, shrunken fist.

Then at last he slumped and fell into the ashes, and the wind began to blow them over what remained of his body, now reduced to a gory mass of blood and fat, his entrails spilling out.

"So die all who sin against God and His sacraments!" came the cry from many throats.

"No man can befoul his lips with such lies and live!"

But Cuthbert wept, and beat his breast until it bled, and swore that he would avenge his friend if it was the last thing he ever did.

1

February 1534

CATCH HER! CATCH HER!"

I recognized the high, shrill voice of Ardith Plumfield, one of the four rockers who looked after my baby sister Elizabeth in the royal nursery at Hampton Court.

Ardith was a tall, gawky girl with long arms and legs who seemed always to be in a state of wide-eyed alarm. She had been holding little Elizabeth, wrapped tightly in a silken blanket woven with gold threads, until a moment earlier when the nursery floor began to shake under our feet and suddenly there was a great deal of noise and confusion.

"It is an earthquake!"

"Run! Run quickly! Before the walls tumble and the roof falls on us all!"

And in fact the walls of the nursery were shaking and swaying, as if their solid bricks were melting into waves before our eyes. Glass was breaking, windows shattering. With a loud crack a heavy roof timber fell near me, causing more panic.

"It is a sign of the Lord's displeasure with those who sin against Him!"

The voices of the rockers were shrill with dread, though others were voiceless, trembling in panic, and could barely cry out at all.

"It is a sign of His judgment against the king's marriage," I heard some say. "He will not let any of us live!

Amid it all I heard Ardith cry out again, even more loudly.

"In the name of all the saints, catch her!" And looking up, I saw that she was about to toss my baby sister into the air—in my direction.

I love babies, all babies. And so without a moment's hesitation I held out my arms, Ardith threw her toward me—wrapped tightly in her gold-threaded cloth—and then ran from the room.

I caught her—and at first, nearly dropped her.

She was tightly swaddled, an infant bundle no bigger than my silver washbowl. And she was as slippery as an eel. It felt to me as if she were wriggling in my arms, trying to escape my grasp as she wailed and howled. Or was it just that the floor beneath me was pitching and rolling? I could not be sure but I was certain of one thing: that my feet needed to be on solid ground—or solid stone.

A stone staircase was just beyond the wide arched doorway of the nursery. I clutched the wriggling bundle as tightly as I could and hurried out through the archway, into the open air.

The chill of that February blast made me shiver even as I heard the blaring of the king's huntsmen blowing their horns, sounding an alarm as they invariably did when there was any sort of danger.

For danger there surely was, with cries of terror and fear all around me and the thudding and stamping of running feet. Little Elizabeth too had begun to cry, first a whimper and then a louder, more shrill cry of distress. Her eyes grew wider as the noise around us increased, and I thought, please dear Lord, don't let me drop her.

I began to climb the stairs, clutching the baby, but she slipped out of my arms. I thought for certain that I had lost her, that she would fall and crack open her head on the sharp stones, and that I and not Ardith Plumfield or the quaking of the earth or any other force under heaven would be blamed.

I gasped, I prayed—"Ah, dear Lord, don't let me drop her!" and then, just as her head was about to strike the stone, I managed to dive down and put my hands under her soft neck and prevent the worst from happening.

How I did this, how close I came to dropping my sister I will never know, but I am certain that it happened, and that it was the Lord's will that the baby survived.

"The princess! She's saved the little princess!"

The royal huntsmen had put down their horns and were shouting, forgetting everything but their relief and delight that the king's baby daughter had not perished. (And well aware, as I now realize only too keenly, that if she had suffered injury, they might have been blamed, along with everyone else near the nursery, so vengeful was her mother the harlot Nan Boleyn!)

At the sound of the huntsmen's shouting the rockers and nursemaids and kitchen boys who had fled when the floor started to shake beneath their feet and the walls to sway were beginning to file slowly back toward the nursery, ignoring the chill wind and the trembling earth in their surprise that the little princess had been spared.

She was, after all, my father's daughter, even if her mother was the accursed Nan. And though she was not the boy my father the king and his paramour had so ardently desired, but only a rather thin, scrawny red-headed little girl—some of the youngest nursemaids called her "the little princess with the pointy head" when they thought no one was listening, and giggled when they said it—still she was heir to the throne, and would remain so until Nan managed to give birth to a healthy prince.

I cringe as I write this, to be sure. I can hardly bear to write my father's new wife's name, let alone acknowledge her as queen. But I must, if I am to tell this story truthfully and in good conscience.

Oh, there was much gossip in the royal nursery just then! And I, having sharp ears and an engaging manner, heard a great deal of it.

Everyone knew that my father King Henry was not a well man, and it was even being said that he might not live much longer. His physicians had long faces and his apothecaries were full of frowns.

He had once been the most handsome of kings, the finest horse-man and champion in the lists. Handsome and energetic though he still was, it was plain to see that he winced in pain with every step he took, and he could no longer heave his bulk into the saddle of his favorite mount Griselda without effort, let alone take on an opponent in the lists.

Bulging sores sprouted from his wide thighs, and though he loudly denied any weakness, even to those who knew him best, I knew that he had other failings as well. His stomach hurt when he ate too much, which he often did. He did not hear everything that was said to him, even when the words were shouted. And it had become difficult for him to read the dispatches and other documents put in front of him, the letters blurred before his eyes.

He squinted when he tried to read, and could no longer form his letters clearly or accurately. Even writing his name, Henricus Rex, gave him difficulty. I, who wrote precisely, forming my letters and symbols with care, took pains not to seem to notice his difficulties. I did not want to put him to shame.

"See here, Crum," he would call out gruffly in his booming voice to his able chief minister Thomas Cromwell, "put your seal on this," or "stamp this, will you?" He was quick to deal out blows to those who served him, even the highest ranking of his ministers, but neither his bullying nor his bad temper could hide his advancing weakness.

He pretended not to need anyone's help with anything, but the truth was that he had reached the age of forty-three, and was no longer the young, vital man I remembered from when I was his Pearl of the World, his sweet blond daughter who was so quick to learn and who could read and write fluent Latin when I was only six or seven years old.

He was so proud of me when I was little! He boasted that I was the wisest princess in Christendom, as well as the loveliest. He ordered his Milanese armorers, the venerable and distinguished firm of Missaglia, to send craftsmen in wood to England to carve a small throne for me, and to emblazon it with my name.

It was as beautifully appointed as any royal throne could be, only in miniature. They used six different rare woods to create my throne, and inlaid it with ivory and gold. When I sat in it, dressed in my royal cape and wearing over my blond hair the small jewel-studded cap that was made especially for me, I was the very image of a future monarch, or so I was told. It did not matter then that I was a princess and not a prince, or that I was delicate and small for my age. All that mattered was that I never cried (so my father said), or made demands in the way unruly children do.

But there was something more, something my father told me when I was older.

"You will not remember this, Mary, you were far too young at the time, but when you were only a babe in the nursery, still in your rockers' arms, and your mother Queen Catherine and I were mourning the sad truth that there was no prince in the royal nursery, but only a small, frail princess, something mystical happened."

It was a favorite expression of his, that something mystical happened. That without warning, the usual order of things was altered, and a wondrous event occurred.

"We awoke one morning to find everything coated in ice," he went on after a pause. "All London was frozen. The outer walls of the palace were white with its thick coating. The very uniforms of the guardsmen were white with frost. I could hear the horses in the royal stables stamping their feet and whickering and neighing their complaint.

"No one knew what to do. We had never seen such a thing happen before. We had had cold weather, to be sure, and frost and snow, but never had there been so much of it, nor had it lasted so long.

"We did not know what to make of it. Many people feared the very sight of all the ice, and murmured that it was a sign of the end times. The dreadful end of the age foretold in the book of the Revelations of St. John.

"I don't mind telling you, Mary, that I was one of those who feared it. I had never heard or read of such a thing happening before, and I was greatly alarmed.

"I tried not to let those around me see how alarmed I was, but I could not hide my fear from your mother. She knew me far too well. She knew that she had failed me in not giving me a healthy son. One who could, in good time, follow me as king."

At this I protested, ever eager to defend my mother, but he swept my protest aside with a wave of his large hand.

"Yes—she failed me, again and again. You, Mary, were our last hope for a prince. Your mother would not have more children, she was far too old by the time you were born, and you were not strong. Everyone knows that when a woman is getting old her womb is weary. If she has a child it will be feeble, especially if it is a son."

He paused once again, and seemed lost in his thoughts. I waited until he went on.

"At last the ice began to melt, and we thought the worst was over. But then it began to rain—a torrent of rain, Mary, with thunder such as no one in the court had ever heard before. As if all the drums in England were being beaten at the same time. And there were great flashes of lightning, and high winds that tore around the corners of the palace, whining and shrieking."

He looked at me then, and I could see the terror in his eyes. He was reliving all that he had gone through in those dreadful months when I was a baby, and he felt his doom descending—not only on him, and on the house of Tudor, his lineage, but upon the very kingdom itself, perhaps for all time to come.

I could not help but frown in disbelief. For here I was, conversing with him, and many years had passed, and the realm had not withered, nor had the fortunes of the house of Tudor been in any way altered. I said as much.

"And do you know why, Mary?"

"No, father."

"Because of you."

"Because of me? And I no more than a small babe in my rockers' arms?"

He nodded. "Because you survived the great affliction we called the 'Lord's Visitation,' and by surviving it, you became our recompense for having no son. You became, for a time, our hope for the future."

Sweeping, epic entertainment from
CAROLLY ERICKSON

"History comes to life . . . thanks to Erickson's amazing talents."
—*RT Book Reviews* (4 ½ stars) on *The Secret Life of Josephine*

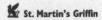 St. Martin's Griffin